Pretty When She Kills

RHIANNON FRATER

PERMUTED PLATINUM

PRETTY WHEN SHE KILLS
Copyright © 2014 by Rhiannon Frater. All Rights Reserved.

ISBN (paperback): 978-1-61868-172-0
ISBN (eBook): 978-1-61868-173-7

This book is a work of fiction. People, places, events, and situations are the product of the author's imagination. Any resemblance to actual persons, living or dead, or historical events, is purely coincidental.

No part of this book may be reproduced, stored in a retrieval system, or transmitted by any means without the written permission of the author and publisher.

Published by Permuted Press
109 International Drive, Suite 300
Franklin, TN 37067

Cover art by Claudia McKinney, Phatpuppy Art.

Follow us online:

Web: http://www.PermutedPress.com

Facebook: http://www.facebook.com/PermutedPress

Twitter: @PermutedPress

Dedicated with much love to all the fans of Pretty When She Dies

Prologue

The girl stood drenched in blood at the center of the graveyard. Languorously, she swayed as the night wind tossed about her unfettered white-blond hair and tugged at the white lace dress that was dangerously close to sliding off her delicate shoulders.

Enormous blue eyes gazed vacantly at the bodies at her feet. The askew forms of the young men foolish enough to dig her up out of her grave bore brutal wounds inflicted by her long, sharp teeth. Tilting her head, the girl gazed past the treetops at the bloated harvest moon ascending in the night sky. The orb spilt light through the branches and cast a bluish glow over the old cemetery. Her pink tongue licked the blood from her full red lips.

Rachoń stood in the dark shadows of the pine trees watching the ghostly figure. Her eyes thoughtfully surveyed the scene before her, her long blue nails tapping against the trunk of the tree she leaned against. Tilting her head, she sniffed the air. The coppery smell of blood mingled with the scents of fresh earth and chemicals.

It wasn't difficult to stitch together what had occurred just a few minutes before she had arrived on the edges of the old cemetery in East Texas.

"She's awake," Rachoń said, her naturally husky voice sensual to the ear.

"Why do you always end up with the messy jobs?" a voice grumbled behind her.

Flicking her gaze in the direction of her companion, she bestowed an annoyed look upon the immaculately dressed man maneuvering over the uneven forest floor. Prosper's skin was as dark as hers, but whereas her afro was shaped into twists, his head was shaved. Despite being blood relations in life, his eyes were black and hers were maroon. He bared his fangs as he grimaced.

"The master calls and I obey," she said, annoyance in her voice.

"You're a stupid woman for loving that pasty man," Prosper said, shrugging.

"He's my master. I obey him whether I want to or not," Rachoń said in a low, dangerous voice. "Whether I love him, or not."

"Kill her and be done with it." Prosper lifted one of his fine Italian loafers out of the dirt and sighed. "We've wasted enough time in Texas. I want to go home."

"Just shut up and let me deal with this." Rachoń returned her gaze to the pale wisp of a figure swaying in the moonlight.

The girl was probably barely eighteen. Her slightly rounded cheeks and arms gave her a very youthful appearance. Her burial garb hung by threads over her mostly nude body. Blood and bits of flesh slid lazily down between her small breasts and over her smooth stomach.

"He's just playing more games with you," Prosper said with a shrug.

"It's what he does best."

"Mayhem, death, destruction," Prosper agreed.

"Exactly."

The so-called Satanic Murders at the local college was the biggest story in the area. It was constantly on the news. Every gruesome detail was recounted in solemn tones by perfectly coiffed reporters to tantalize the audience's morbid interest.

What had really happened at the college was simple: Rachoń's creator and sometime lover, The Summoner, had made a new fledgling and buried her in the forest. Upon her resurrection, the new vampire had slaughtered over a dozen people to satiate her newborn thirst. That fledgling was gone now, having fled the area. The Summoner had followed, tracking her for his own amusement across Texas. It was a sick game he liked to play: create new vampires, abandon them, then see if they survived or not.

Which left Rachoń to clean up after him. Setting her hands on her hips, she stared across the graveyard at the petite woman who had hair the color of moonlight.

"Dammit," Rachoń growled, and stepped out of the tree line.

The ground was soft beneath the soles of her boots as she carefully avoided the consecrated areas of the graveyard. The waves of power wafting up from holy ground repelled her if she drew too near a blessed grave. It was like being too close to a raging bonfire and the heat of the power burned against her skin.

Shuddering, she hurried toward the open grave. The earth had lost its blessing when the men had dug up the coffin of The Summoner's latest victim. She felt her shoulders loosen with relief as she stepped onto the unconsecrated earth. The casket had fallen back into the grave, most likely when it had been shoved aside in the mayhem.

An icy tendril of power rippled across her cheek and she looked sharply toward the blood soaked creature standing a few feet away. The dazed expression on the girl's face had not altered as she slowly shifted her weight from one

PROLOGUE

foot then to the other. Her burial dress continued to slide downward over her body inch by inch as she swayed.

"Did you feel that?" Rachoń asked.

Prosper grunted as he stepped next to her, wiping at his very expensive Italian suit with his hands. He hated being dirty and complained bitterly under his breath before saying, "Feel what?"

Rachoń's eyes searched the darkness enshrouding the trees that bordered the small cemetery. "This had better not be another one of his games." Rachoń did not like the idea of The Summoner turning his perverse attention in her direction. She would not be a pawn in one of his sick games.

Prosper set his hands on his silk-clad muscular thighs and leaned forward to look at the corpses. Rachoń also examined the bodies, wondering what sort of idiots would dig up a dead girl. Of course, the dead girl had been a huge news story, but still she could only wonder at their stupidity.

The young men at the girl's muddy feet wore jerseys from the local collage. Their throats were savagely mangled, their limbs broken, their bodies drained of blood. There were four of the fools.

"They dug her up and she ate them," Prosper decided.

"Grave robbers?" Rachoń was doubtful.

"I bet it was a dare. For a thrill. Stupid people."

The girl's wide, staring eyes were blank, void of emotion, but she was gazing in their direction. Blood slid over her pale skin to pool around her toes. Embalming fluid slid down her thighs, the chemical smell slicing through the cloying scent of drying blood.

"I thought you said she probably wouldn't rise." Prosper grunted as he sat on a gravestone and wiped at his shoes.

"It's been four days since he buried her. She's just slower to rise than some," Rachoń answered. Out of a hidden sheath in her leather jacket she drew a long wicked dagger with a curving blade. It was perfect for decapitation. She would make this quick, then return home to Louisiana. She found Texas distasteful.

"What will we do with these stupid boys, Rachoń?"

"Decapitate them, stake them, bury them with her. The last thing we need is them rising as ghouls."

"Messy, nasty business," Prosper grunted.

Rachoń stepped over one of the bodies and gripped her weapon tightly. She kept her gaze on the creature before her. The girl's blue eyes were empty, staring, and disconcerting. One swift swipe, a stake through the heart, and the girl would be truly dead. Why The Summoner hadn't claimed this victim was a mystery. She didn't like it. He rarely left his fledglings to rise alone. He liked to watch their struggle, their madness, their need for blood.

"This feels wrong." Frustration ate at Rachoń. What did it mean? The Summoner abandoning this fledgling to pursue another?

"Just finish it. I hate Texas," Prosper complained.

Lifting her dagger, Rachoń braced her feet apart.

Just one quick swipe.

The girl's eyes shifted to look upon Rachoń. A spark of intelligence and understanding broke through the blankness.

"No!"

The pale blue eyes flashed to white.

A cold wave of power roared through Rachoń, nearly knocking her off her feet. She stumbled back, trying to keep her balance. The dark power surged around her.

"What the hell?" she cried out.

A hand gripped her ankle in a vise-grip.

"Shit, they're rising!" Prosper exclaimed.

The college boys' limbs jerked and quivered as they struggled to stand. Rachoń glanced down at the one grappling with her ankle, trying to pull her off her feet. As the corpse rose to its knees, she could feel its fingers tightening as it grew stronger. She swept the blade of the dagger through its neck, severing flesh and bone. The head rolled away, tumbling into the open grave.

Yet, the fingers locked around her boot did not relent. A few deft swipes of her dagger and the fingerless hand finally released her.

"Rachoń!" Prosper cried out. "Is he here?"

"It's her! Destroy the zombies!" she ordered.

Whipping about, she glared at the girl with the glowing white eyes. Impossibly, the newborn vampire had the necromantic power of The Summoner. Rachoń had never seen such a thing before in her long life. The pale young woman was trembling with the power spilling out of her. The bone-chilling dark magic clung to Rachoń, trying to grip her, or shove her away. Behind her Prosper grunted and swore above the sound of flesh and bone rending and cracking.

The Summoner had sent her here to make sure the girl did not rise. He considered the new fledgling he was pursuing across Texas his newest prized possession. Apparently, he had not realized that he had imbued his newest fledgling with his necromancer magic.

The girl fastened her glowing white eyes on Rachoń and thrust out her hand. The necromantic magic ripped at Rachoń, trying to pierce her mind and take control. Rachoń laughed with delight as the gris-gris around her neck repelled the attack.

"This is fabulous!" Rachoń exclaimed with pleasure.

"Kill her and be done with it!" Prosper shouted.

Casting a dark look over her shoulder, she saw that her cousin had ripped the zombies to pieces. His fine Italian suit was flecked with shreds of flesh and drenched in blood. Grumbling, he furiously tossed the bodies into the grave.

Rachoń stepped closer to the girl, who thrust both of her hands out at Rachoń, fingers flexing as her lips trembled.

"You can't touch me, little girl. I know how to deal with your kind," Rachoń

x

PROLOGUE

whispered. The fledgling was crazed. She needed more blood and soon, she was also powerful.

Rachoń loved power.

With one quick stroke, Rachoń sliced open her own wrist.

"Come on, little one. Time to eat," she said, holding out her arm.

The girl's eyes faded to blue as they latched onto the blood welling out of the wound. With a hungry cry, the girl gripped Rachoń's wrist and clamped her lips over it. Sucking hard, the girl's eyes closed with pleasure.

Rachoń slammed the dagger through the girl's back, piercing her heart. Instantly, her body tumbled over, blood still drizzling from her lips.

"She's not dead. Finish her." Prosper grunted as he disposed of the dismembered bodies.

"No. I want her," Rachoń answered, a smile unfurling on her dark lips. "She's a necromancer just like him. Her power will be my power."

"How will you control her?" Prosper frowned, his wide brow crinkled with concern.

Rachoń lightly touched the gris-gris hanging around her neck. "Entombment and a steady diet of my blood. He may have made her, but she will belong to me. In a few months, she will do everything I ask of her." Rachoń crouched and rolled the girl onto her back. Pulling off the remains of the girl's dress, she saw the ugly cuts from the autopsy were already healed. The thick thread used to sew her up had been ejected from her flesh and clung to her damp skin. She was fully transformed now.

"Fill in the grave and we'll head back to Shreveport," Rachoń said in a soft voice as she gently stroked the girl's fine white-blond hair that was stained pink by blood.

"Fine. Anything to be out of Texas and out of this mess your master made." Prosper picked up a shovel that the boys had brought to dig up the grave. "Hope you're happy with your new toy."

"Oh, I am," Rachoń said with a bright smile.

"What is her name again? They haven't put in her headstone yet." Prosper started shoveling dirt back into the grave, covering the bodies he had stacked inside.

"Bianca Leduc," Rachoń responded, her fingers resting on the girl's soft cheek. "And she is mine."

Four Months Later...

Part One

Friday Night

CHAPTER ONE

"Fuck you!" Amaliya scowled, feet set apart, hands on her hips.

"Nice language," Cian chided her, smirking as he perched like a bird on a leaning tombstone in the center of the cemetery.

"You call this a nice evening out?" Amaliya narrowed her eyes at him.

She had been lured out of their comfortable spacious apartment to the east side of Austin, Texas under false pretenses. Cian had promised her a nice night away from the hubbub of the downtown area. She had assumed they would be hanging out at one of the dive clubs, or maybe one of the small venues run by theater groups that were located east of I-35. Instead, they were standing in the middle of a very old cemetery at a little past midnight.

"We're away from the hustle and bustle of downtown just like you wanted," Cian said, grinning. His chestnut brown hair was ruffled by the wind. It was not as long as it had been for awhile. He had chopped it off to a more manageable and stylish length, but it looked good on him. His keen hazel eyes, heavily fringed with dark lashes, clearly projected his amusement.

"I even dressed up!"

Well, technically, she really hadn't. The jeans were clean, the black platform heels with lots of straps were not too scuffed up, and her black corset-top had actually been hanging in her closet and not strewn on the floor with the rest of her laundry.

"You look beautiful," he said, flexing his hands. He held a dagger in each one.

"Oh, fuck you."

"Later."

"Ugh!"

"If you don't practice, you'll regret it. You need to have control of your power." Cian stood up on the crooked headstone, easily balancing.

"What if the neighbors see us?" Amaliya looked over both shoulders through the clusters of thick trees dotting the graveyard, then across the street at the darkened houses.

"They're all asleep; the street lamps don't even reach this far, but...if it will make you feel better..." Cian closed his eyes, concentrated, and exhaled.

Almost immediately a thick mist billowed up from the ground, slithering around the old graves, and floating up to form a protective curtain around them.

"Show off." Amaliya dug her heel into the ground, flexing her foot slightly. She was agitated by the whole night. She had wanted a nice evening out with Cian, pretending they were actually a couple, and just not the only two vampires in the cabal of Austin that were under constant threat by outside forces. Ever since her arrival in Cian's city, she had been trouble for him. She knew it, he knew it, but they had fallen hard for one another. In a weird way, they were family because The Summoner had created both of them. Incestuous family, she supposed, since they couldn't keep their hands off each other.

Unless she was mad at him. Then she just wanted to punch him.

"You need to practice, Amal. If we're attacked, I need you to be able to protect yourself."

"I killed The Summoner! That has to count for something!"

Cian stared at the daggers at his hands. "Well, it does. But there are greater monsters in the world."

Amaliya barely saw him move, his action was so swift. She ducked, but the blade nicked her as it passed. Blood trickled from her wounded arm as she crouched in the mist, ready for his next move.

"You hit my tattoo!"

"It'll heal." Studying the tip of the remaining dagger, Cian said, "But the point is, I hit you."

"Grazed me. It's just a flesh wound." The blood sluiced down her arm and dripped from her fingers.

"You should be faster than that." Cian's Irish brogue was seeping through his words. He wasn't happy with her.

Amaliya felt like ripping off her shoes and hurling them at him before stomping home. She never asked to be a vampire. She never asked to be a necromancer. Hell, she had never asked to fall in love with him and shack up in Austin. She hated that she was trapped in the city since she had killed The Summoner. Other vampire cabals had a keen interest in her power. With the threat of The Summoner removed, the other powerful vampires were not very happy with the idea of his progeny remaining alive.

"I am fast," Amaliya protested. "I just don't want to be—"

The blade glinted for a second in the moonlight and she flung her hand up before her. The ground around her gave way as a corpse exploded out of the unmarked grave on which she was crouched. The dagger slammed into its chest

CHAPTER ONE

and the very old, decayed body shuddered.

Amaliya reached out and touched the zombie with her bloodied fingers. The mildewed fabric and desiccated form beneath her fingers didn't disgust her as it once would have. She felt an affinity to the dead now. She felt a kinship with them, compassion, almost a sense of belonging. As her blood touched its flesh, the corpse took on a more human appearance. It was an elderly black man. Inclining his head toward her, the zombie awaited her next command.

Standing, Amaliya gripped the dagger and yanked it out of the zombie's chest. "Sorry. Instinct. Didn't mean to awaken you."

The dried orbs that were once eyes, were slowly taking on color. The longer she touched the zombie, the more he would resemble the living. Her blood was life to a zombie. It was the basis of her necromantic power. The Summoner hadn't needed to shed blood to raise the dead, but she did.

"Sleep," she whispered.

The zombie closed its eyes and the grave swallowed him.

Staring at the dagger in her hand, Amaliya felt both sickened and enthralled with her power.

"You could raise the graveyard," Cian said stepping next to her.

"I don't want to pull a *Night of the Living Dead*," Amaliya said in a sad voice.

Tangling his fingers in her long black hair, Cian lifted his chin and pressed a kiss to her forehead. He was an old vampire and at five foot seven they were almost the same height. In heels, she loomed over him.

"You can control them. Don't ever fear you'll end up making flesh-eating zombies. Those only live in movies," Cian assured her.

"But they'll rip someone apart if I command them." Amaliya distinctly remembered commanding the dead to do that several times before.

"You can control the dead. It's your power. No other vampire has such an ability," Cian reminded her. "You must learn to harness it."

Amaliya frowned at his words, the old urge to run away playing havoc with her nerves. When things got too rough in the past, she had always run. That's how she had found Cian after she was made into a vampire. She had fled to Austin and accidentally found him. In many ways, it was the smartest and best thing she had ever done in her life. Yet, at times, she still felt the urge to bolt when reminded of the enormity of her new position in the world of the vampires. She was the inheritor of The Summoner's terrible necromantic power and the right-hand to the Master of Austin.

Like in Bram Stoker's *Dracula*, the vampires in the Americas tended to call themselves masters if they were old enough and powerful enough to carve out some territory of their own. In Europe, Cian said they called themselves king, queen, regent, and even emperor. Amaliya supposed being a 'vampire president' sounded dull. Cian wasn't particularly enthralled with the title of Master of Austin, and he wore it grudgingly.

Years before, in the Seventies, when The Summoner had been playing games in Cian's life, the creator and fledgling agreed to a pact. If Cian became the master over a city, The Summoner would let him be. Cian had usurped the Austin cabal, sold them out to the vampire hunters, and took over the small college town when the hunters had wiped out the resident vampires. He wasn't even particularly ashamed of his actions and had even friended the head vampire hunter, Professor Summerfield.

Amaliya was swiftly learning that Cian was ruthless and didn't really live with any regrets. He did what had to be done and didn't really worry in the aftermath. She lived with constant regrets and envied him. Her biggest regret was ever going on a date with her professor in college, who ended up being The Summoner in disguise. If she hadn't gone on that coffee date chances are she'd still be in college and would have eventually ended up marrying sweet Pete back home in East Texas. At times like these she was haunted by a life she would never have.

"I don't like being the big bad scary necromancer," Amaliya said at last.

Cian brushed his lips over hers. "I know. But you are."

Leaning against him, her fingers settled on his waist. She loved the way his body felt against hers. He had been a slave in the West Indies in the 1600's when he had been made into a vampire. A sparse diet and hard labor had chiseled his body into lean muscle. She, meanwhile, should have lost a few pounds before becoming a vampire. She hated her long waist, wider hips, and short legs. Cian, though, seemed to love every inch of her.

The thought made her blush.

He chuckled in her ear, most likely sensing the flush of her skin and her arousal. The mist drifted around them in big clumps as it slowly dissipated.

Licking his ear, she pressed herself against his body, her fingers sliding under his shirt to glide up over his back.

"We're here to practice," Cian reminded her.

"Fuck practice," Amaliya whispered.

Cian's lips caught hers in a passionate kiss, his hands cradling her face. He made her crazy for him and it scared and thrilled her at the same time. The caress of his hands, the touch of his lips, the teasing of his tongue, all made her want to throw him down on the ground and ride him until they were both screaming.

His cellphone buzzed between them.

Nipping his lips, Amaliya tried to keep his hand from sliding into his jean pocket to get his phone.

"No, no, no," she complained.

He pressed one last hard kiss to her lips, peered at the number curiously, then answered. "May I help you?"

Amaliya frowned as his expression suddenly became quite dangerous.

"Rachoń, this is unexpected." His Irish accent overwhelmed his voice.

Craning her head toward the cellphone, Amaliya listened in.

"Miss me, dear brother?"

CHAPTER ONE

The woman's voice sent shivers through Amaliya's already aroused body. It was like rich velvet; soft and sensual.

"It's been a very long time," Cian said neutrally.

The throaty laughter was amused and a little cruel. "I would have thought you would give me the courtesy of a phone call when our dear little sister murdered our father."

"You know I had no love for The Summoner, or his ways," Cian responded tersely.

"This is true. The relationship between father and son is always complicated, isn't it?"

"He was my creator, not my father."

Amaliya pressed her hand to Cian's chest and he glanced at her briefly. He was struggling with his emotions.

Rachoń's laughter was cruel with its amusement. "You never could run far enough away from him."

"You never tried."

"Maybe that is why I hold Louisiana in my grasp and you merely have Austin."

"You turned your entire family and made them your minions so you could rule Louisiana."

"I freed them from slavery and made them rulers," Rachoń said sharply.

Amaliya smiled. Cian had hit a sore spot.

"We've both done what we had to in order to survive, haven't we, Rachoń?"

"I will give you that." There was a pause in her voice. "I haven't called to argue."

"Then what do you want?"

"To visit you," Rachoń answered.

Cian lifted an eyebrow as Amaliya raised both of hers.

"I see. May I ask why?"

"I want to see our sister. I want to see where our father died. And I want to make a pact with you. I know you have Santos and Etzli stalking your borders. Word is that they are trying to make pacts with Courtney, the new Master in Dallas and Nicole from Houston. You need me."

Frowning, Cian hooked his arm around Amaliya's shoulders and pulled her along with him as he headed toward his car. "I'm not certain—"

"You need me, Cian. We both know it. The only thing holding off Santos is the baby necromancer. He was terrified of The Summoner and that is why he left you alone before. Now there is your new pet. Santos wants her. The only reason he hasn't attacked is because he still doesn't know what she can or can't do. How much longer do you think the threat of her power will hold him off?"

Unlocking the car, Cian glanced up and down the street warily.

Amaliya didn't sense anything, but she wasn't as powerful as Cian. Nervously, she slid into the passenger seat as he took his place behind the wheel.

"Cian?" Rachon's voice sounded small and distant now that Amaliya wasn't snuggled into Cian's arms.

"What do you know?" Cian asked tersely.

"People talk to me. Powerful people. Sometimes they let things slip."

Cian slid into the car, his brow deeply furrowed. "When?"

"Tonight."

"Where?"

"That I don't know."

"We'll talk later," Cian said shortly. He killed the call and shoved his phone into his jeans. "I'll need you to summon the dead over distance."

"What?"

"Can you do it?" His voice was hard and demanding.

Amaliya bit her bottom lip, glancing toward the graveyard. "Yes. I bled in the graveyard tonight. I can do it."

"We're going to be attacked. Most likely close to home. They won't attack here near the graveyard."

"Are we being watched?" Amaliya knew enough not to look around, but remain casual.

"Yes. Probably by a human servant. They're harder to sense." Cian quickly pulled away from the graveyard, speeding down the street.

"Fuckin' great," Amaliya muttered. She tried not to panic as she watched the darkened streets of Austin stream past the window.

"We should have relocated to another part of the city. I usually move once a year, but I didn't want to uproot you so swiftly."

Cian's car sped over the rolling hills along streets lined with old houses and mom and pop businesses toward the shining glory of downtown Austin. The neighborhood was mostly populated by a large section of the black and Hispanic population of the city and was much older and poorer. In recent years it had started to undergo a renewal as the middle class bought up the old houses and restored them. College students also made their homes in the small cottage style homes. The occasional mini-mansion lurked on quiet, tree-lined roads, and a few Victorians were hidden jewels in the neighborhood.

When Amaliya had been human and attended the University of Texas for one year, she had liked hanging out on the east side. It had small dives that served the best food in town and she had often chilled on the front porches of the rented homes of friends. Watching the darkened houses slid by, Amaliya wondered what it was like to sleep during the night, safe in the thought that monsters didn't exist. She couldn't remember what it felt like to be so innocent and human.

The car was a few blocks from I-35 and downtown Austin when a SUV ran a red light. Amaliya only caught a glimpse of its black shape and tinted windows before it crashed into the car, striking Amaliya's door. The impact slammed her sideways as the air bags exploded, punching into her body like a fist. Glass filled the air as the car spun across the intersection, wheels shredding on the asphalt,

CHAPTER ONE

the smell of rubber and gasoline filling the world. The car smashed to a halt against the metal bench of a bus stop.

Chapter Two

Rubbing the stubble on his chin, Santos glanced at his cellphone expectantly. The Master vampire of San Antonio was in a sour mood. He was always short-tempered when anxious. He did not like waiting. Since he was unable to determine what the end result of his carefully laid out plans would be, he was very much on edge. There were too many unknown variables to be certain of anything when it concerned Amaliya, the vampire-necromancer offspring of The Summoner.

His fingers tapped on the heavy wood of his throne-like chair. Seated in the office of his mansion tucked into the hills on the northwest side of San Antonio, he glared at the cellphone one more time. Outside, Tejano music was pumping into the night air as his cabal partied on the enormous patio he had recently installed after making sure to remove all the corpses he had buried under his property. He did not want Amaliya resurrecting his former victims to attack him as she had in the past.

The door to his office opened and Etzli slipped inside. Wearing a pale blue strapless mini-dress and silver high heels, she looked ready for the club scene. Her lush black hair was shiny and artfully curled around her face. Makeup and bronzer gave her the appearance of a living, breathing young woman in her early twenties. In actuality she was hundreds of years old.

"No word yet?"

"Manny hasn't called," Santos said, shrugging.

"Manny is probably dead," Etzli reminded him with a smirk.

Again Santos shrugged. "He was disloyal to me. If he dies tonight, he will be absolved in my eyes."

Etzli walked languidly toward the desk, her hips swaying side to side. She was very aware of her beauty, sensuality, and ability to mesmerize both men and women. Even though they had spent hundreds of years fighting and loving each other, Santos never grew weary of gazing at her. She was the embodiment of the Aztec people. Her blood was pure. His had been tainted by the blood of the Spaniard invaders.

"Manny was just a stupid thug," Etzli decided as she slinked around his desk, her long red nails lightly skimming over the burnished wood.

"I don't like it when other men touch my women. You should know that." Santos gave her a dark look.

The delight in her smile said it all. She loved to make him jealous. The more he rebuffed her, the more seductive she became until he was mad with his passion for her. She was his weakness and he hated that fact. For all he knew she had encouraged Manny to romance the wicked little witch Santos had been sleeping with. It was exactly the sort of thing she would do. In his rage, he had sent Manny and Irma on a suicide run. He was beginning to regret sending Irma, but Manny was expendable. Hopefully, Cian would send Irma back. Cian usually left one person standing to deliver a message to his enemies.

"Do you really think it was wise to send one of your witches?" Etzli asked. She always had the uncanny ability to know what he was thinking. "She was such a dear little thing."

Santos cast a spiteful look in his half-sister's direction. "Let me guess. You were also sleeping with her?"

"She was delicious," Etzli admitted. Her long lashes threw spidery shadows over her face.

Clenching one hand, Santos growled. "Is no one loyal anymore?"

"I am loyal to you always." Sliding behind his chair, Etzli leaned over his shoulder, her hair brushing his cheek and neck. "I just like to play with your toys sometimes."

Santos shifted his weight so he was leaning away from her. "Why are you here?"

"I'm just curious. When you capture Amaliya, will she be your woman?"

"She'll be my minion, my pawn," Santos said tersely. "I never should have let Cian take her from me when I had her."

"She's pretty. Her light eyes are very alluring," Etzli teased.

"I have no interest in her sexually. She has the power to raise the dead. To control them just like he did. That's why I want her."

Though The Summoner was dead, Santos did not dare say his name aloud. His own dealings with the necromancer-turned-vampire had been the stuff of nightmares. In the early 1900's The Summoner had captured and held Etzli prisoner for nearly a year. Santos had traveled across Mexico and Central America searching for his hideout. Once they had found him, Santos and his band of vampires had lain siege to The Summoner's haven inside a ruined temple for many nights, fighting off hordes of zombie humans and animals. At last he had

CHAPTER TWO

managed to fight his way into the temple to find his sister naked, drenched in blood, and surrounded by dead creatures. The Summoner had fled, leaving her behind. He would never forget the vision of her staring up at him, wounds slowly healing on her flesh. In the aftermath of the battle, he had wanted the power The Summoner had wielded so that none would ever dare touch what was his again. That power now dwelled inside of Amaliya, Cian's second, and he would have it.

"It may be many years before you can use her power," Etzli reminded him.

"I can wait. I can be a patient man. I deal with you," he said shortly.

His plan to bring Amaliya under his control was simple. He would drain her of blood, imprison her in a stone casket, and feed her one drop of his blood each night until she was restored and bound to him and his bloodline. He was uncertain of how long it would take to transfer her bond to him, but he was determined to enslave her.

Etzli laughed as she slid one finger slowly down the side of his neck. He batted her hand away like it was an irritating bug. "Cian is not so easy to kill, you know, my dear brother."

"I know." Santos' voice was testy because he knew exactly how hard it would be to kill Cian. He had tried many times before. "But this is about her. I want to know what she can do away from the graveyards. I need to know if she is capable of doing what he did."

Looping her arms over the back of the chair and around his neck, Etzli leaned over him, her hair a fragrant curtain of black silk. "You're so afraid of her."

Santos pushed her arms away. "I do not fear her."

"Yes, you do." Etzli laughed with delight. "You fear her so much you are willing to kill your own people so you can figure out exactly how much you should be afraid of her."

"Be silent!"

"You let her go and now you regret it. Now you have a much bigger battle to wage."

"Stop mocking me."

Etzli ran her hand over his dark hair then slipped away before he could deflect her touch. "You know I will stand by you no matter what foolish thing you may want to do."

"You expect me to ignore the fact that The Summoner's only fledgling to wield his power is eighty miles away? That I could use her to bring all of Texas under my control?"

"No. Of course not." Etzli rested her manicured hands on the desktop and stared at him. "But I don't want to see you be a foolish man in your pursuit of her."

Slapping his hand down on the desk, Santos rose and glared at his half-sibling. "Do not underestimate my power!"

With a simple shrug, she started toward the door.

Rage engulfed him. He clenched his hands at his side, resisting the urge to follow her and strike her for her impudence. Etzli's ability to enrage him made him feel weak.

With a knowing smile, she slipped out the door and shut it behind her. With a frustrated growl, he dropped back into his chair and stared at the cellphone.

Innocente awoke with a start. Her heart thudding in her chest, she stared into the shadows filling her bedroom. Instinctively, she knew she was being watched.

"Who's there?" she asked, her slight Mexican accent edged with a West Texan twang.

When she was younger, she would have assumed it was a ghostly visitor. Her ability to see and speak to the dead drew specters to her, but now she knew that there were much more dangerous creatures that haunted the night. Just a few months before she had helped kill one of the deadliest vampires to walk the earth. Of course, he had killed her granddaughter Amaliya, so he had it coming.

There was no answer, but a presence filled her room.

Drawing her legs up, she curled against her headboard. Her fingers slid under the covers, closing over the rosary she kept under her pillow. Her other hand found her pistol filled with silver bullets, a gift from Jeff, a vampire hunter in Austin.

"Who's there? Answer me!"

Again, no answer, but she knew she was not alone. She sensed someone lurking in the darkness. The darkness in her room was absolute. She couldn't even make out the outlines of her bedroom furniture. The air was heavy and oppressive.

"I'm armed. I will hurt you," she said in a firm voice. Maybe whatever lurked in the darkness thought she was weak because of her advanced years and the gray in her hair, but she would show them otherwise.

"Can you help me?" a voice asked softly.

It sounded child-like, feminine, and frightened.

"Show yourself!" Innocente ordered. Under her covers she slipped the safety off the gun as she wrapped the rosary around the barrel. All her life she had endured the visitations of the dead, but for a few years she had managed to keep them at bay. It was difficult to hide from the ghosts that were seeking help.

"Help me," the voice whispered. "He hurt me."

Innocente tried to swallow the lump in her throat. Her voice slightly rasped as she said, "Show yourself."

The darkness in her room split like a curtain and withdrew to reveal a young woman dressed in a white lace dress with ribbons woven into her white-blond hair. Her enormous blue eyes gazed at Innocente solemnly. Both of her hands were pressed against her throat. Blood gushed over her fingers and ran like red

CHAPTER TWO

ribbons over the silky lace of her dress.

Innocente gasped, startled by the vision. "Who hurt you, sweetie?"

"The Summoner," the girl whispered, her perfectly shaped pink lips barely moving.

"*Dios mio!*" Innocente crossed herself, but kept her hand with the gun and rosary tucked under the covers. "He's dead!"

Red tears stained the girl's cheeks as she held out one bloodstained hand toward Innocente. "He hurt me. Please, help me!"

"How?" Innocente whispered, giving in to the plea. The young woman looked so fragile, so desolate, it tugged at her heartstrings. "How can I help you?"

"Save me from her," the girl's voice was fading. "She wants me to do terrible things."

"Who does, honey?" Innocente's heart was beating faster and faster.

"The woman with the red eyes," the girl wailed.

The room grew colder as the apparition at the end of Innocente's bed wept. Tears streamed down her cheeks.

"Who are you?" Innocente managed to say despite her dry throat and trembling lips.

"Bianca Leduc," the girl answered. "She's going to kill Amaliya."

"No!" Innocente gasped. "No, not my Amal!"

Bianca Leduc's eyes flashed white as the room fell to freezing temperatures. The moisture of Innocente's breath turned to ice on her lips.

"Help me! Before it's too late!" Bianca cried out then the darkness swallowed her. Her departing scream echoed throughout the room.

Innocente cried out in fear, then the lamp next to her bed flashed on. Sergio, her grandson, stood next to her bed clutching a bowl of cereal. Innocente slowly sat up, startled to realize she had dreamed the entire encounter.

"What's up, Grandmama?" Sergio asked, spooning more cereal into his mouth and crunching it loudly.

"I had a nightmare," she answered, pressing her shaking hand to her chest. Her heart was beating wildly in her chest. She flipped over the pillows revealing the rosary and firearm. "It was just a nightmare."

"What about?" Sergio asked, frowning slightly.

Innocente grimaced, the nightmare already beginning to fade. "I'm not sure. There was a girl in it and she needed my help."

Cynthia, Sergio's wife, appeared behind him. She was bleary-eyed, yawning, and looked half-asleep. "Everything okay?"

Since the encounter with The Summoner a few months before, Innocente had been living with Sergio's family. She had hated losing her independence, but now that she understood the true dangers of the supernatural realm she knew she had to be careful. Sergio had moved his family in with her and there had been some difficult adjustments as the house had become a home to all of them. She had reluctantly allowed Cynthia to redecorate the main rooms of the house and send off boxes full of clothes, toys, and other items she had been storing in the extra rooms in her house. Innocente always found it difficult to let go of objects from the past. She loved to feel the energy of her long dead husband and daughter in their old possessions, but she had finally let those old things go.

"Grandmama had a nightmare," Sergio answered his wife.

Cynthia stole his spoon and ate a mouthful of cereal. "I hate nightmares. Especially the ones with clowns."

Innocente stared at the end of the bed, her mind struggling to hold onto the image of the girl she had seen in her dream. There had also been a name said by the apparition in her nightmare, but she had already lost it. "This one had a ghost. A girl. She needed help."

Arching an eyebrow, Cynthia tilted her head. "You mean...a dream."

With a slight nod, Innocente grabbed the notepad she kept next to the bed. With still quivering fingers she wrote down as much of the dream as she could recall. It was fading fast and it aggravated her. She knew the girl's name was important, but it eluded her.

"Grandmama, is this someone we know?" Sergio sat on the edge of her bed. His tall, muscular body made her mattress dip down. He continued to shovel cereal into his mouth as he stared at her with worry.

"No, no. No one I know, but she..." Innocente's hand froze over the notepad as she remembered what the girl had said. "She said The Summoner killed her."

"But we killed him," Sergio said swiftly, his eyes widening.

"There was a lot of blood and then..." Innocente remembered the girl's eyes flashing completely white just before she had vanished. "I think Amaliya is in danger. We need to call her!"

"I'll get the phone," Cynthia said and rushed out of the room, her long blue bathrobe flowing out behind her like a cape.

"It'll be okay, Grandmama," Sergio said in a comforting tone.

Innocente drew the covers up around her chest as she shook her head. "Something is wrong, Sergio." The dream had been a warning, but she had been too afraid to remember the details. She was angry at her failure.

Cynthia returned with Sergio's cellphone and thrust it at him. He handed over the empty bowl, then dialed his cousin's phone number. As he listened to the phone ring on the other end, he reached out and laid his big hand over Innocente's. He gave her an encouraging smile even though the worry lines around his eyes had deepened.

"Amal, it's Sergio. Call me. We're worried about you," he said at last.

"Voicemail," Cynthia sighed, leaning against the door jamb. Though she had not been a part of the events a few months earlier, she believed the wild story her husband had told her once she met Cian and Amaliya. Cynthia was quite matter of fact about most things in life and had adapted faster than Innocente thought she would. Sergio had married a remarkable woman.

"Maybe they're...uh...hunting," Sergio suggested.

CHAPTER TWO

"Or other things," Cynthia added, a sly smile on her lips.

Innocente pulled her rosary from under her pillow and held it gently in her hand. The pink faceted beads glittered in the lamp light. Reverently touching the crucifix, she sent a silent prayer up to the heavens.

"No, no," she said at last. "Something is wrong." Shoving off her covers, she swung her legs over the edge of the bed. "I might as well get up. I won't sleep until I hear from her."

"She's fine," Sergio assured his grandmother.

Innocente tried not to let tears spring into her eyes. She knew Sergio was wrong. Amaliya was not fine. She felt it to the marrow of her bones.

CHAPTER THREE

Amaliya's face pulsed in pain and her left arm felt broken. The door was lodged into her side and her crushed ribs were in agony. Blood streamed down her face as she attempted to free herself from the seatbelt digging into her torso. White powder filled the air and burned her nostrils. Blinking the blood from her eyes, she glanced at Cian. The driver's side window was shattered from the impact of his head striking the glass and blood covered his face.

"Get ready," he ordered, his voice ragged as he pulled his seatbelt off.

Amaliya's veins burned as she willed herself to heal. The buckle finally popped free and she slid out of the seatbelt. Gasping at the pain, she dragged herself out of the car through the broken windshield. Bits of glass pressed into her palms as she crawled onto the buckled hood of the car.

The first thing she noticed was the silence. The sounds of the city were gone. Not even the whistling of the wind slipping through the branches of the trees was audible. Twisting around on her hip, she saw the SUV was crumpled against a utility pole. Two men were slowly stirring inside. They appeared as stunned as Amaliya and Cian.

What concerned her more than the men in the SUV was the tiny Hispanic girl standing under a street light with both arms lifted upwards. A miasma of purple and black smoke wound around her hands like writhing serpents. Dressed in jeans and a tank top, the girl looked like any other teenager, but the power pulsing out of her was terrifying. Her dark eyes watched Amaliya from beneath her straight bangs and her hair was gathered into two small buns on either side of her head. Her full lips were turned up in a cruel smile.

Cian pulled himself through his broken window.

"It's an—"

His body jerked and fell out of sight as he was peppered with bullets.

Amaliya slid off the hood and crouched alongside the car, hiding from the gunman. "Cian!"

"Stay down!" With surprising speed, he crawled around the car to join her. His flesh expelled the bullets, the tiny bits of metal clinking as they fell to the street. "I'm here. Fuck, silver. Burns like a bitch."

"Come out and play," the girl's voice called out and she giggled.

"They brought a witch. Fuck." Cian shook his head, aggravated. He handed Amaliya a dagger. "Strike to kill. No mercy." He was already weakened from healing himself from the accident and now even weaker after healing from the silver bullets. Which was probably exactly what their attackers wanted.

"Why isn't there any sound?" Amaliya asked, fear strangling her throat.

"Magic. She has us in a bubble. It will keep all the humans away from here, which is a good thing. They don't need to witness what is about to happen."

"Which is?" Amaliya asked fearfully.

"Us killing them."

The crumpled car rose into the air before being tossed up the street. Amaliya cried out in surprise. A slim Hispanic man in jeans, a leather jacket, and cowboy boots grinned as he raised his weapon and aimed. Cian leaped to his feet and ducked away from the barrage of gunfire aimed at him. Scrambling to follow, Amaliya grunted as a massive form erupted from the shadows and tackled her to the ground. The big man straddled her, pinning her to the asphalt.

A meaty fist hit her twice before she managed to grab the thick wrist of her assailant. The big beefy face of one of Santo's men glared down at her. She recognized him from her captivity months before. He was wearing another ugly yellow shirt and his shaved head gleamed in the light from the streetlamp. This was the same asshole who had beat the living hell out of her a few months before.

"What's up, chica?" He hit her with his other huge fist and she lost her grip on his wrist. Grabbing her top, he dragged her upward. Bringing his head down, he head butted her.

Amaliya literally saw stars.

The big man chuckled as she reeled from his blow, one hand drawing out silver shackles from his jeans. "Time to go meet your new master."

"Fuck you!"

Before he could capture her wrist, Amaliya shoved the silver-edged dagger into his thick neck. Gasping, he clutched his throat. Amaliya planted her heels on his chest and kicked him off her. Rolling away, she hurriedly clambered to her feet.

Nearby, Santos's other goon was continuing to fire at Cian. Cian dodged the bullets, moving closer to the attacker.

Meanwhile, the witch continued to maintain the spell that was keeping the human world from seeing the battle as her cold dark eyes watched. "Kill him!" she shouted. "Hurry up and kill him! We need to get the girl!"

Cian was a streak in the night. Amaliya knew he was burning up his power.

CHAPTER THREE

Very soon he'd weaken and be deranged with the hunger. Cian reached the gunman, knocked the firearm from his hand, and hurled him into the SUV. The impact of the man's body caved in the side of the vehicle. Cian stalked after him, kicking away the gun that had fallen from the man's hand.

Amaliya heard a scuffling noise and quickly turned to see the bald guy getting to his feet. He had dragged the blade out of his throat and now held the dagger at his side.

"Nice move, *puta*. Now I got your weapon. Let's see what else you got," he said, grinning. His bloodied teeth and fangs glimmered.

Despite the fear clawing its way up and out of her chest, Amaliya stepped into a defensive position. "Bring it, Pikachu."

"Not such a badass away from the graveyard, are you, bitch?"

Amaliya shrugged. "You shouldn't count on that." She reached down within herself and found the core of her power. Slowly she began to feed it with the remaining blood in her veins, unwinding it.

It took all her willpower not to look behind her and check on Cian. She had to trust him to take care of himself.

The big vampire in the blood-stained yellow shirt smirked as he pulled out a pistol and aimed it at her. "Too easy," he said.

As his finger squeezed the trigger, Amaliya unleashed her power. It sliced out like icy razors, filling the world around her. A cold wind swirled around her as she felt the dead reach out to her, answering her call. It only took a fraction of a second for her to ensnare them and pull them to her along the pulsing waves of her power, drawing them through the earth to her side.

Just before the first bullet was about to puncture her chest, the dead exploded out of the street. Bullets punched into their bodies as Amaliya was enveloped by the throng of the corpses.

The witch screamed in terror.

The hulking vampire gasped. "What the fuck?"

"Surprise, asshole." Amaliya sent the dead after the big vampire in the ugly yellow shirt, urging them to kill him.

The vampire howled, his pistol firing until it clicked empty. "No fucking way!"

Dry, shrunken bodies, moldering clothes, and ratty hair filled her vision as she pushed her way through the zombies. She wanted to reach Cian, but she had summoned more dead than she realized. As she passed by her minions, they touched her reverently, her bloodied flesh infusing them with more life. The big bald vampire screeched in terror, fighting the corpses. Amaliya felt her zombies being torn apart through her connection with them. The vampire was physically more powerful than the zombies. Turning, she reached out and grabbed two of the nearest corpses with her bloody hands. She poured her power into them, and through them into their brethren.

"Kill him," she ordered.

The empowered zombies surged forward.

Weaving her way through the throng of dead, she finally reached the outer edges the horde. Cian stood over the remains of the other attacker. There was pride in Cian's eyes as he surveyed the mass of dead attacking Santo's minion. Covered in blood, his eyes were bright red with hunger. He was ghastly pale and his face was thinned out to the point where he resembled her zombies. He needed to feed soon.

The witch stared in horror at the crowd of zombies ripping into her companion. Her hands shook and sweat poured down her face. Afraid, she began to pull her hands down to her sides.

"Don't you dare drop the spell," Cian said to the girl.

"Fuck you," the witch answered.

Amaliya could feel the witch withdrawing her magic. To her surprise, she felt it tangling with her own necromantic power. Curiosity gripping her, Amaliya closed her eyes and reached out with her supernatural senses to feel the edges of the spell. The magic must have been based on blood or death, because the spell began to absorb into her power. With a grin, Amaliya wrenched the spell away from the witch. Instantly, the purplish manifestation of the witch's power vanished from her hands. It reappeared, swirling around Amaliya's head like a dark halo.

"What the fuck?!" the witch cried out.

"I have it," Amaliya said to Cian. To her amazement, she was able to hold it in place. "I have the spell!"

The witch gasped, her hands falling to her side. Her arrogance was gone as the precariousness of her situation registered. The screams of the bald-headed vampire faded as the sounds of tearing flesh and crunching bones took their place. The corpses were tearing him to little bits.

"Santos sent weaklings to test us," Cian said, scorn in his voice.

The witch suddenly lashed out with one hand, a ball of black energy hurtling toward Amaliya. Amaliya immediately summoned her dead. A zombie erupted from the earth to absorb the blast. Amaliya felt the creature shudder, but it did not fall.

"She can't hurt me! Her magic is full of death and blood. It's mine!" Amaliya said triumphantly.

The witch paled, her breath ragged.

"Then she's not necessary anymore," Cian decided.

The horde of zombies gathered around Amaliya, filling the intersection as she stared at the witch facing her.

The girl's eyes flashed toward Cian, then back at Amaliya. "Send me back to Santos. I'll tell him whatever you want," the witch said at last. "I'll deliver your message."

Cian shook his head. "Unnecessary."

The witch spun about to run, but Amaliya unleashed her power and four

CHAPTER THREE

zombies burst from the street to block the witch's path.

"Don't let her through the spell protecting this area," Cian ordered.

"I have her." Amaliya said confidently. She was flushed with power and laughed with delight. She could feel the magic around her building, growing stronger. Her zombies were looking more human as they clustered around her.

"Let me go!" the witch screamed. Drawing a pistol from the waistband of her jeans, she aimed it at Amaliya. "You let me go, you stupid bitch!"

The four zombies behind the witch seized her, holding her securely. Cian drew close enough to slap the gun out of her hand. Amaliya heard the girl's wrist shatter. The girl screeched in pain.

"What are you going to do with her?" Amaliya asked.

Cian grabbed the girl by her hair, wrenched her head to one side, and bit into her throat.

Startled, Amaliya watched Cian drain the teenage girl as she flailed against him. For a second she considered rushing in to help the girl, but instead turned away. There was nothing she could do for the witch. It was too late for her.

The zombies gently touched Amaliya's body as she walked among them. Each drop of blood imbued them with more life. Yet, they were the empty shells of people long gone. There were no souls inside the bodies, but there were memories. She could feel the whispers of who the zombies once were. The lost hopes and dreams brought tears to her eyes.

Finally, she reached the blood-soaked area where the vampire had died. Only a few scraps of material remained. Stepping into the center of the puddle, she closed her eyes. Her vampire nature called to the blood of the vampire. It took only a few seconds for her to feel the tickling sensation of rivulets of blood sliding up over her heels to touch her skin and absorb into her flesh. Within a minute all of the vampire's blood and what remained of his power was hers. Opening her eyes, she saw the zombies reverently gathered around her. They clutched bits of the vampire's body.

"You did a good job," Amaliya said to them.

The one nearest her was the older black gentleman she had summoned in the cemetery earlier in the night. As her power renewed the corpses, she saw most of them were also black, dressed in the tattered remains of their Sunday best. Touching the cheek of the old man, she said, "Rest now."

Instantly, the corpses sank into the street, vanishing.

The road seemed strangely empty with the zombies gone.

She almost missed them.

Cian tossed the corpse of the witch into the back of the ruined SUV. He shoved the other vampire in after her, then pulled the SUV with one hand down the road. Amaliya ran after him.

"Cian, what are we doing?"

"Hiding this until we can deal with it properly." Cian shoved the vehicle into an alley. The metal groaned as he rammed it into a dark patch away from the street lights."

"And how do we do that?" Amaliya asked.

"We call Jeff." Cian flashed a quick smile at her before striding back into the street to retrieve the car. He was flushed with the blood of the witch and was completely revitalized. Amaliya was relieved to see him looking normal, but slightly disconcerted.

"You drank the witch's blood. What will it do to you?" Amaliya retrieved her purse from the car before Cian began scooting it up the road. She rifled through it, making sure she had all her things. Her cellphone was broken, the face shattered. "Crap."

"Well, a few things." Cian easily pushed the car around into the alley. It was like he was handling a grocery cart. Amaliya rarely saw him use all his power. It was rather intimidating, but exciting.

"Like?" She frowned, looking at him worriedly.

"A black witch's blood can make a vampire a bit more powerful for a short period of time."

"If it was death magic, can't it hurt you?"

"Darling," Cian said, flashing a grin. "You forget. I'm already dead." He set the car on its side and pushed it up against the SUV.

Rolling her eyes, Amaliya shook her head. "Lame."

"There is one other effect it has," Cian said, drawing close to her, the lines in his face becoming somber.

"What?" She hated the way her voice cracked, but she couldn't help but worry.

"It makes a vampire incredibly horny."

Snatching her up around the waist, he shoved her up against the back of a building and kissed her deeply. It was the sort of kiss that rendered her helpless in his arms and lasted so long she was glad she didn't need to breathe.

When they parted, he grinned at her. "Now, lower the spell so we can go home. I need to make some calls, then ravish you."

Flushed with desire, Amaliya nodded. She drew in her power, feeling it coil inside of her, cold, dark, and glittering. It felt stronger than before, more feral. It made her shudder.

The spell came with it, a new sensation as it faded away into her flesh.

The world was suddenly full of sound again.

Amaliya peeked out into the road to see that cars had been turning along side streets to avoid the intersection. A few more turned before the spell completely collapsed, and then the through traffic began again.

"They didn't understand why they had a sudden aversion to taking this road," Cian explained in her ear.

"Because of the spell?"

"Yes."

"Why don't we have a witch?" Amaliya frowned at him.

CHAPTER THREE

"They're rare and hard to find," Cian answered. "Come along. Time to go home." He tugged on her hand, walked into the shadows, and Amaliya felt herself dissolve into nothing.

Chapter Four

Etzli watched Gregorio, one of Santo's many human minions slip out of her brother's home office. It had been several hours since Manny and his ill-fated crew had left for Austin. Only Gregorio had returned. Standing in the shadows of the hallway, she beckoned to him as the door to the study shut. The man's dark eyes brightened at the sight of her.

With a flirtatious tilt of her head, she strolled along the hallway confident that he would follow. She did not stop until she reached her spacious room tucked on the far side of the mansion. Slipping inside, she waited for Gregorio to enter, then shut the door. Unlike the rest of the mansion that was full of Mexican antiques, Etzli's rooms were very modern. There was no dash of bright color anywhere in the tranquil whiteness of the furniture. She stood out starkly against the backdrop of her room, vibrant and beautiful with her dark skin, eyes, and tresses.

"What did you see?" she asked, her fingers lightly playing with the tips of her hair curling over the swell of her breasts.

It was difficult for the craggy-faced older man to tear his eyes from her fingers and cleavage. "I saw the girl bring the dead up out of the street. They were not near any cemetery."

"Ah," Etzli said thoughtfully. "So she can wield her power like The Summoner did. What else?"

"They killed Manny, Art, and Irma." Gregorio dared to take a step toward her. He was hungry for her touch. Her bite was an addiction and she used it to her benefit.

She lightly rebuffed him, enjoying his desperate need. Slowly, she pivoted on her heel and walked to the divan set before the high windows that let in the bright moonlight. Perching herself on the end, she motioned to Gregorio. He instantly followed, fell to his knees, and bowed his head.

"What else did you see?" she asked, her voice a soft purr.

"She took Irma's power from her. I saw it happen. It came to her and wrapped around her," Gregorio whispered.

"Did you tell Santos?"

Gregorio shook his head. "No, I only told him the basics as you instructed."

Her long nails combed through his slick black hair that was laced with gray. "You please me."

"I only wish to serve you."

Extracting her cellphone from her cleavage, Etzli continued to stroke the man's hair. He melted into her touch, his mind drifting in her power. She punched in the numbers manually, remembering them by heart. It was only a matter of seconds before Rachoń answered.

"Cian will be calling you," Etzli said, not bothering with the niceties of conversation.

"And Santos?"

"He's afraid. She can raise the dead away from the graveyards." Etzli couldn't help but smile. "She's everything we feared. She even stole away the black witch's death magic so Cian could drain her. Santos didn't like that, but it will teach him to be more careful with his assets."

"Excellent," Rachoń answered and hung up.

Etzli tightened her grip on Gregorio and yanked him up to her waiting mouth. Biting deeply, she drank in celebration.

Cian listened to the mortal's voice in his ear, rubbing his chin as he watched Amaliya stalking around the loft apartment. She was agitated and it showed. She was energized with the death magic she had absorbed and he could feel it cackling around her as she moved. At the same time, she was terribly afraid. Sweeping her dark hair back from her face with shaking hands, she gave him a wary look.

He shrugged and gave her a slight smile.

"I had the bodies removed. The vampire will burn in the sun, so he's not a problem. But the witch is," Jeff, the local vampire hunter, was saying.

"I didn't leave marks on her," Cian assured him.

"I noticed. But what do you want me to do with it? I handle vamps, not witches. That was our agreement." Jeff was aggravated. His tone was clipped and slightly confrontational. He had been surly when Cian had woken him up and told him about the attack; now he was worse.

Resting his feet up on the edge of his desk, Cian leaned back in his chair. "Can Eduardo move the SUV to the outskirts of San Antonio? We can leave her on a remote road and tell Santos where to find her."

CHAPTER FOUR

Sighing wearily, Jeff answered, "Yeah. He can do that. But he'll want payment."

"I'll pay whatever he wants."

"Your car is toast, you know. Gone."

"I'll report it as stolen. They'll think vandals got to it."

There was a long pause. "Cian, I'm not your henchman."

The vampire had been waiting for that comment throughout the conversation. He was ready for it and said in a very firm, but gentle tone, "You agreed to help me keep the city in order just like your father did."

Another long pause lingered on the other end of the phone.

Cian expected that, too. Other than The Summoner, Jeff had truly never dealt with the dangerous aspects of the supernatural. He was well-read on the subject, but most of his dealings with otherworldly creatures had to do with incorporeal creatures, like ghosts and demons. Cian liked Jeff, but he wasn't about to let the so-called vampire hunter off the hook. If Jeff wanted to live in Cian's city, he would have to face the truth. The supernatural realm was dangerous and deadly, and Jeff was already tied to it.

As if Jeff was reading his mind, the mortal said, "Things are getting more dangerous now, aren't they?"

"Yes," Cian answered simply.

"You do realize most hunters don't play nice with vampires."

"You do realize most vampires don't allow hunters to live."

"Touché," Jeff grumbled.

"Jeff, your father and I kept Austin safe from a lot of very dangerous creatures over the last thirty years. We worked very well together. That is why you don't have to spend your days trying to figure out where the latest nasty is hiding while trying to determine the best way to kill it. We kept the city clean. So you get to have a nice bookstore, go on ghost hunts, and occasionally deal with an ornery spirit. You also get to date my ex-girlfriend, who I would truly like to see live a long and peaceful life. If you're going to live in my city and muddle in the affairs of the supernatural realm, then you had best realize that working with me is your best chance of survival. Otherwise, I'll ship you off somewhere else with your merry band of hunters and deal with this myself. Santos and Etzli are brutal killers and it was only a matter of time before they made their move. Do you understand?" His Irish brogue was thick and he felt both irritated and weary of the conversation already.

Jeff was very quiet on the other end, but Cian could hear him breathing.

"Time to stop playing vampire hunter and become one, Jeff."

There was a long exhalation before Jeff answered. "You're right. I'm just..."

"Scared shitless?" Cian offered.

Jeff laughed. "Yeah, exactly."

Amaliya stomped past Cian again, puffing away on a cigarette. Cian's gaze tracked after her. Her dark looks mirrored his feelings on the situation.

"I have one more thing to tell you," Cian said.

Jeff sighed. "Hit me with it."

"Rachoń from New Orleans will be visiting the city."

"Are you shitting me?" Jeff's voice raised an octave.

"No, I'm not. She may be my best chance to hold off Santos and Etzli."

"Or she might be coming to kill you. She was The Summoner's favorite!"

"I am aware of all that."

Jeff exhaled angrily. "So what do you need from me?"

"We'll talk tomorrow."

"Fine. Where?"

"Your shop. Midnight. Bring your crew."

"Fine."

"I'll see you tomorrow then," Cian said.

"You're a real dick," Jeff grumbled.

"Yeah. It comes with being a vampire." Cian hung up.

Amaliya stalked past him. "She's coming to kill us, Cian."

"We can't know that."

"She's up to no fucking good. Did you hear the fear in Jeff's voice?"

"Jeff is an unproven hunter. He has yet to make his first kill. He's going to be afraid of anything with fangs right now," Cian answered, shrugging.

"Rachoń loved The Summoner. She loved him, Cian! If someone killed you, I would fuckin' rip their gawddamn head off and shove it up their ass."

Cian chuckled. "Nice to know you love me that much."

Amaliya angrily stubbed out her cigarette. "My point is that she's going to want our heads. You can't let her visit!"

"We need her," Cian said, shrugging.

Amaliya leaned over him, gripping the armrests of his chair and glared at him. "Don't be stupid."

Cian couldn't help but observe the swell of her breasts. He didn't want to deal with the business of ruling Austin. He wanted to ravish her.

"Ugh! Stop staring at my boobs!" Amaliya covered her cleavage with one hand and swerved away from him.

Grinning, Cian watched her storm off. "I have important calls to make. Do you mind not stalking around so loudly?"?"

Amaliya kicked off her heels, aiming them in his direction. One sailed over his head, the other nicked one of his computer monitors, toppling it. Cian just smirked as she stormed around him barefooted.

"My phone is toast! I need a new one. Make Santos pay for it!"

"I'm calling Rachoń first." Cian dialed his blood sister's number.

Rachoń answered after a few rings. "Ah, you're alive." She didn't sound surprised, but also not necessarily pleased.

"He sent weak henchmen. It wasn't much of a threat."

"She raised the dead far from any cemetery. How did she do that?" Rachoń

CHAPTER FOUR

asked.

"Santos had someone spying on us, I see," Cian said, not surprised at all.

"Of course. It was a test after all. Now he knows she's dangerous even away from the usual stomping grounds of the dead. Next time he attacks, it won't be his weakest fledglings. He is aggravated about the witch though. Witches are so hard to come by."

"Then he shouldn't have sent her."

"You used to always leave one person standing to deliver your nicely worded messages," Rachoń said, her tone mocking.

"I didn't feel charitable tonight. Plus, I was a bit hungry."

Rachoń laughed heartily. "Ah, maybe you did learn something from The Summoner after all. Now about that visit..."

"You may bring two of your people with you. No more." Cian's tone was brisk, hard, and non-relenting. He knew how to deal with Rachoń. It was best to not allow her an inch from the beginning.

"Just two?" Rachoń sounded annoyed.

"My cabal is small. Two should be sufficient."

"I'll think about it."

"You do that. I'll call you tomorrow to negotiate the terms of your visit," Cian finally said.

"Excellent." Rachoń's voice was cautious. "Until tomorrow."

Terminating the call, Cian stared through the windows toward the state capitol building.

"Are we fucked?" Amaliya asked, her hands on her hips.

"Not yet." Cian tapped the cellphone against his chin. "But Rachoń is up to something."

"Of course she is. She fucking hates our guts! We killed The Summoner!"

"It's something more than that. If she wanted revenge, she would have moved against us by now." Cian frowned, sorting through the knowledge he had of Rachoń and his past dealings with her. "I wish I could figure out what she wants."

Clutching her hair in tight fists, Amaliya growled. "Fuck! We should just run!"

"We'll be fine."

"There are only two of us, Cian!"

"We will be fine, Liya," Cian said firmly.

"But she's dangerous, right?"

"Absolutely."

"How dangerous is she?"

"As dangerous as I am," Cian answered.

"Which means?"

"We're very close to being fucked," Cian admitted.

"Well, shit," Amaliya sighed.

"Come here," Cian said, holding out his hand.

With a frustrated sound, Amaliya slid into his arms. Tucking her head against his neck, she curled up, her feet resting on the armrest.

"We're going to die, aren't we, Cian?"

"Maybe. But not without a fight. We're both powerful. We have the hunters on our side, too."

"They've never killed anything before, Cian."

"No, but I do think they can rise to the occasion."

"Rachoń is coming to kill us. We both know it."

Amaliya's lips were soft against his neck and he slowly stroked her long hair. Cian wasn't sure of Rachoń's motives and he was sure that attempting to kill both of them was not out of the realm of possibility, but she tended to maneuver in ways that were mystifying.

"You're a badass necromancer that can call zombie hordes to your side in an instant," Cian reminded her.

"Yeah, if I spilled blood in the cemetery the same night."

"We'll deal with Rachoń, then deal with Santos and Etzli."

"And live happily ever after?"

"Of course." Cian grinned at her. "What else will we do?"

"Die horrible deaths."

"Pessimist." Cian kissed her soft lips lovingly.

"Realist," she answered.

"Badass," he whispered against her lips. Sliding his hand up under her shirt to rest against the small of her back, he said, "Now, to finish this night properly..."

The fear in her voice faded, replaced by desire. "Yes, please."

Cian pressed her lips to hers and set aside his worries for another night.

CHAPTER FIVE

Rachoń set her cellphone down on the battered kitchen table. A soft breeze ruffled the curtains over the kitchen sink and brushed against her cheek. The checkered dish towels, cracked black and white vinyl floor, and decor heralded back to another era. Rachoń's mother had rather liked the Forties and Fifties and kept the house suspended in time. Her mother, known to everyone as Mother Delia, was in the living room watching the late night talk shows with Prosper.

Outside, children played in the moonlight, their squeals and laughter mingling with the boisterous voices of her neighbors. The Sullivans were having a family reunion that was running late into the night. The smell of the crawfish boil turned her stomach, but she rather enjoyed the sounds of the party. The music made her sway a little as she stood contemplating her conversation with Cian.

When Etzli told her that Santos planned to test Amaliya's power, Rachoń thought it was a foolhardy move, but not unexpected. Santos wanted Amaliya for himself, but he'd have to find a way to capture her. Testing her powers was the best way to determine the woman's weaknesses and determine the best plan to acquire her from Cian. Of course, this meant killing Cian, but Rachoń knew from experience the Irishman would not die easily. He was stronger, older, and more resourceful than most of the vampires in North America.

As Rachoń walked through the kitchen, the floorboards creaked under her feet. She would have to replace the floors soon and have the foundation checked. The old house was a money pit, but her mother loved it. Prosper hated that she and her mother lived among the poor. Prosper lived in the elegance and wealth of the French Quarter along with his brothers. Rachoń couldn't bear to leave the old neighborhood behind until she had to. She loved the sense of community, the beauty of the people, and the strength of will of those who had to work even harder for the simple pleasures of life. She kept her corner of the neighborhood free of crime as payment for the joy she received from watching the people who inhabited the homes around her living their daily existence. Besides, her mother hated being uprooted, so it was easier to alter the memories of her neighbors than actually upset the older woman.

The small house was tucked along the northern edge of the Ninth Ward in New Orleans. It was a simple white clapboard bungalow with a nice big porch surrounded by her mother's lush landscaping. Her mother loved to putter around outside at all hours of the day. The house had survived the terrible wrath of Hurricane Katarina only because of the massive magical wards Rachoń had placed on the property over the course of the previous century. The neighborhood had suffered massive losses though. She'd secretly funded the reconstruction of many of the homes through a dummy foundation. Sadly, there were still destroyed homes slowly rotting away on abandoned lots.

The neighbors thought Rachoń was an artist, living odd hours, struggling to make it big. She sometimes chatted with them, but not very often. They could sense there was something off about her, something not quite right. Rachoń had vivid memories of the many times she had been hunted by her owner's henchmen and by vampire hunters; therefore she tried to keep a low profile.

"Mama, I'm going to check on the girl," she said as she walked into the living room.

Her mother leaned over the arm of her leather recliner, the only new piece of furniture in the house for the last twenty years. The older woman was very tiny, with a delicate face and slim frame. She had been a house slave before Rachoń had rescued her. She had pale green eyes, light brown skin, and her white hair was twisted into a bun on top of her head. Rachoń's father had been black as night with maroon eyes just like his daughter. He had died before she had rescued her family and burned the plantation.

"She's such a quiet thing. I keep forgetting she is back there," her mother admitted.

Prosper grunted at something funny on the TV, not really paying attention to their chat.

"I just want to make sure she's okay." Rachoń pressed her hand against her mother's cheek, feeling the soft warmth of her skin. Her mother had refused to become a vampire, but had agreed to take sips of Rachoń's blood to extend her life. Delia was very devout in her faith and afraid of losing her soul if she became a vampire. She prayed faithfully at church every day for her vampiric family. Rachoń often wondered if God was listening.

"Oh, that girl isn't okay, but she's quiet. So it's all good." Her mother snuggled her face into Rachoń's hand as she raised her own arthritic hand to touch her daughter's fingers.

CHAPTER FIVE

"You tired yet?" Rachoń asked, smiling as her mother kissed her palm.

"No, no. Don't need sleep yet. Besides, that wild party next door won't let me sleep. But they did have some good crawfish earlier. Mmmm..." her mother grinned.

Rachoń lovingly kissed Delia's cheek.

"Rachoń, let's make Rhianna into a vampire," Prosper said from the sofa, grinning.

"Let's not," Rachoń answered.

"Always ruining my fun..."

Delia laughed and playfully slapped his knee. "Always on the prowl for a pretty girl."

"I got a pretty girl right here," Prosper answered, resting his big hand over hers.

"Oh, you're such a liar!"

Rachoń left them to their TV watching and banter. She slipped down the hallway to the room in the back of the house. The walls of the hall were covered with framed charcoal sketches of the family throughout the years. The faces of her cousins, aunts, and uncles were carefully captured with the sure strokes of a charcoal pencil. Over a century and a half of the same faces caught in various eras were lovingly recreated by her mother's hand. Digital photos were framed and carefully arranged in one area of the wall, but they weren't as remarkable or touching as the sketches.

Pushing the door open to the small bedroom, she peeked in at the young woman seated on the floor, her hands in her lap, staring at the TV.

"How are we doing, Bianca?"

As always, the pale vampire just stared at the screen blindly. She rarely showed an inclination to do anything other than to gaze into nothingness except for when Rachoń opened a vein. Then she would mew like a baby and latch onto Rachoń's wrist until she was sated. Though Bianca's eyes never revealed any sign of comprehension when Rachoń spoke to her, the girl had to understand her commands to bring forth the dead. Without fail, every time Rachoń took Bianca into one of the many graveyards around New Orleans, the girl would summon the dead per Rachoń's request. Yet, she never responded to any other order, never revealed a smidge of awareness, and never said a single word.

Rachoń knelt beside the girl, her fingers tracing over the silky, baby-fine white blond waves. Prosper bought her lacy, frothy dresses and Delia put ribbons in her hair. Maybe they did it because they thought of Bianca as doll-like. Bianca was beautiful and delicate, like a perfect human-sized doll.

Staring into the blue eyes of the girl, Rachoń lightly stroked her cheek. "Pretty girl, how would you like to go to meet our brother and your new sister?"

Bianca didn't blink, didn't move, and didn't do anything other than stare.

Kneeling, Rachoń gently took the girl's white hand between her much darker ones. "I have to obey the last order of our creator. His last edict. But I need you

33

to do exactly what I say, can you do that?"

Not a twitch, not a flutter of the eyelashes, nothing.

"Why do you try? She doesn't understand you," Prosper asked from the doorway. His huge body filled the frame.

Rachoń shrugged. "I don't want her to lose her shit when we travel to Austin."

"I think you're developing a soft spot for her."

"Shut your face," Rachoń scowled, standing.

Prosper's grin only widened. "You're one of the most ruthless, bad ass, evil muthafuckin' vampires in the South, and yet you can be sweet as pie when you want to be."

Rachoń placed her hands on her hips and lifted her chin. "I do what I have to do to keep us all safe. To keep us in power."

"I hate that you still serve that pasty nasty master even after he's dead." Prosper shook his head.

Eyes narrowing dangerously, she pointed a finger at her cousin. "If not for him, we would not be here. You wouldn't be what you are, living your grand life. So shut your fucking face."

"You still love him, huh?"

Rachoń sighed, slightly shaking her head. "He was my master. My lover. My salvation. I loved him and hated him."

"You two were always fucked up."

"Yeah, but now he's gone. I at least owe it to him to do as he wished."

Prosper shrugged dismissively. "What are we doing when we go to Austin? Going to kill Cian and that new bitch?"

Rachoń glanced down at Bianca. The young woman was watching the flickering images on the old TV again.

"I have to take care of one last task for The Summoner."

"If you kill them, I ain't taking Austin. I hate Texas. You know, in a way they did you a favor," Prosper said, his voice almost timid.

Narrowing her eyes, Rachoń fought down the swift anger that filled her and fought the urge to punish Prosper for his impudence. Her long fingers flexed, the need for violence making them tingle.

Ducking his head in subservience, Prosper stood cowed before her.

"Don't speak ill of the dead," she said at last, blinking her eyes so the heat in them would fade.

"Forgive me," Prosper murmured.

"You may hate him, but I loved him." And she'd feared him. Maybe that had been part of the allure of The Summoner. She had courted death and found love in his arms. The swath of destruction they had left in their wake when she had liberated her family had been glorious. She still remembered how the flames engulfing the plantation mansion had reflected in the fresh blood covering their bodies.

Crouching next to Bianca again, she stared at the pale creature thoughtfully.

CHAPTER FIVE

"Maybe he made her because she looks a little like him," Rachoń said.

"Pasty," Prosper agreed.

Rachoń swept the whitish hair away from the lovely face. "Ghostly."

Bianca turned her blue eyes toward Rachoń. For a moment, Rachoń thought she saw a sliver of clarity in their depths, then it was gone in the blankness of her stare. Slicing open her wrist with one long fingernail, Rachoń watched the girl's face. It did not alter as the girl gripped her arm and fed.

"You should have killed her, you know," Prosper sighed, shaking his head. "She's brain dead."

Tenderly stroking the girl's hair, Rachoń just smiled slightly. "No, no, she's much more than that. She's his power incarnate. She's now an extension of me. She gives me power as I give her life."

With a grunt, Prosper wandered back down the hall to the living room.

Pressing a kiss to the silent girl's head, Rachoń whispered, "We will do great things together, won't we, my little ghost?"

Part Two

Saturday

CHAPTER SIX

The sun was barely a sliver of gold over the tops of the trees and it was gearing up to be an exhaustingly warm day. Despite the early hour, the humidity was already thick and gross against her skin.

Samantha jogged at a steady pace, keeping to the path that wound around Lady Bird Lake (formerly known as Lake Travis) in the shadow of downtown Austin. The new high rise buildings were close to completion and she still couldn't get used to the radically changed skyline. Austin was growing in leaps and bounds, much to the disgust of her family.

Austin was once a small college town with a quirky personality. Now it was a burgeoning metropolis with an identity crisis. Keep Austin Weird bumper stickers and t-shirts had been common for years, but Samantha had seen far too many Make Austin Normal memorabilia of late. In just a short period of time, the whole city had changed dramatically.

But then again, so had her life.

Her blond ponytail swung back and forth behind her head as she jogged. She actually liked its rhythm. It was like a pendulum clock. The beat helped her focus on her breathing and pace. Dressed in the burnt orange and white colors of the University of Texas, Samantha ran past other early morning exercisers. Her green eyes glanced toward the tall apartment building where her former fiancé, Cian, and his new slut girlfriend were sleeping through the daylight hours. The sting of his betrayal still remained, even though she tried very hard to ignore it.

She was kind-of-sort-of dating Jeff Summerfield, the owner of the local occult bookstore and part-time vampire hunter. They got along very well and her family adored him. Jeff and Samantha saw each other a few times a week and always had a great time. They had yet to share a kiss, let alone anything more intimate. She was technically on the rebound from her broken engagement with Cian. Though she told everyone it was a good thing they had called off the wedding, that she was fine, and that Cian and her just weren't suited for each other, she had cried like a baby when she had dropped her wedding gown off at Goodwill. The worst thing is that everyone believed her. They all believed she really was okay.

Except for Jeff.

Somehow, he knew she wasn't moving on yet. It almost made her mad how sweet Jeff was to her. He was so perfectly understanding it was annoying. She didn't want to admit that she was still heartbroken over Cian. She wanted to be stronger than that, but maybe she wasn't. It was hard to accept that a piece of her still hurt whenever she heard his voice or saw his face.

An early morning mist hovered over the lapping waves of the dark waters of the lake and clung to the trunks of the juniper trees. The birds called out from the high branches as small squirrels darted around on the ground, evading the early morning walkers and joggers. The wide pathway was sparsely populated this morning. A few bikers rode past her, the wheels spitting up small bits of grit. She frowned after them. Some turtles rested on rocks near the water, soaking in the early morning sun. She waved at them. They ignored her.

Legs aching, side stitching, lungs straining, Samantha plowed through her discomfort. She was just getting back into running and it was not welcoming her back like an old friend. It was a struggle to get up every morning and get out the door, but she was determined to be a stronger, healthier version of herself. She had even enrolled in self-defense classes. Jeff joked she wanted to be Buffy. He was sort of right.

Though she had known Cian was a vampire, she hadn't realized how dangerous he truly was. When she first met him, he seemed like just a sweet, ordinary guy with beautiful eyes. She never truly understood that there was so much more to him beneath the surface. Maybe she had read *Twilight* one too many times, but she had secretly adored the idea that a vampire was in love with her. It had been like some sort of modern day fairytale until she realized he really *was* a monster and she had never truly known him. She hadn't even considered that there might be other vampires out in the world until Amaliya had shown up. Now she was afraid of what else might lurk in the night. Maybe she couldn't fight the monsters, but she could try to outrun them and if they caught her, she would do her best to make them hurt.

The morning mist was heavier near the Mopac footbridge. The early weekend morning traffic roared overhead as she trudged along. She was tempted to buy a new iPod to replace the one she had broken a week before. The sounds of nature in the early morning were calming, but she missed the steady beat to keep her on track. Trying to keep an even pace was growing more difficult as the stitch in her side worsened.

Running onto the footbridge that sprawled under the very busy Mopac

CHAPTER SIX

Expressway, Samantha plunged through the misty shadows dwelling beneath the rumbling traffic. It was cooler under the bridge and refreshing. She slightly slowed her pace, trying to catch her breath.

"Help me," a female voice called out.

It was somewhere ahead in the misty gloom.

"Hello?" Samantha answered.

"Please, help me," the voice repeated.

"Hello? What's wrong? I can call 911." Using the plea as a reason to drop to a walk, Samantha nervously fished her phone out of her fanny pack. 911 was on speed dial. She activated the screen and walked forward, her finger poised over it.

A soft, desperate sob drifted out of the mist. "He hurt me."

"Oh, shit!" Samantha yanked out her pepper spray from her short's pocket as she tried to call 911. To her dismay, her phone registered a dead battery and turned off. "Crap, the phone is dead. Where are you? I can't see you!"

"Please, he hurt me," the woman whispered.

The thick mist and dark shadows clouded her vision, making it hard to see anything. Samantha held the pepper spray out in front her, ready to deal with any attackers. Shoving her phone into her pocket, she warily advanced toward the voice.

"Please, help me!"

"I'm coming!" Samantha swept her arm back and forth in front of her. Her breath was puffing out in cold wisps as the air turned from warm and humid to cold and prickly. The world suddenly felt far away. Even the overhead traffic was a distant drone.

"Please..."

The air had turned frigid and Samantha shivered as she pressed forward. The shadows appeared thicker and darker as the mist shrouded the path.

"Where are you?" Samantha whispered, suddenly very afraid.

She almost tripped over the jogger lying face down across the path. Gasping, she caught her balance and knelt next to the woman.

"My phone is dead. I can't call 911, but maybe I can help you up and we can try to find someone to assist us." Samantha timidly stretched out her hand to turn the jogger over.

"He hurt me," the woman cried out in agony, rolling onto her back, and thrusting a bloody, straining hand toward Samantha.

"Oh, my God!" Samantha gasped and drew back in shock.

"He hurt me!"

Samantha felt her breakfast trying to crawl up her throat and leap out of her mouth. The woman's chest was a ruin of flesh and long ropey, fleshy strands of intestine lay on the ground. Blood splattered the woman's face and arms, and her eyes were wide with terror.

"Help me, please!" the woman sobbed. "Please, Samantha."

Overcoming her repulsion and fear, Samantha held out her hand to touch the woman's shoulder. Just as her fingers could touch the jogger's arm, the woman vanished in a swirl of mist.

"What the hell?"

Samantha stared at the empty spot on the jogging path as several runners sprinted past her. There was no sign of the woman who had cried out for help. No blood, nothing.

Samantha scurried out from under the bridge and ran toward the nearest rest station. Trembling from terror, she hugged herself as she leaned against a streetlamp, trying to compose herself. What she had seen had been horrifying, but what was even more frightening was that the woman—the apparition—had called her by name.

Chapter Seven

Samuel Vezorak was in a good mood all things considered. The family was drinking all his beer and had devoured most of the barbecue he had cooked up earlier in the day, but he had a good buzz going and he could ignore the barbecue sauce smeared all over his leather sofa.

Outside, the radio was pumping out old country classics into the warm summer air. The porch was crowded with family, kids were in the yard chasing after each other, dogs begged for scraps and attention, and the menfolk swilled down beer while they told tall tales.

Samuel was hitting the buffet table one last time. Though he was leaner than a blade of grass, he could eat any man under the table. His wife, Kelly Ann, had made some of her killer potato salad and he heaped a mountain of it on his plate next to some barbecue chicken and brisket.

"Looks like trouble," Kelly Ann muttered, entering the kitchen of their double-wide trailer. Her long blond hair was plaited into a braid down, and her back and her cheeks were rosy from the heat. She guided their youngest, John, to the sink to wash off a mixture of grease, dirt, and sauce from the six-year-old's face.

Samuel had two sets of children. The first set was Samuel Raymond Vezorak, Jr., who went by Ray, Damon, Amaliya, and Rachel from his deceased wife Marlena. Ray and Damon worked with him and lived in the trailers on either side of his with their wives and kids. Rachel had died of cancer when she was very young. Amaliya was...gone. The second set was with his second wife, Kelly Ann. John and Betsey were his pride and joy.

"John, what were you doing out there?" Samuel asked, cocking his head to gaze down at the little tow-head.

John giggled in response.

"Not talking about him, Samuel. Out there. I think it's another one of those reporters." Kelly Ann gestured out the window.

"Dammit. Not another one," Samuel growled.

Mae, his mother in law (and previous sister in law when he had been married to Marlena), carried Betsey into the kitchen. The four-year-old was just as messy as her brother.

"They're looking for Amaliya, you know," Mae said. "That girl's trouble. Pure and simple."

"Amaliya is dead," John said, scrunching his face as his mother wiped at it with a kitchen towel. "She wented to heaven."

"Yes, your sister Amaliya is an angel now looking down on you when you sleep, taking care of you," Kelly Ann said with a forced smile. She gave her mother a warning look and started to clean Betsey's face, too.

"Yeah, of course," Mae said, rolling her eyes, her head turned so the kids couldn't see.

Mae was drunk and ready to fight, but Samuel shut her down with a stern look. Kelly Ann looked up nervously. They did not discuss Amaliya's visit from beyond the grave in front of the children. Samuel would never forget the way his daughter's eyes had glowed red as she casually tossed him and her brother Damon around like they were toys. Mae and Kelly Ann were convinced she had been possessed by demons, but Samuel feared it was something much worse. Though Amaliya was legally declared dead, Samuel still feared for her. And feared her.

Sometimes at night he would wake up in a cold sweat convinced she would be standing in the doorway of his bedroom, her eyes glowing, her teeth sharp, ready to take revenge on him for his shitty parenting.

His chest hurt at the thought of her. He remembered her as a beautiful blond child with blue-gray eyes, dancing and singing out in the backyard, not the surly young woman covered in tattoos with dyed black hair. It was difficult for him to reconcile the two images of his daughter.

Samuel shifted his over-burdened plate to his other hand and moved to look out the window.

"Where'd you see the reporter, Kelly Ann?"

"Out near the fence," his wife answered. "He's wearing a cowboy hat."

"A local maybe?"

"Never seen him before if he is."

The screen door screeched open, then snapped shut as someone else entered the trailer.

"Hey, Dad, got some reporter type out by the end of the drive. Want me to shoo him off?" It was Ray. Tall, lean, and weather-beaten, the oldest of his children was the spitting image of him at the same age.

"I'll take care of it," Samuel decided. "A man can't even enjoy a decent meal

CHAPTER SEVEN

around here without those jackals coming around."

"Damon went to get his shotgun. A good shot over his head will get that reporter's ass moving," Ray said, grinning.

"I don't want the police out here again," Mae said shrilly. "They give me hell about the dogs running around loose."

"Calm down, Mama." Kelly Ann frowned at her mother. "Let the menfolk take care of it."

Samuel glanced down at his plate, sighed, and set it on the counter. Plucking a fresh beer from the cooler, he gestured to Ray with a jerk of his head to follow him, and headed into the living room.

The living room was just as crowded as the porch. A few people were watching a race on the TV. The barbecue was a monthly event at his house and neighbors always showed up in droves for his award-winning brisket. He liked showing off his culinary skills and hanging out with the people he thought of as true friends. They were not fancy uppity types.

Pete Talbert was lingering near the doorway, keeping a watch on the stranger outside. Pete was a good guy in Samuel's estimation. He had hoped that Amaliya would gain some sense and marry the guy, but that had not come to pass. Lately, Pete was withdrawn and a little jittery. Samuel suspected he was mourning Amaliya's death. Pete had never stopped crushing on his daughter, even when she had turned weird. Pete had suffered a bizarre stroke a few months before and was still recovering. Though Samuel didn't like to admit it to himself, he wondered if it had to do with Amaliya's mysterious visit on Easter.

"He's just hanging out by the gate taking photos," Pete said as Samuel stepped next to him.

"The road is public land," Ray said, frowning. "Not much we can do if he doesn't come on our property."

"I can go check it out," Pete offered. He scratched at his black goatee, his blue eyes nervous. "Maybe I can get him to leave."

"Nah. I'll go set him straight," Samuel responded. With a weary sigh, he shoved open the screen door.

Their boot heels thudded across the porch as the men headed toward the stairs. Samuel knew that Ray and Pete were right behind him. They were good guys and he was glad for the company. He was getting too old to do all the ass whooping. If he was lucky, the reporter would shove off without any trouble and he could get back to his plate of cooling food.

Strutting up the gravel drive toward the gate, he hooked his thumbs onto his belt and fastened his blue-gray eyes on the man snapping photos of his home. Damon quickly caught up with them, holding his shotgun casually in one hand.

"Should we call the police?" Damon asked.

"Nope. Gonna handle this ourselves," Samuel answered.

The man on the other side of the fence noted their approach, but didn't seem concerned. His cowboy hat was pulled low on his forehead and his eyes were hidden by dark sunglasses. In his hands was a very fancy, very expensive camera. On the road behind him was a big black truck with a small travel trailer attached to it. Samuel didn't like the man's long duster that flowed in the warm summer breeze. It could hide all sorts of weaponry.

"Good afternoon," the man said, just as Samuel started to open his mouth. "Lovely homestead you have here." The accent was Southern, but not Texan.

"Thank you, sir, but I need to ask you what you're doing taking pictures of my place," Samuel answered, folding his arms over his chest.

It was difficult to tell what the man truly looked like. His face was hidden by the shadow thrown by his hat and his sunglasses. The one thing that did show clearly was his wide smile. "Oh, I'm an investigator. I'm just taking photos for my files."

"You're a policeman?" Ray asked skeptically.

"Private investigator. I've been hired to look into the so-called Satanic Murders."

"Police closed that case when they found Professor Sumner's body. He killed himself," Samuel answered. He didn't believe the official story he had been fed, but he didn't like strangers hanging around his property.

"They never found your daughter's body, did they?" The man tilted his head and Samuel caught a glimpse of the man's dark eyes.

"She's dead, sir. We had a funeral. Maybe one day we'll find her body, but the police said they found the spot where she died. Lots of blood, too much lost to be alive," Samuel answered gruffly.

The policeman had shown Samuel the pictures of the bloodstained wall. Amaliya had been killed behind the dorm. The foundation and bricks had been dark brown with her blood and the ground had been saturated with it. The police were convinced that the killer had temporarily buried her body and later retrieved it, storing it in her dorm room. The police weren't sure why Professor Sumner had taken Amaliya's body with him, but Samuel suspected the truth. His daughter had woken up buried in the ground and found her way back to her dorm room before trying to come home.

The stranger nodded his head. "That's what the newspapers said. Don't you think it's odd that Professor Sumner took her body?"

"He was obsessed with her," Ray said defensively. "All the papers said so. They even said he was trying to date her. He was a sick bastard and I'm glad he killed himself."

Beside Samuel, Damon shifted uncomfortably, casting his eyes downward. Samuel hoped his younger son would keep it together. He knew for a fact Damon still slept with a shotgun next to the bed ever since the night he last saw his sister.

"That's what they said, true," the stranger said.

"Sir, what is your name? I'd like to see some identification," Pete said briskly.

With a wry smile, the man reached into his pocket.

CHAPTER SEVEN

Samuel automatically stiffened while Damon slightly lowered his shotgun.

"Ethan Logan, Private Investigator." The man flipped open his wallet then extracted a few cards from the well-worn leather. He handed one to each of the men standing on the other side of the fence.

"Who hired you, Mr. Logan?" Samuel asked, curiosity getting the best of him.

"That is private, Mr. Vezorak. Let me just say that you were not the only family to suffer a loss that terrible weekend. Other families are grieving as well. The bodies of their loved ones were recovered, but yours was not." Ethan snapped his wallet shut and shoved it back into a pocket inside of his long duster.

"She's dead, Mr. Logan," Samuel said, fear beginning to claw at his insides.

"What are you insinuating?" Pete asked defensively. "Amaliya died just like everyone else."

"She was a suspect for a short period of time because her body wasn't found," Ethan said in a voice that was both accusatory, but nonchalant.

"Hey now, my sister had nothing to do with those murders!" Ray took a threatening step forward, his hands clenched into fists.

Samuel gripped his eldest by the shoulder, his fingers digging into the other man's flesh as a warning. "We don't need trouble, Mr. Logan."

"I'm not trouble, Mr. Vezorak. I'm looking for the truth. There is one person in this whole mess unaccounted for. That's your daughter. Now, the police think she might be dead, but what if she's not? What if she escaped and she's in hiding? What if Professor Sumner didn't kill all those kids?"

"My sister did not kill anyone!" Ray shouted.

Out of the corner of his eye, Samuel saw Damon's hands shaking. Both of his sons were at the point of falling apart in one way or the other and Samuel didn't like it. He did not need more trouble on his hands because of Amaliya.

"Amaliya is dead. She's not hiding nowhere. She didn't escape. She died. You had best be moving on before I call the police and report you for harassment," Samuel said in a cold, terse voice.

Ethan slung the strap of his camera over one shoulder, letting the expensive piece rest against his back. "Let me ask you, Mr. Vezorak, did you see Amaliya that Easter weekend? Did she come back here looking for help?"

Samuel narrowed his eyes on the man before him. He could be very intimidating when he wanted to be, but the stranger was unaffected by the glower.

"Why would you say something like that?" Ray asked defensively.

"I talked to a few at the college. They said she drove around in your pickup. When she disappeared, so did the pickup."

The blood drained out of Samuel's face as he stared at the man. "Damon and I picked it up after she was reported missing."

Ethan stared at Samuel thoughtfully, then finally said, "I'm sure you did."

Next to Damon, Pete was staring at his feet, not saying anything. Samuel's discomfort grew. He was afraid that maybe Pete had seen Amaliya that night.

Damon would keep his mouth shut, but would Pete?

"So none of you saw her Easter weekend?" Ethan's gaze swept over the four men, but his eyes rested on Pete much longer than on anyone else.

Or was Samuel just imagining it?

"You know, if she's alive, in hiding, she could go to the authorities and tell them what she saw. Maybe Professor Sumner didn't commit suicide in Louisiana. Maybe there is much more to this story, huh?" Ethan finally took off his sunglasses. His eyes are dark brown and somehow frightening. They were so intense that Samuel felt he was peering straight into his very mind, seeking out the truth.

"She's dead," Samuel said at last. "Dead and gone. And you best be gone now. Ray, call the police."

Immediately, Ray obeyed his father, pulling out his cellphone.

The man named Ethan Logan slid his sunglasses back on. "If one of you remembers seeing her, call me. I'll be in the area." He slowly turned and sauntered away, his duster flaring out around him dramatically.

"Fuck," Damon whispered.

"Keep it together, son," Samuel said, gripping his shoulder and squeezing it hard enough to inflict pain.

Ray clicked off his phone without dialing, watching the departing stranger. "I don't like it, Dad."

"She's dead and gone," Samuel said firmly. "She ain't coming back."

Pete glanced sharply at Samuel, his blue eyes watery. The boy had it bad for Amaliya his whole life and now she was gone. Samuel hoped to God that Pete hadn't seen her that night. If Amaliya was the reason for his strange stroke, it only confirmed what Samuel feared.

Amaliya was now something unnatural and evil.

Dust billowed up and drifted over into the yard when the big black truck pulled around and roared down the road. Samuel didn't like people sniffing around in his business and he felt unnerved by the stranger's visit.

"Let's get back to eating," he said at last and strode back toward the trailer.

CHAPTER EIGHT

Jeff Summerfield, sometime vampire hunter and fulltime occult book store owner, stared at the spell with some confusion. Standing behind the checkout counter in his store, he studied the book in front of him, squinting slightly. Rubbing his hand over his brown hair, mussing it up, he reread the spell for the sixth time.

"Uh, I don't get it."

"It's screwed up, right? There is no way an ice giant can deflect that spell!" Benchley's voice was adamant, his fists curled up at his sides. His friend and sometime vampire hunter sidekick, Benchley, ran the shop next to the occult book store. It specialized in gaming and was packed with books, figurines, collectibles, and huge tables that took up the back area of the shop where gamers played massive battles with tiny armies all day and night. "The DM totally made a bad call! That's the last time I play with that sixteen year old twerp."

"I don't play these games, you know that. I have no idea if an ice giant can deflect this spell, but if you say so, I'll side with you."

Benchley rubbed his dark blond goatee, shaking his head. He was wearing his usual long, baggy khaki shorts, a faded t-shirt advertising an obscure band, and worn sandals. "I got screwed. Now I have to make a new character and start over. My whole day is trashed."

"I would like to say I feel your pain, but I'm an uber-geek of another variety," Jeff answered, handing back the rulebook for the latest fantasy tabletop game.

"Yeah, yeah. PC gamers suck."

"Says the former WoW addict," Jeff quipped.

"I detoxed when they made it too easy to level to sixty," Benchley retorted.

"I know, I know. You played it since the beta. You did the grind to level sixty when it actually meant something. Yada, yada, yada," Jeff teased.

"Don't mock me," Benchley said defensively.

"I don't mock. I observe. Sarcastically."

The bell over the door chimed as it swung open, a blast of hot air and a blinding flash of sunlight announcing the arrival of a customer.

"Fuck it's hot," Benchley gasped, cringing.

The door clanged shut.

As Jeff's eyes readjusted to the cool, refreshing gloom of the bookstore, he saw Samantha standing just inside the doorway. Wearing a white skirt, a cute pink tank top, a white flower tucked in her hair, and obscenely high, pale blue wedge heels, she whipped off her sunglasses dramatically.

"Fuck my life," she declared.

"Girlfriend trouble," Benchley whispered, hiding his mouth behind his hand.

"She's not my girlfriend," Jeff muttered back.

"Did you hear me?" Samantha's high heels clicked against the wood floor as she approached.

"Uh, fuck your life is what I heard," Jeff responded.

Samantha swung her enormous Betsey Johnson purse adorned with pink skulls and sequins onto the counter, then dramatically flopped forward onto it, burying her face in her folded arms. "Fuck. My. Life. In. The. Asshole. Without. Lube."

"That sounds...painful," Jeff said, lightly touching her blond head.

"Hi, Sam," Benchley said, awkwardly waving at her though she couldn't see him.

Samantha lifted one hand, gave a short wave, then let it drop back on the counter. "Hi, Shark-boy."

Benchley blushed, trying not to stare at Samantha's ass.

Jeff thought Benchley's crush on the blond was rather sweet. He wasn't worried about any competition. Though he and Samantha weren't an official anything yet, he felt fairly certain that things were developing nicely. Leaning over Samantha, he pulled her bangs aside to try to see her face. She tilted her head just enough so that he could see one eye peering out at him.

"Bad day at the office?" he asked. "Did you work today?"

"I wish! And no."

"Uh, Cian giving you hell?"

Samantha shook her head, lifting it. She rested her elbows on the counter and cradled her face in her hands.

"Amaliya being a bitch?"

"I hate her."

"I know."

"But it's not her. Though it's usually her."

Benchley leaned against the counter, nearly toppling over the pens in the jar next to the cash register.

CHAPTER EIGHT

Jeff saved it just in time.

"So, uh, what is it? I can maybe...uh...help." Benchley attempted to look nonchalant.

Samantha blew out a puff of air, her bangs flipping upward.

"Sam, maybe we can both help." Jeff lightly touched her cheek. "C'mon, talk to us."

"My life sucks, Jeff," Samantha said, her eyes filling with tears.

"No, it doesn't, Sam."

"My ex-fiancé is fucking Vampira and I've gone all *Sixth Sense*! My life sucks!"

"Okay, I get the Vampira reference, but not the *Sixth Sense*," Benchley said, clearly confused.

"Me, too. Sam, honey, can you be a little clearer?"

Samantha wiped at her eyes irritably. "I'm so not going all Patricia Arquette. I refuse to! Because the next thing you know I'll be all John Edwards-y and people will be banging on my door wanting the deets of their dead granny's peach cobbler recipe!"

"Still lost," Jeff said, wincing.

Samantha grabbed his t-shirt and hauled him toward her. Staring at him in the eye, tears streaking her face, she said, "I see dead people!"

"Cian and Amaliya?" Jeff queried, arching an eyebrow.

"No! *Dead* dead people!"

"She's not real good on the being clear thing is she?" Benchley observed.

"She speaks Samantha-speak. It's a variation of English," Jeff admitted.

"Don't mock me, Van Helsing!" Samantha fumbled with her purse.

"How many espresso shots did you have today?" Jeff asked, watching her shaking hands.

"Uh, four." Samantha jerked out a folder and slammed it onto the counter. "And two margaritas at Polvos."

"Did you drive here?" Benchley exchanged a worried glance with Jeff.

"No. I got a cab. So, Jeff, you have to take me home." Samantha flipped the folder open and shoved it toward Jeff. "I am seeing dead chicks. Okay? Like... really dead." She pointed adamantly at a printed article from the *Austin-American Statesman*.

Jeff picked it up and read it swiftly. It was a story with which he was passingly acquainted. A young woman went jogging one morning a few months before and disappeared. A picture of a pretty brunette was included and Sam kept poking it with one finger as he tried to read.

"Her! I saw her!"

"Cassidy Longoria?" Jeff glanced up at Samantha. "You found her body?"

"No, Jeff! I saw her Casper!"

"I think she's saying she saw her ghost," Benchley offered helpfully.

"Don't say that!" Samantha shushed him with her hands. "If you say it like that they'll hear you and start bugging me like they harassed Whoopi Goldberg in that one movie!"

"You mean *Ghost*?"

"Ugh! Shhh." Samantha pouted, clenching her fists. "I don't want this to be real!"

"If you're seeing ghosts, that kinda makes it real," Benchley answered.

"Oh, fuck you." Samantha scowled.

"Sam," Jeff said gently, touching her hand and getting her attention. "You saw the ghost of this jogger, right?"

She nodded, tears still tracing down her cheeks.

"Where?"

"The jogging trail. Under the Mopac Bridge."

Jeff didn't doubt Samantha had seen something very upsetting. It was clear that she was distraught and very rattled. Also, a little drunk and on a caffeine high. "Tell me what happened."

In rather disjointed and sometimes incoherent string of words, Samantha related all that had happened that morning.

"Sounds like a sentient ghost," Benchley said, his tone very serious. Benchley was the best ghost hunter Jeff knew. He took ghosts very seriously.

"But that's not the worst of it, Jeff," Samantha continued. "It was really scary, gooey, and bloody, but I think I felt her there before. Today is the first day I saw her, but I always feel this really super-cold breeze under the bridge. And... and...I've been seeing things out of the corner of my eye around my house. When I drove by the cemetery the other day, this old man was sitting on a gravestone and he waved at me. And now I think he's a ghost. Then I realized that the other day I said hello to this woman walking down my street and my friend, Giselle, who was with me, didn't see her. I thought she was jerking my chain, but now...now..."

"You think you're a medium?" Jeff offered.

"Uh huh. Just like that *Lost Highway* chick," Samantha said with a solemn nod.

"Got that reference, and Patricia Arquette is hot," Benchley said.

"Tell me I'm not going all Allison Dubois, please, Jeff. Please!" Samantha clutched at his hands, her big eyes imploring him.

"Have you ever sensed or seen anything before the last few months? In your childhood?" Jeff asked. He plucked a pen from the jar and began taking notes on the cover of her folder.

"No, never."

"When did you start noticing things? Like maybe cold spots, shadows, flashes of people out of the corner of your eye, that sort of thing?"

Samantha stared at him as she pondered his question. Slowly, her eyes grew larger. "That whore!"

"Amaliya reference, right?" Benchley asked Jeff.

CHAPTER EIGHT

Jeff nodded.

"I'm catching on." Benchley looked proud.

"After I drank from her! When I almost died and you made me drink her blood!"

"Good thing you don't have customers right now because that would be really hard to play off," Benchley said.

"Jeff, you made me drink her blood! You said it would heal me! You didn't say it would make me go all *Ghost Whisperer*!"

"Sam, are you sure? You never experienced anything like that before?"

"Dude, I'm Baptist. We believe in God, the devil, and angels. Not ghosts."

Jeff rubbed his brow, pondering everything she had told him. "A lot of people do end up coming into their abilities with a near death experience. That could be why you're now seeing things."

Samantha rubbed the spot where the sword had skewered her a few months before. "Yeah? You mean it's not the skank's fault?"

"Not sure. Let me check on something."

Sliding out from behind the counter, Jeff headed into the back of the store to where he kept his private collection of books written by previous vampire hunters. The fire safe was tucked into a corner of his office. After unlocking it, he pulled out a few of the leather bound journals.

Benchley and Samantha lingered in the doorway to his office, watching. He sat at his desk and started flipping through the tomes. Rubbing his leg, he rested his artificial leg on a rest under his desk. Every once in a while his stump would give him issues. Today, he was having phantom pains in a foot he no longer possessed.

"So you think it's really because I almost died?" Samantha pulled on her bottom lip with her teeth.

"It's totally plausible. Near death experiences place you at the veil between the living and the dead. You hover between the two. So you begin to see both," Benchley explained as he darted into the office to sit on a stool near Jeff's desk. He craned his neck to see the journal in Jeff's hands.

Opening up one of his father's old journals, Jeff scanned for an entry that had been made soon after his mother's death. His father's obsession with vampires had increased tremendously after his wife had been murdered and his son maimed by one particularly nasty vampire. Flipping through pages, he listened to Samantha and Benchley chatting back and forth, but really didn't pay attention to what they were saying.

He was concerned that Samantha's abilities appeared to be growing, not receding. Some people had very clear visions of the dead soon after a near death experience, but would eventually lose the ability.

"And you didn't see her until today? Not even a passing glimpse?" he asked, cutting off Samantha's summarization of all the seasons of *Medium* to Benchley.

She adamantly shook her head, her blond hair whipping about. "Nope.

Never."

Returning his gaze to the book, Jeff continued to scan entries. He had a sick feeling in the pit of his stomach and it was only growing worse.

"Oh, shit." Benchley sat back, his expression fading to solemn. "Jeff has that look,"

"What look? There's a look?" Samantha leaned over to peer into Jeff's face. "What's that look?"

Jeff swatted her pointing finger away. "Uh, my concentrating look."

"No, that's his 'oh, we're fucked' look."

"Bench, you're not helping," Jeff said irritably. He found the passage he was looking for and started to read it.

"Lemme see," Samantha said, lunging for the book.

Jeff caught her hand and gave her his sternest look. He really, really liked her, but no one messed with his stuff. "Samantha, let me do this. Give me a sec. Okay?"

With a frown, tears still in her eyes, Samantha gave him a curt nod.

"Thank you," Jeff said, then returned his gaze to the elegant scrawl of his deceased father's handwriting. The sick feeling inside worsened. Rubbing his brow, he glanced toward Samantha. Her green eyes were fearful and she was chewing on her bottom lip nervously. "Okay, there may be a problem."

Samantha fell back against the wall, clutching her stomach, close to hyperventilating. "Tell me."

"Apparently, when a vampire gives a human their blood, it can have a variety of side effects."

"It *is* her fault!"

"Samantha, listen to me!"

"Okay, okay. Listening."

"When a vampire gives a human their blood it can imbue the human with vampiric abilities in a greatly diminished capacity. Only if the vampire has some sort of unusual ability. My father documented that the mortal servant of a vampire he encountered could toss balls of fire. The vampire master was a pyromancer. Another vampire hunter reported a mortal servant that could control animals." Jeff paused, waiting for Samantha to say something. Her eyes had widened to the point that there was white all around her irises. "Sam?"

Turning on her heel, she stalked toward the front of the store.

"Sam?" Jeff hurried after her, slightly limping much to his consternation.

Samantha whipped about, breathing heavily, gripping her cellphone in one hand.

"Say something?" Jeff winced.

"Sam, you're kinda scaring us," Benchley added coming up behind Jeff.

Pointing at Jeff, Samantha fumed in silence. At last, she let out a cry of frustration.

"Samantha, let me look into it further. Maybe it will fade away." He lightly

CHAPTER EIGHT

took her by the shoulders. Her skin felt soft and warm under his touch.

"That whore!" Samantha screamed. "Oh, my gawd! She did this to me! As if she hasn't fucked up my life enough!"

Jeff gently brushed her hair back from her face and guided her over to a couch to sit down. "Sam, sit down. Your face is so red."

"I'm so fuckin' pissed off!" Samantha cried out. "I don't want to see..." she paused "Will they all bug me if they know I can see them? Like in that movie?"

"Possibly," Jeff said.

"Probably," Benchley said at the same time.

Flopping back on the couch, Samantha stared at the ceiling, her phone cradled against her breasts. "Fuck. My. Life!"

"Let me do some digging, okay, Samantha?" Jeff was worried she was about to blow a blood vessel.

With a soft sob, Samantha threw herself into his arms, her wet face pressed against his neck.

Rocking her gently, Jeff said softly, meaning every word, "I will help you with this. I promise."

Chapter Nine

The sky was a magnificent panorama of purple and pink as the sun set beyond the tall green pine trees enclosing the campground. Pete sat in his old Mustang staring at the big black truck attached to the camper, pensively stroking his black goatee. Glancing down at the card the mysterious stranger had given him earlier in the day, he pondered once again if he was doing the right thing.

The comments from the man named Ethan Logan had made Pete very uneasy. For weeks after he suffered from what the doctor had finally labeled a stroke, he'd experienced difficulty remembering the night he had collapsed in the Dixie Motel. He didn't even remember why he'd been in the motel room, let alone naked. It was suggested by a few of his friends that Pete had been slipped a drug by a woman in a bar. There had been no drugs in his system and no one had seen him at his regular bar, so that theory was shot. It bothered him that there wasn't a real explanation for his loss of memory. It had been embarrassing to be questioned by the police. Even more embarrassing that it was evident he had sex with someone he couldn't even remember. Without being able to recall the event, he wasn't even sure if a crime had been committed against him.

That whole night had been a blur until he had started to dream. Each time he dreamed, he'd wake with a hearty erection and tears on his face. At first the visions had been hazy with no real discernible details. It was disconcerting to lie alone in his bed sobbing like a baby, but not know why. Then as the weeks turned into months, the dreams began to gradually become clearer. That was when he saw the face of the woman he had loved most of his life emerge out of the murk. He had even started to wake crying out her name.

Amaliya.

Ever since Easter weekend the Vezoraks had all been acting oddly. At first he thought it was because Amaliya had died and her body had not been recovered. But as his dreams continued to gain coherency, he started to wonder.

Tapping his fingers against the steering wheel, he exhaled sharply. "What the hell am I doing?"

Maybe he was being a fool, but he was seriously beginning to wonder if Amaliya was still alive. Maybe Ethan Logan knew more than he was letting on. Pete had mourned her with the rest of her family, but if there was a chance she was out there in hiding, he wanted to find her. Maybe she needed him.

So many maybes.

"Pete, you're a damn fool," he uttered, shoving his car door open and climbing out. Pocketing the card, he kicked the door shut and sauntered toward the camper.

Ethan Logan must have been watching him, because the side door of the trailer opened and the tall man stepped out. The cowboy hat and duster was gone, but the man was still imposing. He had strong features and broad shoulders that made Pete believe that Ethan could deliver a crippling punch in a fight.

There was an old grill, a folding table, and a cooler set out on the patio. The coals in the grill were bright red. Ethan's shirt sleeves were rolled up and his hands appeared damp and freshly washed, so Pete guessed he had arrived at dinner time.

"You found me," Ethan said in a somber voice.

"Only camping ground around here. I figured you'd be here or parked at Wal-Mart. You weren't at Wal-Mart, so..."

The corner of the investigator's mouth quirked up in one corner. "Not bad detective work."

"Is that what you are? Truly?" Pete asked stepping onto the cement slab the trailer was parked next to.

"Sure am," Ethan said, slightly shrugging.

"That a Georgia accent?"

Ethan gave him an even bigger smile. "Who's investigating who?"

"Plates are Georgia," Pete confessed.

Ethan glanced briefly at the license plates on his truck, folding his arms over his chest. "So they are."

There was an uncomfortable silence between the two men. Pete fidgeted as he listened to the sound of the insects buzzing in the trees. Shoving his hands into his jean pockets, he said, "Do you really think Amaliya is alive?"

"Do you?"

The man's keen brown eyes had a way of making Pete feel like he was somehow guilty of something. They were piercing and intense.

"Uh, not sure."

"But you think she might be. That's why you're here, right?" Ethan reached inside the camper and dragged out two folding camping chairs.

CHAPTER NINE

Pete shifted on his feet, his gaze darting around the nearly empty campsite. He was vastly uncomfortable, yet he couldn't say why. "Yeah. That's why I'm here."

"Have a seat." Ethan patted the back of one of the chairs he had set up and vanished back into the camper.

Slumping into one of the blue cloth chairs, Pete leaned forward, rubbing his hands together anxiously. His dreams felt closer than ever, more vivid, now that he was actually entertaining the thought that maybe they were somehow grounded in reality.

Ethan reappeared with a plate loaded with slices of onion, a few hotdogs, and two hamburger patties. "You hungry?"

Pete shook his head.

"Well, there will be enough if you want some. I've had a full day. I'm starving." Ethan flashed a disarming smile at Pete before placing the food on the grill.

"Why do you think she's alive?" Pete asked.

Ethan rolled one shoulder. "No corpse."

"That's it?"

"Do I need more?"

"So you think she didn't die?"

"I didn't say that," Ethan answered.

"That don't make no sense if you think she's alive."

"There are all types of being alive, Pete."

"You know my name?"

"Yep. I did a little research on you."

Pete frowned, uncomfortable with the thought of being part of any investigation. He watched Ethan finish laying the food over the hot coals. The smell of cooking meat and the grilling onions filled the air. The investigator flipped open the lid of a cooler set next to the grill and tossed Pete a beer before claiming one for himself.

"I don't get it. Why would you care about me?"

Ethan settled into the chair next to Pete, popped the can, and took a long drink of the ice cold beer. "I educated myself on everyone out here before I set out. I like to know who I'm dealing with. You're good ol' Pete, the guy who had a bad crush on my missing girl."

"Who told you that?" Pete asked a bit defensively.

"Everyone in town." Ethan flashed his teeth as he flung out his arms. "And I do mean everyone. The general consensus is that you were lovesick."

"It's true that I loved her," Pete conceded, his brief moment of anger fading. He pried the beer open and took a swig. "I loved her most of my life."

"Did she return it?"

An image from his dream flitted through his mind. It was of Amaliya leaning over him, her eyes hooded with desire.

Ethan's brow slightly furrowed as he waited for an answer.

"I don't know."

"You're an interesting guy, Pete. The same weekend your lady love went missing, you ended up in the hospital with a stroke. The hospital paperwork said you suffered from a sudden loss of blood pressure. Digging a little deeper it said you had also lost a lot of blood."

Pete looked at the man sharply. "You went to the hospital?"

"Like I said, I did my research. So, Pete, the weekend the love of your life supposedly was murdered and buried out in the forest outside of her college, you end up in the hospital from a severe loss of blood. They cover it by calling it a stroke. Meanwhile, her body goes missing, but her dorm room is filled with signs that she may have crawled out of her grave and went home for a nice shower."

"How do you know all that?"

"Police reports."

Pete gulped down the rest of his beer. His hands were shaking. He suddenly felt the need to be shit-faced. As the blackness of the night settled into the trees around the campsite, the fireflies flickered among the branches.

Ethan reached over to snag Pete another beer from the cooler.

"The police said she's dead, Mr. Logan."

"The police cover things up that they can't explain. Especially when higher ups tell them to." Ethan handed him another cold beer.

"They said that the professor dug her back up for Satanic rituals or something. That he was all obsessed with her and wanted to use her for black magic."

"Yet, Professor Sumner kills himself outside of Shreveport. Kind of convenient don't you think?"

"He felt guilty?"

Ethan guffawed. "Sure. Guilt. He kills fourteen people and feels guilt. I seriously doubt a man capable of so much death could feel guilt."

"You think he didn't kill them?"

"Nope." Ethan nodded. "He didn't."

"Then who did?"

"Amaliya."

Pete stood up so fast, his chair skidded back and toppled over. "Bullshit!"

Ethan wasn't affected by Pete's explosion and slightly shrugged. "Think about it. She dies. Is buried in the forest. But she climbs out, goes and takes a shower, a room full of college kids ends up dead, she disappears. The truck she was using shows up at her dad's house, and you end up in the hospital. Mr. Rusk from the Dixie Motel tells me that you arrived at the motel with a dark-haired woman in the car. He never saw her face, but we both know who that was, don't we?"

"I don't recall," Pete mumbled. He finished the beer in three hard swallows. His head began to buzz, but he liked the feeling.

CHAPTER NINE

"But you're starting too, aren't you? You're starting to see her face. You're starting to remember that she was the one in the room with you."

Pete ran his hand over his numbed features. To his embarrassment, he was getting an erection as random images from his dreams drifted over his mindscape. "Uh. Maybe."

"In your dreams, maybe?" Ethan stood up to check on his dinner. The taller, bigger man didn't seem at all fazed by the things he was saying. It made the whole evening feel even more surreal.

"I dream about her," Pete admitted in a weak voice. The wall that had kept that evening from his waking mind was beginning to crumble. He could clearly see Amaliya's smiling face as he pulled her close for a kiss.

"In that hotel room with you, right?" Ethan continued to flip the meat and placed the onion slices on top of the burgers.

"What are you saying?" Pete demanded. He felt dizzy, a little sick, and terribly afraid.

Ethan set the tongs he was using on the plate on the folding table, then turned around slowly. "Amaliya did die. But she came back. She came back as something different. Maybe she was afraid, not understanding what she was, and she came home. I'm guessing from my encounter with her father and family today that they drove her off. But you, Pete, you loved her. If you saw her wandering around out here alone, what would you do?"

A strong memory unfurled inside of his mind. He saw Amaliya walking along the roadside in the darkness, her bag over her shoulder. Her beautiful face had been illuminated by the headlights of his Mustang as he stopped his car beside her.

"I picked her up," he whispered. It was a statement. Not a question.

"And took her to the motel," Ethan continued for him.

"Yeah."

Pete staggered backwards. Ethan swiftly moved to shove the still-standing chair under him. Pete fell into it heavily. A cascade of memories overwhelmed him. He remembered confessing his love to Amaliya and his hopes she would one day settle down with him. He recalled sneaking her into the motel room and then what had followed. He had been joyously happy as they made love for hours and then...

The beer in his hand fell to the concrete, its contents splashing over his boots, but he didn't even notice. He cradled his face in his hands, overcome.

"What happened, Pete?" Ethan asked in a low voice.

"She had no reflection," Pete whispered.

As clear as day, he recalled looking into the mirror over the vanity and seeing only himself, yet he had held her in his arms, had still been inside of her after their latest sexual romp across the room. "And I was afraid."

Ethan righted the other chair and sank into it. The sun was so low the stars were now flooding the East Texas sky. In silence, Ethan handed Pete another beer.

"She...started to cry. She was upset. Her tears were bloody. There was blood in them. I tried to get away from her, but she kept begging me to not be scared. I...saw her teeth."

"Sharp, huh?"

"Yeah, then she just threw me like a toy across the room. The rest is still hazy."

"She tried to remove the memory from your mind."

The second that door shuts forget about me. Understand? Amaliya's voice whispered in his mind.

"Yeah. She did. With hypnosis or something."

"She was new to it all. Didn't know what she was doing. You're lucky to be alive, Pete. Others were not so lucky," Ethan said.

Combing his hands slowly through his dark hair, Pete shook his head. The images filling his mind combined with what Ethan was insinuating was too much to fathom. The tranquility of his surroundings was at odds with the maelstrom inside his head.

"What you're saying, it can't be real," Pete said at last. He popped the beer and drank it swiftly. He wanted to be numb. He didn't want to feel. He wanted to be fuzzy. Ethan's words were weaving Pete's memories together into a tapestry he did not want to look at, let alone accept.

"Why not?" Ethan returned to the grill. The fat sizzling onto the hot coals filled the air with smoke and the stench of burning flesh.

"Because...if she died, she couldn't come back. Dead is dead."

Ethan chuckled, shaking his head. "Oh, if only that were true."

"You think she's some kind of...vampire, don't you?"

Glancing over his shoulder, Ethan gave Pete an incredulous look. "Think? I know she is." Ethan shoveled his food onto the platter and opened up the Tupperware bins he had on the folding table. Inside were bread, condiments and chopped up lettuce and tomato. Building his hamburger, Ethan continued, "I have no doubt that she was killed and buried in that forest. She rose a few days later, probably hungry and very disoriented. Coming back does that to them sometimes."

"Them?"

"Vampires." Ethan finished making up his sandwich, covered up the remaining grilled meat, and settled back in his chair.

"It can't be. It just can't!"

"Think about it. It all fits together. The massacre at the college, her coming here and seducing you, feeding off you, then trying to wipe your memories so you won't remember. She then heads on down the road and kills a trucker in a motel, and some crazy bitch on her way to kill her husband. I have figured that much out."

"Amaliya would never kill anyone!"

"She did, and she will. She will do it for blood. She needs it to survive. Right now she's out there, hiding, probably afraid." Ethan bit hungrily into his burger, chewing swiftly.

"Why are you looking for her?" Pete asked. His blurry gaze fell over the camper and truck again. He had missed the silver crosses worked into the rims of the wheels. Glancing around the area, he saw small silver cross stakes pressed into the ground around the truck and camper. "You're a vampire hunter."

Ethan shook his head. "Paranormal investigator."

"You gonna kill her?" Pete felt his throat constricting at the thought of Amaliya dying again. Her face filled his mind, so beautiful, so sweet.

"Nope." Ethan mopped up some ketchup with his bun and took another big bite.

"Then what? You said someone hired you to investigate the murders. Is that true?"

Ethan bobbed his head and wiped off his mouth with a napkin. "Absolutely. I know Amaliya killed those people, but I want to know who killed her. She can tell me that."

"Then what are you going to do?"

"Kill the one who made her," Ethan said matter-of-factly. "She can lead me to him."

"You won't kill her?" Pete asked, his voice slurring with beer and fear.

"Nope. I can save her." Ethan shoved the rest of his hamburger in his mouth, annoying Pete.

"You can make her be alive again? Human?"

"Absolutely," Ethan said around his food as he chewed.

"For real?"

"She's only been a vampire a few months. There is this old ritual that the Catholic Church used to restore vampires to life."

"You're shittin' me?" Pete stared at the man incredulously. The entire conversation was insane, but he couldn't make himself get up and leave. Despite everything, Pete believed every word Ethan was saying.

"No, I'm not shittin' you. But it can only work within the first year of the vampire's life. After that, the monster inside of them becomes too strong and they are lost. So my plan is to find Amaliya, find out where her master is, use his ashes in the ritual, and restore her to life."

Pete shook his head in disbelief. "But why?"

"It's what I do. It's what my family has always done. We make sure that the vampires never grow strong enough to overthrow humanity. We kill the old ones, restore the young ones."

"And you came here to figure out if we know where she is?"

"You're my first stop. After this, I head west."

"Her family outside of DeLeon," Pete sighed.

"Yeah."

"They won't talk to you. Same as the Vezoraks. They're not going to trust you if they do know where she is."

"That's why I'm hoping you'll go with me, Pete," Ethan said staring into Pete's eyes. "How much do you love Amaliya, Pete? Enough to try to save her from eternal damnation?"

Pressing his lips together, Pete nodded mutely. The fingers clutching the beer were numb. He felt adrift, disengaged from the world around him.

"So what do you say, Pete? Will you help me find Amaliya and save her?"

"Yes," Pete said, knowing he had no other choice. "I'll do anything I can to save her."

Ethan flashed a wide smile, his dark eyes glittering. "That's what I was hoping to hear."

Part Three

Saturday Night

Chapter Ten

Cian could barely hear himself think. The pounding, growling music filled the loft, causing his chrome and glass desk to vibrate. Seated at an array of flat screen monitors, he glanced over his shoulder at Amaliya. She was at her drum kit pounding away with a fervor that was almost terrifying. Her black hair flew around her face, whipping back and forth, obscuring her rapturous expression.

"You're going to break another one!" Cian shouted at her.

Either she didn't hear him, or she ignored him. Wielding the drumsticks like a rock star, she was lost in the music. The loud booms made Cian cringe. Every time she smacked a cymbal, he fought the desire to duck. He had barely escaped decapitation a few weeks before when she had hit a cymbal too hard and sent it spinning across the apartment. Amaliya had already gone through five different drum kits. Caught up in the music, she'd forget her vampire strength and destroy them.

Rubbing his temples, Cian wondered how the horrendous racket pouring out of the speakers could even be considered music. It was loud, chaotic, frantic, and primitive. It had taken him awhile to realize that the growling was actually words. He sighed. To think he had installed the sound system to listen to his favorite composer, Brahms.

The doorbell was barely audible, but he caught the insistent buzzing noise on the fringes of his hearing. He glanced at the monitor streaming the feed from the security cameras.

Samantha stood in the hallway outside his apartment. She was tapping her foot and had her hands on her hips. She didn't look happy. He unlocked the doors with a few keystrokes and slid out of his chair to go greet her.

The door opened and the petite blond barreled into the foyer with a look of determination on her face that gave him pause. That particular expression was never a good sign when it came to his former fiancé. He leaned against the wall and raised an eyebrow. Samantha had a penchant for dramatic entrances and it was best to let her have her moment.

Yanking out a small box from her purse and thrusting it in his direction, she said, "Here's the replacement phone for the whore."

Cian inclined his head. "Thanks for picking this up, Sam."

"You should give me a raise," Samantha said to him in a distracted tone, but her eyes were not on him. Her attention was directed up the hall toward the living room where Amaliya was lost in her drum solo.

"I just gave you one."

"I should totally get hazard pay," Samantha said, her eyes flicking toward him. Her hands were clenched at her sides and he realized she was barely containing herself.

"What's wrong, Samantha?" he asked at last, deciding to bite the bullet.

She swiveled about on her scarily tall wedges and finally truly looked at him. Her eyes were shimmering. She was close to tears.

"Samantha?" Now he was truly worried.

"I told you to send her away and you insisted on her staying. You totally fucked up my life."

His eyebrows lifted. Cian was surprised by her outburst. He thought they had worked things out between them. "Sam..."

"Don't try to charm me. You made a choice and I'm paying for it!" Samantha shook her head, her pain evident on her face.

"I'm sorry."

"I know you are. But I'm still pissed!"

"I really believed that I could somehow reclaim my humanity," Cian said in a gentle tone. "I believed you could save me from myself. I did love you. I still care for you."

"I know that!" Samantha dabbed at her eyes with a well-used tissue. "Honestly, Cian, I get it. I do! Hell, I know that I was living a stupid dream. I thought I was Bella Swan to your Edward Cullen, but it was all a stupid dream."

Cian lightly touched her shoulder. "Samantha, we were both foolish to believe in that dream. We lied to ourselves and each other because it was a lovely, beautiful dream."

"I know! We were so stupid!" She slid easily into his arms and laid her head on his chest.

Cian rested his head on her soft blond hair, gently rocking her. He still cared deeply for her. Samantha was a very special person. Her heart was so open, her loyalty so fierce. Samantha had been brave enough to try to save him from The Summoner. That was the most amazing act of love anyone had ever shown him.

"You may be a good person, Cian, but you're a dumbass."

CHAPTER TEN

Cian laughed. "Maybe."

They pulled apart and he lightly touched her cheek. Her flushed skin was warm under his touch. He always loved the warmth of her flesh. She burned a little hotter than most humans. It always made him feel a bit more alive, but today she felt downright feverish.

"Samantha, what is going on?" He started to wonder if she was ill.

"I'm..." she shrugged.

"You're not here just to tell me what a cheating jerk I am, are you?"

"No, I gave you that speech already. And you still suck for it." Samantha took out a fresh tissue from her purse and blew her nose. "I'm here to talk to Morticia."

"Sam..."

"Look, fucker, I have a right to hate her for more reasons than you know. Okay?"

Cian started to protest, but stopped himself. He had betrayed Samantha with Amaliya. Instead of getting married to Samantha in a few weeks, he was living with Amaliya. How could he deny Samantha the right to be angry?

"Samantha, do you really think it wise for you to continue this argument with her?"

"Oh, I have a whole new thing with her. I need to talk to her like right now."

"We're waiting on an important phone call. This is not the best time."

"God, how can you think with that music?" Samantha glared toward one of the speakers, changing the subject.

"She's practicing." Cian shrugged.

"She gonna be a vampire rock star like Lestat?"

Cian snorted. "No, no. She loves drumming. It's her thing, I guess."

"Whatever." Samantha stalked toward the living room.

"Samantha, could we avoid a fight tonight?"

"No," she snapped.

Amaliya was just finishing a very dramatic drum solo when she spotted Samantha. She pointed a drumstick in the blonde's direction. "Don't interrupt!"

"Fuck you!"

With a growl of frustration, Amaliya continued playing, her blue-gray eyes glowering at the blond stalking toward her.

"We need to talk!" Samantha shouted over the music.

"Why? You hate me."

"Yeah? So? I still need to talk to you!"

Amaliya hissed, snatched up the remote for the stereo, and killed the music. Standing, she twirled the drumsticks around her fingers. Dressed in a tight black tank top and skinny jeans, Cian found her insanely sexy. Her feet were bare and she had painted her toenails and fingernails a bright red the night before. Dyed black hair hung in wild disarray around her face and Cian had the sudden urge to drag her off for a quickie. Instead, he folded his arms and stood to the side ready to referee.

"Okay, talk, little bitch." Amaliya tapped the drumstick against her thigh, waiting impatiently.

Surprisingly, Samantha seemed at a loss for words. Hesitantly, she shifted on her feet.

"Well?"

"Gimme a moment, slut. I'm trying to gather my thoughts."

Amaliya rolled her eyes.

Cian reached out and lightly touched Samantha's shoulder. "Just talk to us."

"This isn't easy to say!" Samantha exclaimed.

"What isn't easy to say?" Cian asked, knowing that she'd answer. He knew her very well and how to get her to respond.

"I'm seeing ghosts and it's vamp-bitch's fault!"

Amaliya blinked rapidly, surprised. "What?"

"I drank your stupid blood and now I'm seeing ghosts! *You* did this to me! You made me a fucking ghost whisperer!" Samantha stomped over to the couch and sat down, clutching her purse.

"Is this making sense to you?" Amaliya asked Cian.

Stunned by Samantha's words, Cian was trying to process the revelation. He had heard that servants of some vampires absorbed power through the transfer of blood over time. It usually took many years for those abilities to manifest. Of course, nothing about Amaliya had been the norm so far, so maybe there was something about the infusion of the necromantic power into her vampiric nature that had altered her blood.

"Cian?" Amaliya narrowed her eyes.

"It might be, though it would be very unusual for her to have abilities leeched off of your power after just one time imbibing your blood," Cian answered.

"Well, I am seeing ghosts. And it's her fault. I never had this before." Samantha pointed at Amaliya with an accusing finger. "Thanks for fucking up my life once again!"

In silence, Amaliya walked over to the couch and sat down on the opposite side of it. Drawing her knees up to her chest, she set her feet on the leather and stared at Samantha with a completely blank expression on her face.

"Your fault," Samantha repeated.

"Samantha, are you sure you're seeing ghosts?" Cian asked. Afraid of the close proximity of the two women, Cian moved to sit on the coffee table. He could easily keep them separated if he needed to.

"Oh, yeah. Damn sure." Samantha wrenched a folder out of her purse and thrust it at him.

"What's this?"

As Samantha explained all that had occurred, Cian flipped through the notes Jeff had made and the information on the dead woman Samantha had seen.

Amaliya was quiet, her arms folded on top of her knees. She was obviously listening, but wasn't saying a word.

"And these are?" Cian held up a list with dates and times.

"Well, Jeff and Benchley asked me a lot of questions and I realized that I have been seeing ghosts since I drank from her. I just didn't realize it because they weren't all gross and mucked up like Cassidy." Samantha dabbed at her eyes again. "Jeff thinks I'm getting stronger and that's why Cassidy asked me to help her."

Thrusting out her hand, Amaliya gestured for the folder. Cian handed it to her, then leaned toward Samantha.

"Samantha, Amaliya saved your life that night. You would have died. None of us knew this would happen to you." Cian lightly touched Samantha's trembling hand.

Beside them, Amaliya was looking through the folder.

"You know what, Cian? I was really freakin' happy before she showed up. My life was pretty good. Except for that bitch Roberto, our life together was really great. Then she came along and everything went to hell. The Summoner showed up and what else was I supposed to do? Let him kill you? I did what I could to save you and now..."

Amaliya slammed the folder down on the table and leaped off the couch. Shaking her head, she stormed off toward the balcony. "I need a fucking smoke."

"This is your fault!" Samantha shouted after her.

Amaliya whipped about, her hair falling around her face. "Oh, fuck, no, it's not! Look, little bitch, I did what I had to do to save your stupid ass even though I knew you hated me. I did you a goddamn favor!"

"I was trying to save you and Cian!"

"You were trying to save Cian!" Amaliya snagged her cigarettes off the dining room table and searched her jean pockets for her lighter.

"Because I loved him! I didn't want him to die! I would do it all over again!" Samantha jumped to her feet, dropping her purse on the floor. She didn't even seem to notice.

Cian sat quietly, letting the two women vent. They needed to do it so all of them could figure out what to do next. Though the women in his life had been hurling insults at each other for the last few months, they had not actually spoken about what had occurred. Amaliya was the queen of avoidance; Samantha was the queen of righteous indignation. It was not the best combination.

"Then don't scream at me for saving you!"

"This never would have happened if you hadn't come to Austin and fucked everything up!"

"This never would have happened if The Summoner hadn't fucking killed me and buried me in the fucking forest!"

Samantha started as if she had been slapped. Amaliya raised a trembling hand and pointed at Samantha. "Don't you fucking dare act like you're the only victim in all of this." Blood-tinged tears slowly slid down Amaliya's cheeks.

Lowering her eyes, Samantha said nothing.

"We're all fucked because of him. Because of The Summoner. Cian is what he is because of that asshole. I am what I am because that shit decided to play a game with my loser life. You're...a ghost whisperer because of him. Don't lay this on me!"

"If anything, it's my fault for not sending her away," Cian added, guiltily.

"No, it's not," Samantha said at last. "None of this is your fault." With a bitter laugh, she handed Amaliya a fresh tissue from the wad she was clutching in one hand. "You're so totally right. I'm being a complete bitch to you when it's not your fault."

"It's about fuckin' time you realized that," Amaliya growled, shoving the door to the balcony open and escaping.

Cian slid to his feet and moved to comfort Samantha. She held up a hand, warding him off.

"Please don't."

"Samantha."

"No, don't, Cian. I'm so sick of you being nice to me. I'm tired of the guilt in your eyes. You've said your piece." With that, Samantha followed Amaliya, shutting the door deliberately behind her, cutting him out of whatever came next.

Behind him, his phone began to ring.

CHAPTER ELEVEN

The sparkling beauty of the Austin skyline usually calmed Amaliya. Seeing the UT Tower lit up beyond the glowing white countenance of the state capital building was always a reminder of her happiest days in Austin as a young, hopeful college student. But tonight, staring at the bright lights and listening to the hum of traffic only made her feel like running away. The city felt claustrophobic and her skin crawled with the desire to flee.

When the door opened and slammed shut behind her, she knew who it was. It wasn't the smell of margaritas on Samantha's breath or the scent of her perfume, but the anger she felt pouring out of the woman she had usurped.

"I'm sorry," Amaliya said, exhaling a puff of smoke. She surprised herself by apologizing, but her rage had left her as quickly as it had come. The Summoner had wrecked all their lives to some degree, but Amaliya couldn't ignore the guilt pricking at her.

Samantha stepped up to the rail and curled her hands over the cool metal. She didn't respond, just stared outward, sniffling.

"You're a fucking annoying bimbette, but I really am sorry." Amaliya sighed.

"For what?"

With a shrug, Amaliya flicked ash into the wind. "All of it. I should have bailed. Left you and Cian to your lives."

With a strangled laugh that was mixed with a sob, Samantha shook her head. "It wouldn't have mattered. How much longer do you think we could isolate ourselves from the truth?"

Tilting her head, Amaliya scrutinized the tear streaked face of the woman beside her. "What do you mean?"

"It was all going to fall apart anyway. I can see it now. I mean...what would've happened? Cian and I would have had our pretty candlelight wedding and then what? Be happy for a few years? And then what would happen? I told him I didn't need to have kids to be happy, but that's only because I had this glamorous idea about one day being a vampire, too. He'd change me on my twenty-ninth birthday and I'd be fabulous forever. I was in love with the whole fairytale of living forever with him. Being forever young. Never dying."

Amaliya finished off her cigarette and reached for another one. "But you were happy."

"I didn't know him, bitchface," Samantha said wearily. "I know that now. In fact, I have known since you showed up that we weren't meant to be. If Cian and I were really as solid as I thought, you wouldn't have landed in our lives like a nuclear bomb."

Amaliya couldn't argue with that point. She had shattered the illusion that Cian and Samantha had constructed by their mutual desires. Cian's to be human again; Samantha's to be an eternal creature.

Glancing back into the apartment at Cian, who was talking on the phone, Samantha sighed. "I still believe Cian's a good guy, but I look at him and it's like I'm seeing a different person. I miss the image I had of him in my head. The fantasy I was in love with. I don't know him. Who he is now...he's yours."

Lighting up, Amaliya shrugged. "For now."

"What do you mean 'for now?'" Samantha narrowed her eyes.

"We live forever. Maybe one day we won't be able to stand each other." Amaliya lifted her shoulder dismissively. "We have the now. The future is..." She waved her hand toward the horizon. "The future is unknown." Cian and she had made no promises to each other. What they had now was great, but they didn't talk in terms of forever like mortals did.

Samantha stared at her with disbelief, then gradually understanding bloomed in her eyes. "It really is different for you, isn't it? Being what you are?"

Amaliya gave her a brief nod. "We could possibly live forever, or get murdered brutally tomorrow by Santos and his crazy half-sister. Fuck, The Summoner's favorite kid is sniffing around. We could be fucked so many different ways. Why talk about forever? I want the now. Whatever it is that Cian and I have, I want it for the here and now. It could be gone tomorrow." It felt good to say the words, to acknowledge the truth. No matter how desperately she wanted to run away, she also wanted to stay.

Watching Amaliya with a very thoughtful look in her eyes, Samantha was silent for a few minutes. Amaliya left her to her inner musings and enjoyed her cigarette. Surprisingly, talking to Samantha was making her feel better, but she had more yet to say.

"Did it hurt a lot when you died?"

Samantha's question was unexpected. Amaliya responded with a quick incline of her head.

"In the movies, the bite doesn't usually hurt."

CHAPTER ELEVEN

Amaliya laughed. "The Summoner ripped my throat out. It hurt like hell, but what was scarier was my blood pouring out of me. I remember thinking that I needed to stop the flow of blood. But there was no way to stop it. I knew immediately, even though I didn't want to accept it, that I was about to die. And he...was so happy to watch me die." Amaliya shuddered at the memory. She distinctly remembered the kiss he had placed on her forehead as the world had grown dim. "He told me I was pretty when I died."

"That's messed up. When I was dying, it hurt, but it felt peaceful, too. Like the world was just growing dimmer."

"I felt that, too." Amaliya hated the memory of The Summoner forcing his blood into her, watching her with delight as she choked. "But he ruined it."

"Do you wish you had stayed dead?"

"No." That was one thing Amaliya was sure of without a doubt. "No, I'm glad I'm here. I'm glad I found Cian. I know we hurt you, but I do...love him."

"You're such a whore," Samantha said, rolling her eyes.

"Fuck you." The words didn't hold the malice they usually did.

"I'm glad I'm alive, too. I'm...scared though."

Leaning her elbows on the railing, Amaliya stared out over the hills in the west. "I am, too."

"What am I?" Samantha asked fearfully. "Do I belong to you now or something?"

"I don't think so." Amaliya glanced over at the other woman. "I honestly don't know." She was secretly terrified that she was now somehow responsible for Samantha.

Samantha rubbed her face with her hands and let out an exasperated sound.

"Sam," Amaliya said, trying to gather her thoughts and fashion them into a sentence that would make sense and not piss off Samantha. "Sam, I'm sorry that you're different now. I know how fucked up it is. I fucking hate The Summoner for making me into a vampire the way he did. He didn't give me a choice. He just killed me. But I'm okay with what I am now. I like being a vampire. Now, ironically, I have made you into something...different...against your will. I feel like an asshole."

Amaliya tilted her head downward so she wouldn't have to see the speculative gaze of the other woman. She did feel guilty about a lot of what had happened, but at the same time it wasn't really her fault. Their lives were all totally fucked up because of The Summoner. He had abandoned her to struggle to survive. Now Samantha was transforming into something new and Amaliya instinctively wanted to duck any responsibility that might land on her shoulders. Yet, how could she do that? Wasn't that what The Summoner had done to her?

"I can call my grandmother to come and help you," Amaliya added.

"I'd like that. Even if she hates me."

"She doesn't hate you. She just doesn't like it when you call me names."

"Well, you deserve it," Samantha sniffed.

"I am sorry."

"You're still a whore."

"You're still a bitch."

They both laughed and smiled. Samantha rubbed her brow wearily and turned her focus toward the interior of the apartment, where Cian was on the phone.

"It's going to get worse, isn't it?"

Amaliya nodded. "Yeah."

"Will we live through it?"

"We'll try." Amaliya answered with grim determination in her voice.

"I'd like to fall in love, get married, and have a family one day," Samantha admitted. "I'd like to not be always afraid."

"You and Jeff dating still?"

"Kinda." Samantha sighed.

"Rebounding is a bitch."

"Not for Cian," Samantha said, sadness more than bitterness filling her words.

"We're vampires. We're..." Amaliya shrugged. "We're assholes."

Samantha busted out laughing. "Oh, yeah. Definitely."

The door opened behind them. Amaliya twisted around to see Cian. His expression was grim.

"What's up?"

"I plugged in your new phone and there are around thirty messages from your cousin and grandmother. You better check it out. The phone is still charging."

"Shit!" Amaliya shoved past him and ran to the kitchen where she always plugged in her phone. A shiny new one was sitting on the counter next to the box it had come in. Snatching it up, she quickly scanned the list of missed calls, then hit the screen to dial voicemail. Listening to the first message, fear punched her in the gut.

"Something is going on. Grandmama had a visitation," Amaliya blurted out to Cian and Samantha who were standing nearby, but not so close as to be obviously eavesdropping. Amaliya quickly dialed her cousin's number.

Sergio answered on the second ring. "About damn time."

"Sorry. My phone was busted in a...in an accident. I just got my new one. What's going on?" Amaliya's fingers were trembling. One sentence from the voicemail had stabbed her through with fear.

"Let me get Grandmama," Sergio answered.

Amaliya heard him calling out for their grandmother. The TV was playing in the background and his kids were talking loudly. It reminded her of the better times in her childhood when her mother had still been alive. That sort of normalcy was a dream of the past. It made her rather sad for just a moment.

"Amaliya," her grandmother said breathless. "You're in danger!"

It was so like her grandmother to cut straight to the point and ignore the small talk of conversation.

"Tell me about her," Amaliya said in a worried tone.

CHAPTER ELEVEN

"She was very pale, not just because she was a ghost, but because her hair was that blond that is almost white. She looked young, maybe in her late teens. Blue eyes. Very fair."

"She said The Summoner killed her," Amaliya's voice sounded weak and fearful even to her own ears. Her hand was shaking even more violently now. That one sentence in her grandmother's voicemail had struck through her like a bolt of lightning.

"Yes, she did. She gave me her name, but I forgot it when I woke up," her grandmother confessed.

"Was it Bianca Leduc?" Amaliya felt Cian's hands gently rest on her shoulders and she leaned back against him.

"Yes, that sounds right. I think so. Do you know who she is?"

"She was the girl that was buried in the forest. He killed her, too," Amaliya said, looking over her shoulder at Cian. "She's the one that didn't rise up to be a vampire."

Her grandmother was silent on the other end of the phone, but Amaliya could hear her breathing.

"Grandmama?"

"I'm trying to remember more about the dream, but it's very hard. I know she said you were in danger. But, I think she said something about a woman with red eyes. I can't remember," the older woman wailed.

"Do you think she will come to you again tonight?" Amaliya hated the sense of foreboding that was filling her.

"Yes, yes. I do. But I'll be ready this time. I'll remember what she says."

"Call me if she does, okay?"

"I will. You better answer your phone this time!"

Amaliya smiled despite the sick feeling in her stomach. "I promise I will."

After a few words of endearment, she hung up.

"Who is Bianca?" Samantha asked in a worried voice.

"She was in my class with Professor Sumner, aka the asshole. He killed her, too, but they found her in her grave. She didn't rise like I did. My grandmother says that Bianca visited her and said he'd killed her. That was my grandmother's voicemail. She couldn't remember much else other than I'm in danger from a woman with red eyes."

"All vampires have red eyes when in a rage or hungry," Cian said, frowning.

Clutching her phone, Amaliya leaned against the counter. She felt sickened by the thought of Bianca roaming the afterlife as a ghost, but was grateful that she was trying to help Amaliya. "I bet this is about Rachoń coming to Austin."

"Or it could be Etzli." Cian rubbed her back gently.

The memories of her death were flooding her mind's eye and Amaliya closed her eyes, pressing her palms against her eyelids. "I hate to say this, but I hope she visits my grandmother again."

"This is really bad, right?" Samantha's voice sounded weak, but close.

Amaliya looked up as Samantha opened up a cabinet, grabbed a glass, and filled it with water. The other woman's hand was shaking, too.

"I doubt it is anything significant. We already know that Etzli and Santos are intent on killing us. Rachoń is coming because she has a hidden agenda. I hate to say it, but the ghost of Bianca isn't really saying anything we don't know," Cian said.

"It has to be significant though," Amaliya protested. "If she's haunting my grandmother, her warning has to be important."

"I'm not saying that it's not, Amaliya. I'm saying that it's not anything we don't already know," Cian said. He appeared quite calm as he gazed down at her. His touch was gentle, but she could see by the look in his eyes he wanted her to calm down.

"I'm pretty sure this is really bad," Samantha said, daring to defy Cian. Amaliya could see the fear in the blond woman's face as she gazed at the male vampire. Cian was imposing in the moment. He was exuding calm and strength, but also a dangerous violence lurked underneath his exterior.

"I agree with her," Amaliya said.

Cian lifted his eyebrows, chuckling. "Oh, really?"

"Ghosts don't haunt unless they have a reason. Unfinished business, that sort of stuff," Samantha insisted. "I've been reading up on it all day since I saw that ghost this morning. This Bianca chick is trying to warn us about something through Innocente. You can't ignore that! You can't say, 'Oh, well, we know everyone wants us dead.' Yeah, maybe they do, but this is a very specific warning. A woman with red eyes."

Cian started slightly, his hazel eyes growing distant as he folded his arms over his chest. "Huh."

"What?" Samantha and Amaliya chorused.

"Rachoń has maroon eyes. It's a trait that runs in her family."

"She's not coming here to help us then. She's coming here to kill us," Amaliya exclaimed.

"She is The Summoner's favorite kid. She's totally going to be gunning for both of you. You can't let her into the city!" Samantha protested.

Cian stared off at some distant point in the horizon, then shrugged. "I'd rather she come here and get it over with then."

"What?" Samantha screeched.

Amaliya shoved him. "What the fuck, Cian?"

"Listen to me. I would rather she come and make her move now instead of joining forces with Etzli and Santos. We can handle her and her minions, but we can't go up against her, Santos, Etzli, and the San Antonio Cabal. Let Rachoń come. If she attacks, we kill her. And that will be a warning to anyone else out there that wants to attack us." Cian's voice was firm. His mind was clearly made up.

"Why don't you have more vampires in this cabal? There are only two of

CHAPTER ELEVEN

us! We're so fucked!" Amaliya shook her head, agitated. "Why don't we have a witch?"

"Yeah, what she said," Samantha said.

"Because I didn't want to deal with all this bullshit! All this political maneuvering! Dealing with the fuckin' dynamics of the undead world!" Cian responded in a gruff voice.

"Well, you're having to deal with it now!" Amaliya shouted at him.

"Because of you!" Cian snapped.

Amaliya sputtered she was so furious in that second.

"Fuck you, Cian!" Samantha said, stepping in front of Amaliya. "Fuck you! You decided to shelter her! You brought this on yourself! On all of us!"

"When did you two become best friends?" Cian looked amused and pissed at the same time.

Samantha threw Amaliya a dark look over her shoulder. "Yeah, why *am* I defending you? Is this that blood thing?"

Amaliya shrugged. She was still angry. They were all fucked.

"Rachoń is coming. We need to deal with that. Then we deal with Santos and Etzli," Cian said in a firm, authoritative voice.

"You're not the boss of me!" Samantha set her hands on her hips and glared. "I think we should vote on this."

"This isn't a democracy," Cian shot back.

"Well, you're a shitty dictator!"

Amaliya reached out and snagged Samantha's arm and drew her to her side. A surge of power swelled up between the two women for a moment, startling Amaliya, but Samantha didn't seem to notice. Recovering, Amaliya said, "He's not going to listen."

"We're so fucked," Samantha sniffed.

"Could you just trust me?" Cian asked.

"No," Amaliya said.

"Nope," Sam answered.

Cian frowned. "Why not?"

"Because you're not listening to the warning!" Amaliya exclaimed.

"Ghosts don't show up for no good reason, Cian!" Samantha added.

"Oh, so you see a few ghosts and now you're an expert?"

Amaliya and Samantha exchanged looks. Cian may be the badass vampire master of the city, but he was being an idiot and they both knew it.

"I would think that a good leader would recognize the assets he has around him and utilize them," Amaliya said, trying not to sound too sarcastic.

"I agree with her!"

Cian frowned as he pointed back and forth between them. "I'm older, stronger, and wiser than both of you."

"I see dead people," Samantha insisted.

"I make them into an army," Amaliya added.

Cian sighed.

"Don't let her come, Cian." Amaliya glared at the man she loved with all her heart, but wanted to toss off the balcony.

"It'll be bad if you do. Really bad," Samantha agreed.

"It's done. I already gave my word. You are both going to have to deal with it," Cian said in a tone that was firm.

"Fuck me," Amaliya sighed.

"You're being a stupid man!" Samantha shifted her purse strap onto her shoulder and strode toward the door. "A complete stupid man!"

"I am the vampire mast-"

"Oh, shove it up your ass," Samantha snarled and disappeared down the hallway.

Cian swiveled about to gaze at Amaliya evenly as Samantha slammed the door behind her as she exited the apartment.

She met his stare, raised her hand, and extended her middle finger. Clutching her phone, she darted past him and headed upstairs. She'd hang out in the TV room until she heard back from her grandmother.

"Amaliya!"

"Fuck you," Amaliya answered.

CHAPTER TWELVE

Cian stood in the dark, staring out over the sparkling lights of downtown Austin. After Amaliya and Samantha had stormed off, he had considered following Amaliya upstairs to speak to her reasonably. It had only taken the sound of the door upstairs slamming repeatedly for him to realize that he had best let Amaliya calm down before speaking to her again. Instead, he had turned off all the lights in the downstairs area and pondered the cityscape.

The change in Austin was dramatic. When Cian had arrived in the city, the tallest buildings had been the UT Tower, the capitol building, and the Westgate Tower. Now, towering buildings were rising up all around downtown. Construction sites dotted the area. Deep foundations were being dug behind hurricane fences and tall cranes hovered over the city.

Even in the residential neighborhoods, older houses were being torn down in favor of more modern structures. Lamar Boulevard was under transformation as well. Older stores were gone, replaced with new modern buildings that were reminiscent of other cities far away from Austin.

Yet, he couldn't mourn the past of Austin like others did. He was a vampire and during his long life he had watched the entire world change. Every decade was vastly different from the one before. Technology leaped forward every year now. Cian remembered his fascination with electricity, phones and automobiles when they had first appeared on the landscape, but now he updated his cellphones and computers without a second thought.

Everything changed as he remained the same. Forever twenty-seven, he would never see himself age, sicken and die. When his time came, it would be violent. There was no other form of death for a vampire.

When he had arrived in Austin, he had come with a purpose. The challenge laid down between The Summoner and Cian had been simple: If Cian could acquire a city, The Summoner would leave him to his own devices. Roberto and Cian had chosen Austin because it was a small city with a low population of supernatural creatures. The coyotes had run off any other type of weres and a war between black witches and white witches had destroyed their population. The vampire cabal had consisted of fairly young vampires who were more interested in living an extended youth with endless partying than being any sort of powerhouse among the supernatural world.

Christian, the vampire Master of Austin, had welcomed Cian warmly. Too young to realize Cian was centuries older than he was, Christian had considered Cian an asset to his cabal. It was Cian's wealth that had seduced Christian, and Cian made sure to spoil the vampires with everything they desired.

It was among them that Cian had found what he desired: a lovely woman with a kind heart and gentle soul who loved him. A Russian exchange student who had never gone home, Galina had been incredibly beautiful with vivid blue eyes, long dark hair and pale skin. She was the mortal lover and blood minion to Christian. Despite the danger of upsetting the Master of Austin, they had fallen in love and had a torrid affair behind Christian's back.

Pushing open the door to the balcony, Cian gazed toward the lake. It was there that he had betrayed the vampires. He had killed humans, deliberately leaving the telltale signs of a vampire. The police had quickly had a paranoid public on their hands. The Son of Sam murders and the Zodiac Killer had the population primed for a panic.

Roberto had helped Cian locate the local vampire hunters and Cian had brokered a deal with Jeff's father. The vampire hunters would destroy the cabal, and Cian, Roberto, and Galina would be spared. In exchange, Cian would take over the city and help keep it vampire free.

Cian still remembered awakening in a house filled with dead vampires. He had taken a risk remaining in the house with the cabal when the vampire hunters had come during the day to stake them and take their heads. Cian was confident that he could read people, and James Summerfield had been a man he felt he could trust. Crawling out of his coffin, he had found Summerfield sitting among the dead cabal.

"It's done," Professor Summerfield had said in a weary voice. He had been splattered with vampire blood and still held a machete.

"And the girl?" Cian had asked.

"Alive."

Cian found Galina huddled in one of the bedroom closets. Terrified, she had screamed when he opened the door. Galina clung to him as he took her from the house they had shared with the cabal. She had been inconsolable for days, mourning Christian despite the fact she had been sleeping with Cian for some time. Cian had hoped she would regain her senses and stay with him, but one night he had awoken to find she had fled.

He had been alone for years afterward until Samantha stumbled into his life.

CHAPTER TWELVE

Just as he had hurt Galina, Cian had also hurt Samantha.

Frowning, Cian leaned against the railing of the balcony. Over the years he had made plenty of mistakes, but he was determined not to repeat them. He recognized now that he should have built up a cabal of vampires and other supernaturals. He should have anticipated that one day The Summoner would be gone and with him the protective veil that kept Cian from attack.

Without realizing it, Cian had wasted time and endangered not only himself, but the woman he now loved. The last few months had been the best he could remember in a very long time. Amaliya had not only reawakened the vampire in him, but the true man. He had been foolish to believe he could return to the man he was before The Summoner had seized him, killed him, and turned him.

Perhaps Rachoń was coming to kill him, but his years with her caused him to believe it was not so simple. Rachoń was clever and deceptive. She would never attack him outright. He believed that without a doubt. Perhaps it was because he shared those very traits with her. Cian was a master at manipulation from his years dealing with The Summoner.

Rubbing his face, Cian sighed. The city was alive below him, filled with life and excitement. It was his city, yet he had failed it. Only he, Amaliya, and an inexperienced crew of vampire hunters could protect it from whatever Rachoń, Etzli and Santos were planning.

Though his mistakes were now haunting him, he knew he would not fall without a fight. No matter what their enemies conspired, Cian believed that he and Amaliya could withstand their attacks.

If they died, he was consoled with the thought of being with her until the very end.

"No more morose thoughts," he chided himself.

Turning, he slipped back into his apartment.

Snuggled into a recliner he had dragged into his grandmother's bedroom, Sergio kept a wary eye on her tiny form on the bed. The whisper of the A/C unit in the window mingled with her soft snoring into a comforting sound. Burrowing deeper into the old worn quilt his wife had tucked around him, Sergio wished his grandmother didn't like to sleep in such a cold room. The quilt wasn't quite big enough to cover his large frame and he kept having to readjust his limbs to keep his feet and elbows from being exposed to the chilly air.

The glow of his cellphone screen was hidden under the quilt as he watched the fourth season of *Dr. Who*. As a precaution, he wore only one ear bud. Watching the antics of the Doctor and his companions, he stifled a yawn. He had already called into work and hoped that he wouldn't end up on the bad end of his boss' temper. Cynthia had volunteered to keep watch in Innocente's room, but Sergio didn't want to put her in danger. He wasn't too sure where ghosts were on a scale of scariest monsters, but he wasn't looking forward to one showing up in his grandmother's bedroom.

Sipping the watered down remains of the soda in his glass, he swept his gaze over the room, scrutinizing every inch of it. Nothing seemed amiss.

The clock on the bed stand next to his grandmother's big king-size bed said it was nearly three in the morning. Yawning again, Sergio fought the urge to close his eyes and sleep. He stared intently at the tiny screen before him as the Doctor ran about with Donna on his heels.

Lifting his glass to sip the very last bit of his drink, he gasped as the icy surface felt like it stung his flesh. He briefly glimpsed the soda frozen solid at the bottom of the glass just as his phone went dead, cutting off the Doctor in mid-sentence and plunging the room into darkness.

The blackness that filled the room terrified him. It was absolute. He couldn't even make out his own hand in front of his eyes. Forcing his limbs into action, he set his phone and glass aside on the floor and slid to the edge of his chair.

The temperature was dropping fast and he was certain the dinky little air conditioner wasn't the cause. Wrapping the quilt tightly around his broad shoulders, he rose to his feet. The dark was unwavering in its intensity. The digital clock's red numbers weren't even visible in the thick miasma of black.

Out of the gloom, his grandmother's voice was a soft whisper. He couldn't discern her words for it was difficult to hear over the chattering of his teeth. The piercing cold enveloped him and his body violently shivered.

Sergio couldn't recall the distance between the bed and the chair. Cautiously, he inched his way toward the sound of his grandmother's murmuring. Just as his knee bumped the edge of the bed, Sergio was engulfed in the clutch of an icy pillar of air.

"Fuck!"

Stumbling, he tripped over the corner of the bed and fell with a mighty thump. The wood floor shivered beneath him. Gasping in the frigid air, he grabbed onto the mattress and hauled himself onto his knees.

At the end of the bed stood a young woman with white-blond hair and incandescent white eyes. Dressed in a white lace dress, she glowed in the blackness that surrounded her.

"What the hell?" Sergio gasped, his big hand reaching out for his whimpering grandmother.

The girl slightly tilted her chin, her terrifying eyes appearing to gaze at him.

"Grandmama," Sergio hissed. "Wake up! She's here."

The bedroom door banged open and the overhead lamp sprang to life. Cynthia stood in the doorway clutching a shotgun. "I heard a big crash!"

One look at the end of the bed informed Sergio that the apparition was gone. Yet, his grandmother remained asleep, clutching her pillow.

"I tripped," Sergio answered. He gripped his grandmother's hand. It was terrifyingly cold.

"It's freezing in here," Cynthia exclaimed, her breath a mist.

"It was here. I saw the ghost." His heart was beating so fast in his chest

CHAPTER TWELVE

it almost hurt. He bundled his grandmother into his arms, gently shaking her. "Grandmama, wake up. C'mon. Wake up."

Cynthia set the shotgun aside, quickly slid onto the edge of the bed, and reached out to touch the older woman. "She's so cold!"

"C'mon, Grandmama. C'mon, wake up." The old woman lay limp in his arms as he continued to shake her. Her lips were slightly moving, but there was no sound coming from them.

With tender motions, Cynthia rubbed Innocente's hands and arms, trying to warm them. "Wake up, Innocente. Please wake up."

Eyelashes fluttering, Innocente muttered, "Bianca..."

"Yes, she was here again. I saw her," Sergio said.

"...she's..." Innocente struggled to open her eyes. "...she's what Amaliya is..." The old woman sank back into unconsciousness.

"What does she mean?" Cynthia asked, her dark eyes seeking solace in Sergio's.

"I don't know." Fearful, Sergio shook the older woman with a little more vigor. "Grandmama, wake up!"

Innocente's eyes gradually opened. "Stop shaking me..."

"Then wake up!"

Her tiny, veiny hand slapped his arm. "I'm awake..."

"Sit her up, Sergio," Cynthia ordered. She grabbed some decorative pillows from the chair in front of the small vanity where Innocente set them before crawling into bed. In the morning she always made her bed and arranged the colorful pillows against the headboard.

Sergio helped Innocente sit up as Cynthia propped the embroidered pillows behind her. "Go get her something to drink, honey."

Cynthia hurried out of the room.

"Grandmama, talk to me." Sergio shook her again as her amber eyes closed.

Visibly forcing her eyes open, Innocente focused on her grandson's face. "I saw Bianca in my dreams again."

"I saw her standing at the end of your bed."

"Her eyes were white like Amaliya's when she calls the dead," Innocente continued.

"I saw that."

"She's what Amaliya is."

"I don't understand. What do you mean by that?"

Cynthia returned with a glass of water and Innocente took it gratefully. After several small sips, Innocente nestled back on the pillows. She looked a little more lucid, but also very troubled. "Bianca is like Amaliya. She can call the dead."

"Even though she's dead?" Sergio asked, confused by her words.

"No, no. She's not dead. I was wrong." Innocente rubbed her brow. "She's a vampire, too."

Cynthia inhaled sharply as Sergio squinted in confusion.

85

"You're not making sense. I saw her standing in this room. Vampires can't get in the house, Grandmama. We had the house blessed by the priest."

"She's astral projecting," Innocente explained.

"Spirit walking?" Cynthia asked.

Innocente nodded. "Yes. She's somewhere else. Trapped. She's seeking help because the woman who captured her is very evil and wants to kill Amaliya."

"So this vampire girl can astral project to you? How does she even know about you?" Sergio didn't like what he was hearing in the least. It sounded wrong to him.

"She heard her captor talking about Amaliya and about me. Bianca is stronger than her captor realizes. Since she can communicate with the dead, she was able to finally find her way to me." Innocente smiled sadly. "The dead do talk to each other."

"We have to call Amaliya and warn her, Sergio." Sergio hated the way Cynthia's lips were pale and slightly trembling. She was afraid, but trying to be strong. He was very proud of her.

Taking her hand, he gave it a gentle squeeze. "I'll call her now."

"Please, hurry," Grandmama urged him.

Tenderly, Sergio laid the quilt around his wife's shoulders. It was slowly warming up in the bedroom, but she was shivering. Sergio snatched his phone off the armrest of the chair he had been sitting in and tried to turn it on. To his relief, the loading screen flashed brightly as it booted back up.

"Should we have the priest come and bless the house again?" Cynthia wondered aloud.

"No, no. She can only come here in spirit. I need her to talk to me, to tell me what this evil woman with the red eyes is planning against my Amaliya," Innocente answered.

"Why is she trying to help Amaliya?" Sergio watched the cellphone screen, waiting for it to finish the startup process.

"I think because they were in a class together when they were mortal. Bianca knows that *puto* killed Amaliya, too." Innocente rubbed her head again. "I have such a bad headache now. I was trying too hard to hold on to what she told me."

Cynthia dug around in the drawer of the bed stand until she came up with a bottle of aspirin. She carefully doled out a few pills and hurried to refresh Innocente's glass of water. Sergio watched her depart to the kitchen clutching the glass, a sad pang in his heart. He hated seeing his wife stressed and afraid. None of them had asked to be a part of the world of the supernaturals, but they were not the type of people to turn their backs on family. Sergio knew that Innocente would not back down from trying to protect Amaliya.

Finally, the phone finished rebooting and Sergio dialed Amaliya's number. She answered almost immediately.

"Bianca came again tonight," Sergio said.

"And?" Amaliya sounded testy, but also anxious.

"I'll let Grandmama tell you." Sergio handed over the phone and settled on

CHAPTER TWELVE

the bed next to his grandmother. In silence, he listened to her explain to Amaliya what she had told him and Cynthia. When she finished, she handed the phone back to Sergio.

"What are you going to do, Amal?" Sergio asked.

There was a beat of silence, then Amaliya said, "I don't know. I have no fucking clue. I have to talk to Cian."

"Keep us in the loop, okay?" Sergio tucked his arm around his grandmother's shoulders and she leaned her head against him.

Amaliya sighed. "I will, but you guys keep safe."

"We'll do our best." Sergio clicked off and snuggled his grandmother. "There, we warned her."

"We should go to Austin," Innocente decided.

Cynthia returned with a fresh glass of water. Her eyes were red and it was clear she had been crying. "You already helped kill one vampire. Don't go picking fights with more."

Innocente frowned as she took the glass and swallowed her pills.

"Listen to my wife, Grandmama. She's right. We need to stay out of it. Let Cian and Amaliya deal with it."

"They might need us," Innocente protested.

"If they do, they'll call," Sergio assured her.

With an exhausted sigh, Innocente nodded, relenting. Maybe she was more afraid than she was letting on. In all truthfulness, Sergio hoped that they would never get a call from Amaliya asking for them to go to Austin. After what Sergio had seen the last time they had fought the powerful undead, he wasn't sure he would survive another encounter.

Amaliya shoved her cellphone into her pocket before stalking through the apartment seeking Cian. Frustrated and unnerved by all her grandmother had told her, Amaliya was ready to resume her argument with Cian. She heard him moving about on the second floor of their apartment, so she started opening doors. She rarely ventured into the smaller guest bedrooms. They were tastefully decorated, but rarely used. Her grandmother and Sergio had stayed with them only a few times, but otherwise the rooms remained empty. The maid service that came twice a week changed the bedding, dusted, and swept, but Amaliya didn't really see the need for even that.

Opening the fourth door, she found Cian standing in the center of the room. The mattress was off the platform bed and leaning against the far wall. Cian was leaning over the base of the bed, which was basically a big flat box made out of polished wood. A secret panel revealed an array of weapons, some appearing quite ancient, tucked into foam inside.

"You and your secret compartments," Amaliya grumbled.

Cian glanced up at her, slightly smiling. "I'm always full of surprises."

Leaning against the door jamb, Amaliya rested one hand on her hip and glowered at him.

"We're still fighting?" Cian asked.

"Yes."

Squatting next to his secret stash, Cian withdrew a sword and studied the blade. "All right. You go first."

"Do we have to get physical? My sword-fighting skills aren't all that great." She quirked an eyebrow at him.

Cian rolled his eyes at her joke. "Amaliya..."

"I talked to Sergio and my grandmother. She had another visitation."

"From Bianca?"

"Yeah. From Bianca. The other chick The Summoner killed."

Cian set the sword down and withdrew a wicked-looking dagger that appeared to be made of black stone. "And?"

"She's not a ghost."

Flicking his gaze toward her, curiosity bloomed in his expression. "Go on."

"She's a vampire, and she's astral projecting."

Amaliya smiled triumphantly as Cian stood up abruptly. His slightly sarcastic demeanor was gone. He looked deadly. "Go on."

"She's like me. She's a necromancer. She raises the dead."

"How do you know that?" Cian crossed the room swiftly to stand at her side.

"Sergio saw her eyes glowing when her apparition appeared in my grandmother's room. My grandmother saw it in her dream when she spoke to Bianca. Bianca begged her for help. She said that the woman with the red eyes is holding her and planning to use her to kill me."

"Rachoń..."

"Yeah. Probably. Bianca is terrified and begging for help. My grandmother said that the girl has been seeking her out for months and finally found her." Amaliya poked Cian in the chest with one finger. "I can't astral project, fucker, and she can. What the fuck, Cian? What is she?"

"I haven't the slightest. Astral projecting is quite complicated. I've known a few witches who could do it, but I never heard of a vampire doing it." Frowning, Cian glanced down at the blade in his hand. "This is disconcerting."

"Oh, fucking yeah, it's disconcerting! I told you that Rachoń is coming for us to kill us. I don't know why the hell you can't accept that. She has her own gawddamn necromancer, Cian. She doesn't need to make a pact with you. I'm not so rare now, am I?"

"It makes no sense. Why are there two of you?" Cian brushed past Amaliya and headed down the hall. "He never passed his power on before to anyone. At least not that I know of."

"Well, The Summoner did and now there are two of us!' Amaliya stalked after Cian. "Can Rachoń make her try to kill me?"

Glancing over his shoulder, Cian gave a short nod.

CHAPTER TWELVE

"Uh, could you, like, give me some details?"

"If Bianca rose shortly after her burial, Rachoń has had four months to feed her blood. Rachoń's own blood, therefore, binding Bianca to her. She can use that bond to force Bianca to do her bidding."

"Wait. I drink your blood." Amaliya stopped dead in her tracks just as they reached the staircase. She suddenly felt ill, not physically, but emotionally. "Fuck you. You bound me to you!"

Gripping the rail, Cian turned toward her. "I drink your blood. You bound me to you. Plus, we were made by the same master, so that adds to our bond. You and I had no choice but to be drawn to one another, Amaliya. That is why we..." he hesitated.

"What?"

He ascended a few steps to stand below her, his hand reaching out to touch her. She pulled away from him, horrified that she might be under some terrible spell he had cast on her. If he had robbed her of free will, she was going to kill him.

"That is why we lusted for each other, why we were entangled so quickly. But that isn't why I love you. Lust is lust. But I do love you and that is because of who you are."

Gazing into his hazel eyes, so earnest and full of adoration, Amaliya felt her fear starting to fade. "And who am I?"

"An infuriatingly hard-headed woman who lives her life with an intensity that I find exhilarating and frightening. Who is kind even though she won't admit it. Strong, despite her desire to sometimes run away. Intelligent. Talented. Beautiful."

Amaliya went into his arms and clung to him. "Fuck you, Cian. You're going to make me cry."

"That's my girl."

He pressed a kiss to her cheek, then took her hand. "C'mon. We need to talk to Jeff and his vampire hunters. We're supposed to be meeting them at midnight anyway, but we need to meet now. "

"So I was right and you were wrong."

"Somewhat," Cian said, flashing a smile at her.

The emotion that swelled inside of her at the sight of his smile didn't feel like some magical bond. It felt like love. Maybe they were bonded to each other, but there was something more going on between them. Something real, and Amaliya clung to that truth as Cian drew her along behind him.

She just hoped they survived long enough to enjoy it.

CHAPTER THIRTEEN

Exhausted, Jeff was not in the mood to deal with the gathering of people in the back room of his bookstore. It was a little past ten and the only thing making him feel alert was the caffeine and sugar he was pouring into his system. He had hoped for a nice nap before his midnight meeting with Cian, but that had not come to pass. Cian's urgent phone call had come right after Jeff's head had hit the pillow.

The hot steam from his black coffee tickled his nose as he took another sip, his eyes watching the people gathered around the long table over the rim of his Bela Lugosi mug.

Cian, Amaliya, and Samantha had been the first to arrive. Now the vampire Master of Austin lurked in the back of the room, leaning against the wall, arms folded over his chest. Jeff often wondered how humans couldn't tell when they were in the presence of a vampire. Cian was unnaturally alluring to both sexes with his keen hazel eyes and magnetic gaze. Jeff often felt himself wanting to give in to a need to make Cian happy. He saw Benchley react in the same manner. They wanted to be his buddy, to please him. It made Jeff very uncomfortable to recognize the power Cian had when he wasn't even attempting to wield it.

Yawning, he glanced toward Amaliya and Samantha. They were seated next to each other at the opposite end of the table. They were being surprisingly civil to one another. That fact made Jeff extremely nervous. Samantha's earlier rage was gone, replaced by a quiet surrender that he wasn't sure he liked.

Benchley had arrived next with his sister Alexia, who resembled a teenage boy with her short brown hair and unisex way of dressing. She was slumped down next to her brother wearing a hoodie, skinny jeans, and Converse sneakers. She was the tech-girl of their outfit and wickedly smart.

Eduardo had arrived last. He was the only one of the hunters who looked remotely alert. Then again, he was nocturnal by nature. His specialty lay with his dual nature, part human, part coyote. Dark hair slicked back from his recent shower, his lean body was clad in a tight black T-shirt, jeans, and battered cowboy boots. He was short, but powerful. When he had entered the store, he had acknowledged Cian with a low bow of his head. Cian policed the vampires entering the city and Eduardo kept an eye out for weres.

Despite Austin being a hotbed for pagans, Wiccans, and other alternative religions, there were no actual magical witches in the city. Jeff had been on the lookout for years. He could really use one on his team, but the supernatural world was very good at hiding itself. There was always the possibility of other supernatural creatures in Austin riding under the radar.

It was Benchley who broke the uneasy silence that followed Cian, Amaliya, and Samantha's rundown of all the recent developments.

"How does this even make sense? She's supposed to be the oddity. The freak!" He pointed at Amaliya with an accusing finger.

"Gee, thanks," Amaliya grumbled.

"I didn't mean it like that!" Benchley combed his hands through his already-messy hair. "I mean, how can there be two of them? Two necromancer vampires? What the fuck is going on? Why are all the rules changing?"

"Rules are made to be broken," Eduardo said with the flash of a smile. "So now there are two of them. Who cares?" He gave a dismissive shrug of his impressive shoulders.

"But there was one necromancer vampire for how long? Thousands of years and then suddenly, we have two?" Benchley stared at Amaliya with a mixture of awe and fear. This was only his second time meeting her and his nerves were showing.

Jeff wished Benchley hadn't drunk most of the pot of coffee on his own. The guy was jittery as hell.

"I blame The Summoner," Sam declared. "It's his fault! He did something to Amaliya and this girl, Bianca."

"The question is why and how?" Alexia's voice, like her appearance, was very boyish.

Amaliya shrugged and hooked her legs over the armrest of her chair. She was wearing very sexy leopard print high heels with red soles. "He's dead. Not like we can ask him."

"Can't say I'm not glad to see that bastard dead." Benchley tapped his fingers on the table. "But he did change things. Somehow."

Jeff nodded as he flipped through one of the books his father had kept on The Summoner. "Cian, there is no other record of this happening. Are you sure you haven't heard of him making necromantic vampires before?"

"Positive. I would have heard about it. Hell, he would have boasted about it." Cian unfolded his arms and sighed. "This is very unexpected."

CHAPTER THIRTEEN

"I got the impression he was surprised by my powers." Amaliya tugged on the ends of her long hair, studying them for split ends. "But then again, he never said he was surprised that I was a necromancer like him. Maybe he was surprised that my powers manifested the way they did. He could call the dead without shedding blood like I have to."

The frown on her face deepening, Samantha asked, "But why did he leave Bianca behind?"

"She didn't rise when expected." Cian finally joined them. He snagged a chair and dragged it to the end of the table, sitting near Jeff. "He may have thought that she wasn't going to change. Sometimes the blood transfer doesn't work. The person never transforms, or only partially transforms."

"Which is where ghouls come from, right?" Benchley asked.

"Ghouls are gross," Alexia grumbled.

"Yes, that's where ghouls come from." Cian leaned forward to look at the book Jeff was flipping through. "Ghouls are the bastard children of vampires."

"What's this ghoul thing?" Amaliya asked, arching her eyebrows.

Benchley raised his hand as though he were in school, realized what he was doing, then awkwardly put it down. "Uh, they're really nasty looking. Kinda like zombies meet the Gollum. They eat dead bodies."

"And sometimes live bodies," Alexia interjected.

"We saw one once. In a graveyard in Fredericksburg," Benchley continued. "Really nasty."

"They have a taste for vampire blood. I had to fight a pack once. They nearly took me down." Cian frowned and stopped Jeff from flipping pages.

Jeff looked at him curiously, but Cian had bent his head to read something.

"So, maybe he thought she was a ghoul?" Benchley looked dubious. "So he leaves her behind and goes after Amaliya because he thinks she's the experiment that worked?"

Samantha eyeballed Amaliya thoughtfully.

Amaliya returned the look with her eyebrows raised. "What?"

"Maybe he's been trying to do this kinda thing for a long time but it didn't work until you because of your grandmother," Samantha said breathlessly.

"Huh?" Amaliya glanced toward Jeff curiously. "Is she making sense?"

"I think she might be," Alexia said, sounding impressed. "Isn't she, Jeff?"

Samantha looked pleased with herself.

Jeff suddenly felt a lot more alert. Cian was studying a news article on Bianca Leduc that Jeff had added to the back of the book when her body had been discovered during the Satanic Murders coverage. Jeff scooted his chair closer to Cian and craned his head to read the article.

"Well? Is she onto something?" Benchley asked, sounding cross.

"They're looking at something. Calm down." Eduardo slid to his feet and prowled around the table to the coffee and muffins set up nearby.

"I'm right, aren't I?" Samantha excitedly jumped to her feet and scurried around the table. She nearly crawled onto Jeff's lap trying to see what they were looking at.

Jeff gave up and slid over on his seat, giving her a corner to perch on.

"I'm so right!" Samantha stabbed at the article excitedly.

Cian's gaze met Jeff's. "This is disconcerting to say the least."

"Disconcerting is his favorite word tonight," Amaliya informed Samantha.

"Spill it! Suspense! Killing us!" Benchley cried out.

"Two words: Josephine Leduc." Jeff glanced up at the two primary ghost hunters.

"Oh, wow!" Alexia exclaimed. "That chick was hardcore! A freakin' legend!"

"Wasn't she the one who solved actual murders? They could never prove her to be a fake. We've got a whole book on her!" Benchley loudly scooted his chair back and rushed into Jeff's office.

Amaliya glanced over at Eduardo. "You have any idea what the geek squad is talking about?"

"Nah." Eduardo slid into the chair that Samantha had abandoned next to Amaliya and smirked. "They all talk in riddles. I'm just the muscle."

Poking one of his impressive arms with her finger, Amaliya said, "I can see that!"

Eduardo flexed for her benefit while Cian loudly cleared his throat.

"Bianca Leduc has a similar bloodline to you, Liya," he said. "Which means that The Summoner may have been experimenting on both of you."

"Still in the dark here." Amaliya shrugged.

"Bianca Leduc is the granddaughter of a very famous medium from the Shreveport area," Jeff explained. Rubbing his chin, he looked at Samantha and Cian. "This is what we missed all those months ago. The connection between Amaliya and Bianca."

"We didn't know Bianca was important until now. She was just another body, another victim," Cian pointed out.

Samantha slid onto Jeff's lap to better read the article. He happily wrapped an arm around her waist, enjoying the feel of her so close to him. Her hair smelled of shampoo and her skin of flowers. He must have been obviously staring at her because she blushed as she stole a look at him. He returned it with a shy smile.

"Okay, found the file!" Benchley dropped a leather book onto the table. Alexia immediately bent over it with him.

Cian sat in the chair next to Amaliya, giving Eduardo a warning look.

Eduardo just smirked.

Amaliya settled her legs onto Cian's lap and grinned at him teasingly. "So someone explain this to me. What the hell are you talking about?"

"If both of you are descended from mediums, he may have been trying to see if your power would connect with his." Cian gently swept Amaliya's hair back from her face. "He made you with a purpose in mind."

"Well, I don't know if that makes me feel better or not. Knowing there was a

CHAPTER THIRTEEN

purpose to what he did to me kinda freaks me out."

Samantha slid into the chair Cian had vacated and Jeff instantly missed her in his arms. She leaned her elbows on the table and stared at the article. "So I'm right, right?"

"It does make sense. His necromantic power has to do with the dead. If the affinity to see and talk to the dead is in your bloodlines, then he could have been hoping that you would inherit his power. So Samantha is probably right."

"Ha! Score! See, I can figure this shit out!" She smiled triumphantly at those gathered around the table.

"Color me impressed," Alexia muttered.

Benchley leaned over the table to high-five Samantha. "Way to go, Sam!"

Jeff returned Samantha's smile when she glanced at him. She looked a lot more peaceful than she had earlier in the evening. He hadn't been too happy to hear she had gone to confront Amaliya, but it seemed to be just what she needed to do to get a grip on the situation.

"Josephine Leduc's daughter would have been a primo target for him," Alexia decided. "He got lucky finding two descendants of famous mediums in the same place."

"It would have been irresistible to him," Cian noted.

"But Grandmama isn't famous," Amaliya protested. "She kept all that on the lowdown on purpose."

"Not true," Alexia said, looking up. "After your grandmother killed The Summoner, I did a little digging. She was in the newspapers when she was a teenager. There was a devastating tornado in her town and she helped find the survivors buried in the rubble. When they asked her how she knew where the living were located, she said the dead told her. She was thirteen at the time, so she probably didn't realize the reporter would actually put that into his article."

"Are you serious?" Amaliya sat back in shock. "She did that?"

"Yeah. There was just one more follow up article where there was a backlash from the local churches against her. Her dad, your great-grandfather, said that the reporter hadn't told her who he was and that she had misspoken," Alexia explained. "I told Jeff all about it."

"Oh, really?" Amaliya tilted her head toward the end of the table. "Really, Jeff?"

Jeff could feel Amaliya's eyes boring into him. "Hey, it was just two articles. I didn't think it was important enough to bring it up to you. I mean you know what she is, right?"

Amaliya shook her head, annoyed. "So sick of people not telling me shit."

"It wasn't on purpose," Jeff said defensively.

"So he could have found out about Amaliya's grandmother pretty easily?" Samantha asked, obviously trying to move the conversation on.

"It wasn't hard to find actually," Alexia confessed.

"It was on a website about the supernatural. It was filed under unexplained paranormal events with mediums." Benchley shrugged. "Of course, Josephine was a much bigger story. She was so good at what she did cops from all over the country would come to her."

"So why didn't he just turn her. Josephine Leduc?" Amaliya looked cross and her eyes flashed slightly red.

"Maybe because she died in a horrible fire," Alexia answered Amaliya's question. "They could never prove it was arson, but it was strongly suspected that someone deliberately killed her. There was a lot of hostility aimed at her. People accused her of being in league with the devil."

"Give me a freakin' break," Amaliya muttered.

"Humans fear what they don't understand." Cian folded his arms across his chest. "That's why the supernaturals remain hidden."

"Yeah, my people were nearly hunted to extinction," Eduardo agreed. "There aren't a lot of us left. I admit that a few of my ancestors did some shady things. Personally, I don't think dragging off a few babies is really a good excuse to wipe out all of my people."

"They ate babies?" Samantha looked aghast. "Gross!"

Eduardo shrugged. "They were hungry."

Jeff gave Eduardo a warning look. Eduardo loved to instigate arguments. It was part of his shifter nature to like a good fight, but it wouldn't be helpful in the moment. Eduardo just shrugged and flashed his teeth. Jeff knew better than to interpret it as a smile.

"So back to the subject at hand," Jeff said, trying to redirect everyone's focus. "Rachoń, The Summoner's favorite child, is coming to Austin tomorrow night supposedly to create a pact with Cian. She's bringing Bianca, who apparently is a necro-vamp like Amaliya."

"Necro-vamp?" Amaliya raised her eyebrows even higher.

"I just made that up. Don't like it?"

Amaliya gave a dismissive shrug. "Whatever."

"Okay, so we need to be prepared for trouble," Jeff continued.

"Don't *they* need to be ready for trouble?" Eduardo said. He pointed to Cian and Amaliya. "We're not their minions."

Jeff saw the flash of red in Cian's eyes. "No, but we're their allies."

Benchley and his sister exchanged looks, then looked toward Jeff. "Uh, Jeff. What are you saying?" Benchley's voice quavered.

"Uh, what I'm saying is that we need to figure out how to deal with this situation. Remember, if Cian falls as Master of Austin we're fucked. Because whoever takes over is going to come looking for us." Jeff folded his arms across his chest. This was the conversation he had been dreading.

"But how can we help?" Alexia asked. "We're humans...except for Eduardo."

Jeff sat forward, resting his elbows on the table. He tried not to look as scared as he felt, but to project confidence like his father would have. "We need to prep like we would for a vampire hunt. We also need to study everything we can

CHAPTER THIRTEEN

about necromancers. We didn't have a chance to do that when The Summoner was in town—"

"You actually never called us in on that," Benchley reminded him.

"Yeah, you stiffed us on that one," Alexia said, her voice shaded with hurt feelings.

"Oh, yeah." Jeff winced.

The glares from his team said it all. Jeff admitted they had a right to be mad at him, but he was still adapting to being a leader. It was hard following in his father's footsteps.

"You could have used us. Especially me." Eduardo glanced briefly at Amaliya. "I could have helped rescue this beautiful lady."

Amaliya smiled at Eduardo as she laid a restraining hand on Cian's arm. The vampire was looking tense enough without Eduardo needling him.

"So we have two major vamps gunning for Austin out of San Antonio and Cian's—" Benchley made quotations with his fingers "'sister' coming to Austin with a necro-vamp minion to kill Cian and Amaliya. And we're stuck in the middle because if either one of those groups takes out our friendly vamps, we're next on the menu."

"It's worse than that," Cian said.

"What can be worse than everyone trying to kill us, me going all *Sixth Sense* and Amaliya being a bitch?" Samantha asked.

Amaliya gave Samantha a sly wink.

Samantha giggled.

Jeff sat back in his chair, his gaze darting back and forth between the two women. This newfound truce between them was a little eerie. He saw from Cian's facial expression he felt the same way.

"Um, what's worse is that Bianca has powers that Amaliya doesn't have. She can astral project," Cian pointed out. "Or did all of you hunters miss that point?"

Benchley squirmed on his chair as Alexia opened her mouth to protest, then resorted to just glaring at Cian. Eduardo chuckled.

"Uh, that was missed," Jeff admitted. "Amaliya can't do that, I take it?"

Amaliya shook her head.

"So, we have a necro-vamp who is the daughter of one of the most powerful documented mediums of all time," Alexia said, twisting the corner of her mouth, "and she's coming here."

"We're boned, huh?" Benchley rested his forehead on the table with a small thump.

"Grandmama is pretty sure that Rachoń is coming to kill me," Amaliya said, shrugging. "The Summoner and I did have the same power, but his worked differently. I have to shed blood to make the dead rise. He didn't."

"But that worked to your advantage," Benchley remarked, his head still resting on the table. "You took the zombies from him when you sprinkled them with blood."

Samantha made a face. "Ugh. Blood. Why is it always blood with you guys?"

"Because we're vampires?" Cian gave her an amused look.

Samantha wrinkled her nose at him.

Jeff rubbed his chin. "So if Bianca can astral project, maybe the way she summons the dead will be different, too."

"Aren't we all ignoring one important fact?" Alexia scowled at everyone, tugging at the strings of her hoodie.

"What is that?" Cian asked curiously.

"She's asking for help," Alexia said. "Duh."

"But the blood bond with Rachoń will force her to obey, right?" Amaliya tilted her head to look at Cian. "Right?"

Nodding, but looking a little unsure, Cian answered, "There is a distinct possibility the answer is yes."

"But she's defiant enough to astral project to Innocente and beg for help," Alexia said, her finger tapping the table. "She wants our help. So if that's true, we have to just deal with Rachoń and whoever else she brings."

"You're assuming that Rachoń will not be able to rein her in," Cian responded, slightly shaking his head. "We have to assume the worst. That Rachoń will be able to control Bianca. We may have to kill them both."

There was a long silence.

"I think I have a problem killing someone that is asking for our help," Alexia said at last.

"Me, too. It seems kind of shitty," Samantha agreed.

Amaliya raked her fingers through her long hair and sighed. "I don't want to kill her, Cian. She's asking for help. He fucked Bianca up just like he did me."

"You're making this a lot more complicated." Cian sighed.

Jeff tapped his fingers on the table. "Benchley, Eduardo, what do you think?"

"I'm with my sister. It seems like a dick move."

Eduardo shrugged. "I say kill her. She's a danger to our pack."

Cian exchanged glances with Eduardo that indicated very clearly they were on the same page.

"You're such an ass," Alexia grunted.

"I'm a fine piece of ass," Eduardo corrected her.

Jeff stared at the newspaper article in the book before him, his hand lightly stroking the page. "Fine. We try to save Bianca. It makes things harder, but…"

Cian's snort indicated his contempt for the idea.

"If we're allies, Cian, then we have a say in this, too. We're not your minions," Jeff said boldly, and was relieved when his voice didn't crack.

Cian gave Jeff a terse nod.

"So we have to determine ahead of time what her powers might be. Benchley, you need to dive deep into our information on Bianca's mother. Compile a list of her known abilities and then we'll try to ascertain what we should be ready for."

Benchley inclined his head. "Okay."

CHAPTER THIRTEEN

"Alexia, please get all our gear in order. We'll need the surveillance equipment and the van ready. Also, pull all the weapons and stock the van."

Alexia gave him a thumbs up.

"Eduardo, you might be the muscle, as you like to put it, but I need you to work with Amaliya." Jeff glanced at the shape shifter to see him grinning. "And, what I mean by that is please make sure you pour her blood in all the cemeteries in Austin every night. That's how she can call the dead to her. Right?"

Amaliya nodded. "Yep."

Eduardo sighed. "I thought it would be more exciting than that."

Cian narrowed his eyes at the coyote. "I'll need you to act as a guard the night we meet with Rachoń. Think you can handle it?"

"I've eaten your kind on more than one occasion," Eduardo said, shrugging. Fastening a charming smile on Amaliya, he said, "In many different ways."

Amaliya rolled her eyes, but looked amused.

"And what about me?" Samantha asked.

Jeff leaned toward her. "I think we'll have to test you and see what you are capable of. We may require your help."

"Only three can meet with Rachoń and her entourage," Alexia reminded him.

"But a few of us could monitor nearby," Jeff responded with a wry smile. "Right?"

"Considering we're anticipating a betrayal, yes," Cian agreed.

"Where will the meeting take place?" Samantha asked.

"Zilker Park. In the open, but away from human activity," Cian answered. "It's best to not allow her near my haven."

"Location doesn't matter if she's going to attack you anyway," Alexia said, shrugging. "I can probably rig up remote cameras if you can pinpoint the exact location for me. I can snag you guys on the digital cameras."

"I long for the days when film rendered us invisible," Cian said, winking at Alexia.

She blushed.

"What if Rachoń is in cahoots with Etzli and Santos?" Benchley ran his hands through his hair. "Oh, man. That could be bad."

"Santos hates Rachoń. He hates anyone associated with The Summoner. Etzli does speak with Rachoń, but I have a feeling that it's her way of keeping tabs on both Rachoń and me. Etzli is..." Cian fell silent, his hand gently rubbing Amaliya's leg.

"Well?" Benchley prompted.

"Duplicitous," Cian finally finished.

"So basically we're just fucked every which way, huh?" Benchley rubbed his face vigorously.

"I plan to survive it," Eduardo said with a shrug. "Vampires are pussies."

Cian gave him a dark look.

"Oh, yeah?" Amaliya looked ready to throw down with the coyote.

"Eduardo, stop causing shit," Jeff said in a weary tone.

"What?" Eduardo had the audacity to look hurt.

"We have less than twenty-four hours to come up with a way to deal with all of this crap coming down on us," Jeff said. "We need to not fight with each other."

"The plan should be simple," Cian said, his voice taking on a dominating tone.

The table fell silent as all eyes turned to him.

"If Rachoń attacks, we kill her and her entourage. If we can save Bianca, we'll do so, but if not, she dies, too. If Etzli or Santos interferes, we will have to deal with them as well." Cian glanced at Jeff. "We could really use more people."

"This is it," Jeff said with a shrug.

"We need more vampires," Amaliya decided. "Any volunteers?"

"Ha, ha," Benchley retorted.

Samantha reached out and touched Jeff's hand gently. "I can shoot, you know. Give me silver bullets."

"We're all going to have to be armed for this," Alexia agreed.

Eduardo lounged in his chair looking bored. "Vampires die just like everything else."

"We're harder to kill," Cian responded.

"Eh, not that hard," Eduardo shot back with a sardonic smile.

"Enough!" Samantha said, surprising everyone. "This isn't a time to be arguing over who is more of a bad ass! Okay? Fuck me sideways! Do what Jeff said! We make a plan. We do it! I don't want to die, okay? I almost did it once and I don't want to do it again!"

"At least we have an idea of what we're dealing with," Jeff said at last. "There shouldn't be any surprises that we can't anticipate."

Amaliya busted out laughing.

"What?" Jeff felt defensive at her outburst.

"Now that you said that, we're fucking doomed to have something come out of left field and knock us on our asses," Amaliya answered.

"I'm not that superstitious," Jeff answered shortly.

"I am," Benchley said, holding up his hand.

"Me, too," Alexia said, holding up hers.

"You fucked us," Eduardo agreed.

"Yeah, honey, you kinda did," Samantha said, joining the traitorous crew.

"I agree with Jeff," Cian said firmly.

"Well, thanks," Jeff grumbled.

Considering what they were facing, at least he had the support of the master vampire.

"Meeting adjourned," Cian said.

"Yeah," Jeff said, feeling a little swept aside as the chairs were shoved back

CHAPTER THIRTEEN

and people rose to their feet.

Samantha leaned toward him, her fingers brushing his hand. "It's okay, Jeff. If we all die, we know it's not your fault."

"Gee, thanks."

She pressed a quick kiss to his cheek, then joined the others in gathering around the donuts and coffee maker.

Jeff stared at the open book in front of him, dread filling his heart. Nothing felt right. Nothing was really making sense. They were missing something vital, but he was hard pressed to figure out what it was.

PART FOUR

Sunday

Chapter Fourteen

The heat shimmered over the highway edging the gas station as Pete climbed out of Ethan's truck and stretched his long legs. Tucking his cowboy hat on his head, he glanced toward the bigger man. Ethan was already messing with the gas pumps, preparing to fill up after their long haul from East Texas to just inside Eastland County.

It was almost six hours since they'd left in the very early morning and the sun was still trekking upward in the cloudless pale blue sky. The hot summer air was scorching as it brushed over his face and tugged at his clothes.

Holding his cowboy hat in place, he stared off down the road that would lead to the home of Amaliya's grandmother. His head was still throbbing from his hangover, but his stomach had finally settled down. He was starting to feel hungry. It was nearly ten in the morning, but he was hoping he might be able to snag a leftover breakfast taco. Amaliya's grandmother was an awesome cook.

"I should call them and see if they went to church," Pete called out.

Ethan glanced over his burly shoulder and gave him a brief nod. The other man's long duster danced and snapped around his tall form. Somehow his cowboy hat remained firmly on his head in defiance of the hot gusts of wind. "Go ahead, but don't tell them too much. Keep it simple."

Pete dug his cellphone out of his pocket. His brain still felt a little mushy and his eyes grainy from what little sleep he had snagged during the trip. Ethan wasn't much for talking as he drove, so Pete found himself trying to start up a conversation with unsuccessful results. He'd finally given up and dozed off to sleep away his beer haze. Yawning, he quickly scanned his contact list and found the number for Innocente.

The phone rang three times, then a small voice said, "Hello? Ottmer-Guerra residence."

Pete hesitated, surprised to hear a child on the phone. But the name was correct: Innocente Ottmer. He knew Guerra was the name of one of the family tree offshoots, so he said, "Hey, this is a friend of Innocente. My name is Pete Talbert."

"I'll get her," the child said, and noisily lay down the phone.

A second later a female voice said, "This is Cynthia Guerra. Who's calling?"

"Uh, hey, Cynthia. It's Pete Talbert."

"Hey, Pete! How are you?"

"I'm good. You and Sergio visiting Innocente?" Pete tugged on his goatee, not really wanting to interrupt a family event.

"We live here now. She's getting older and with the economy like it is..."

"Yeah, that makes sense. Hey, I'm in the area. Would you mind if I dropped by?" Pete glanced toward Ethan. The other man was still pumping the gas, but his body was slightly angled toward Pete. The dark sunglasses hid his eyes, but Pete knew he was under scrutiny.

There was a pause, then Cynthia said, "Sure. Come on by. Shouldn't be a problem. We got up late so we're just now eating breakfast. How far out are you?"

"Uh, I would say about fifteen minutes."

"Great. That gives me time to get the kids dressed. We'll see you soon."

"Talk to you in a few," Pete answered, then hung up. "They're just getting up, so it's all good."

"No church today, huh?" Ethan finished up at the pump and holstered the nozzle.

"Yeah," Pete said, realizing how odd it was for the family not to be at church. Innocente was very devout and so was Sergio.

"Wonder what's up." Ethan tucked his credit card away in his wallet as he let his words hang in the air.

Pete shifted uncomfortably on his feet, gazing at Ethan through the gloomy interior of the truck. He had a feeling that the mysterious man knew a lot more than he was letting on. "You know something?"

"Nope. Just wondering." Ethan slid behind the wheel of the truck and yanked his door shut.

Pete climbed back into the cab. In the few short minutes the vehicle had been standing still, the interior had already heated up. He tilted the air conditioning vents toward him as Ethan started up the truck and blinked the sweat from his eyes. As Pete shut the passenger door, he tilted his head to regard the man next to him thoughtfully.

Ethan caught his look and gave him a slight smile. "I haven't the faintest idea why they aren't at church. I'm just trying to track down Amaliya."

"Okay. Because if you need me to help you there needs to be some measure of trust between us," Pete said in an even voice.

CHAPTER FOURTEEN

Pulling out onto the empty highway, Ethan shrugged. "Trust has to be earned, don't you know that?"

"I'm trusting you to do what you promised. Cure Amaliya," Pete pointed out.

"No, you're hoping I will do what I promised. You're scared shitless that I'm lying to you, but you love her enough to put aside your worries and hope for the best. There's a big difference," Ethan answered. His tone wasn't confrontational, angry, or mocking. He said it simply and plainly.

"Okay, you got me there. I'm hoping that you're being forthright with me and not giving me a heap of bullshit."

Ethan nodded once. "Exactly. Now you're being honest with me."

Pete sank back in his chair and exhaled through his teeth. "Are you being honest with me?"

"I'm looking for Amaliya because I'm tracking her master. I need your help to convince her family to help me locate her. There is a cure for young vampires to return to mortals."

Pete mulled over his words, wiping the beads of moisture form his face with his fingers before rubbing his hands on his jeans. He felt like a fool, but he was a desperate fool. He kept seeing images in his head of Amaliya on that night: the elusive memories he had lost for so many months. Now that he had recollected the events, he wished with all his heart that he had reacted differently. If he hadn't been so afraid, he could have helped her, kept her safe, until the mysterious stranger had arrived to turn her back.

"You know, Pete, there ain't no shame in loving someone. None at all."

"I'm ashamed that I was afraid of her," Pete admitted.

"Well, vampires are scary as shit. Especially when they first come back. They are usually out of control and extremely dangerous. It's only after they learn to control their hunger and use their powers to survive that they become much more cunning creatures. She's still a fledgling vampire. We can save her."

Pete gave a solemn nod of his head. "Then that's what we'll do."

Innocente's house was surrounded by a well-tended yard filled with flower beds and statues. The house was painted a pale shade of pink with dark blue trim. The last time Pete had visited there hadn't been a jungle gym in the backyard or an above-ground pool. The water was bright blue and the steel-frame and blue vinyl liner were in tip-top condition. Pete had the sudden urge to run and throw himself into it.

"A vampire would have a hell of a time just getting to the house," Ethan said with admiration. "Look at all those relics."

"Think she knows what Amaliya is?" Pete wondered.

"Nah, I think she's just a nice Mexican old lady," Ethan answered. He killed the engine and shoved open his door.

Pete slid out of the truck and lifted his cowboy hat so he could smooth down his hair. He felt rumpled and a little out of sorts after being on the road so long.

The front door swung open and Sergio leaned out. He was in Dallas Cowboy pajama bottoms and a blue t-shirt. "C'mon in!" He waved to them, then disappeared back inside, leaving the front door open behind the screen door.

Pete ambled up the front walk and glanced down at the small stone vases set along the path. Each one was filled with water and he briefly wondered if it was Holy Water. A little girl with dark curly hair peered out at him from behind the screen. She was smiling at him sweetly.

"Hey, Emma Leigh. How are you today?" Pete asked.

The four-year-old giggled and dashed away from the doorway.

Pete edged the door open and slipped inside, Ethan right behind him. The air inside of the house was fresh, cool, and smelled of chorizo. As Ethan shut the door behind them, the refreshing gloom was a relief after the hot Texas sunlight. Both men took off their hats and ran their fingers through their hair.

"C'mon!" Cynthia motioned to them from the hallway. "We're in the kitchen."

Sergio's little boy, Alex, darted into view long enough to wave hello, then dashed away.

"Cute kids," Ethan said with a grin.

"They have four of them." Pete's voice held more of a wistful tone than he had intended. "Hopefully after this is all said and done I can get down to making some of my own."

A pretty girl with dark green eyes and curly dark hair walked down the hallway from the bedrooms. "Hey, Pete."

"Hey, Jackie. When did you get so tall?"

The girl looked like she was at least three years older than twelve. It unnerved Pete. Kids grew up so fast nowadays.

Jackie shrugged, giggled, and gave him a brief hug. She glanced toward Ethan suspiciously. "Who's that?"

"A friend," Pete answered.

"You shouldn't lie," Jackie chastised him, shaking her head.

Ethan arched both of his eyebrows as he pocketed his sunglasses.

Jackie regarded Ethan suspiciously.

Pete felt uncomfortable suddenly. He had the eerie feeling that something was going on that he didn't understand.

Rolling her eyes, Jackie shook her head. "Remember where liars go," she said, and headed toward the kitchen.

Realizing the comment was not directed at him, Pete cast a wary look at Ethan.

"Interesting," was all Ethan said, and followed the girl.

The kitchen was cramped. Emma Leigh and Alex were seated at the kitchen table watching the small TV set on a counter while eating some very colorful cereal. The baby, Anna Belle, was drinking her bottle in her highchair, regarding everyone with dark eyes. Sergio and Cynthia were huddled behind the stove cooking breakfast.

"Hey, sorry to be a bad hostess, but I don't want the chorizo to burn," Cynthia

CHAPTER FOURTEEN

said, leaning in to kiss Pete's cheek as he greeted her with a hug.

Sergio was on tortilla duty. "Hey, guys. The kids are almost done. We'll shove them out the door in a sec."

"Dad, that's rude!" Jackie declared.

Sergio grinned at her and continued his duty.

"Well, it's good to see everyone," Pete said. He was a little more nervous than he expected. "This is my friend, Ethan." Pete quickly made the introductions.

"Good to meet you," Cynthia said, casting a smile in their direction as she poured diced potatoes into the big black skillet where the spicy chorizo was sizzling. "You guys on a hunting trip or something?"

"You could say that," Ethan said with a wide grin. "Smells really good in here."

"I'm making chorizo, potato, and egg tacos. I can make you some bacon and eggs if you'd prefer that."

"No, ma'am. Those tacos sound great." Ethan slid off his duster and laid it over the back of a chair before settling onto it. "The kids don't like tacos?"

"We get to eat cereal on weekends, because then we can run all the sugar out of our systems," Jackie said tartly.

"Ah, I see." Ethan nodded his head with understanding.

Jackie continued to regard him suspiciously as she poured herself some cereal. "Sure you do."

"Jackie, be nice to our visitors," Sergio called out.

With a frown, the girl tucked into her sugary flakes.

Pete also took a seat at the big breakfast table. Alex and Emma Leigh ignored them, staring at some horrible kid's program on the TV. Anna Belle was also watching as she slowly slurped on her bottle, but her eyes kept flicking toward him. Pete gave her a slight smile and her eyes narrowed.

"Do you want some coffee? Or some orange juice?" Sergio asked.

"Uh, coffee would be great," Pete said. "I can get it though." He quickly busied himself with collecting mugs and snagged the coffee pot from where it sat steaming. He was surprised to see that his hands were trembling. Glancing over his shoulder, he saw Jackie glowering at Ethan and baby Anna Belle twisting around in her seat to look toward Pete. Maybe the kids were just curious, but he felt uneasy.

Casual small talk started between Ethan and Cynthia, lessening the tension in the room. Or maybe Pete was just imagining it. Sergio finished his tortilla duty and checked on his kids. Pete set a mug before Ethan and poured the coffee. Watching Sergio fussing over his kids made his own heart pang with an unexpected sadness. How many times had Pete imagined this sort of future for him and Amaliya?

Wrangling the kids out the back door was easier than expected. Jackie nearly drowned herself gulping down the last of her sugary milk and hurried out after her younger siblings. She gave Ethan one last dark look before banging the backdoor behind her.

"No slamming the door!" Cynthia shouted after her.

Sergio gathered up the cereal bowls and boxes to clear the table. The baby finished her bottle and set it down on the tray of the highchair with a loud thump.

Ethan laughed. "Like she's just finished a good beer."

Anna Belle regarded him thoughtfully.

"She's always like that. I think she got it from Sergio," Cynthia said, laughing. She set a plate of steaming tacos before Pete and another in front of Ethan. "Here you go."

"Thanks for the meal," Ethan said with a charming smile.

Cynthia returned it. She was obviously less suspicious than her kids.

Pete hungrily bit into a taco, almost devouring half of it. It tasted so amazing he wanted to shove the other half in after it.

A sharp intake of breath and a whispered prayer in Spanish drew the eyes of all in the room to the doorway. Innocente stood in the doorway looking furious.

"You!" she said sharply.

Then all hell broke loose.

Chapter Fifteen

Trying to shift her purse around while searching through it, Samantha muttered irritably. Wearing a short white skirt, pink tank top, and white flip-flops with big pink stones on them, she was cutely dressed, but the dark circles under her eyes were evidence of her sleepless night. Samantha fumbled about inside her packed purse as her cat, Beatrice, regarded her coolly from the back of the sofa. The gray tabby was stretched out in a patch of sunshine, the white bib under her chin practically glowing in the light.

Finally, Samantha located her sunglasses and house keys. She held up both triumphantly, but Beatrice didn't appear impressed. The cat closed her eyes dismissively.

"Well, fine." Shifting the big pink bag onto her shoulder, she yanked open her front door. "I'll be back later. Don't scratch the couch!"

Beatrice ignored Samantha with her usual cat aloofness.

Shoving open her screen door, Samantha nearly whacked Jeff in the face as he stepped onto the porch.

"Whoa!"

"Sorry, Jeff!" She hurriedly shut the door and locked it while he took several cautious steps back onto the walkway. "I'm all crazy this morning. I slept through the alarm clock."

"No problem. It was hard for me to wake up, too."

Jeff gave her his usual kind smile and she hugged him tightly.

"You're so sweet!"

"If you insist," he answered, snuggling her.

Giving him a quick kiss on the cheek, she slid out of his arms, feeling self-conscious. He just smiled and held out his hand to her. Happily, she took it and they walked down the walk to his beat-up Land Rover parked at the curb.

"Did you eat anything?" Jeff asked, holding the passenger door open for her.

"I didn't. I got up too late."

"Good thing I snagged some coffee and some kolaches then," he said with a grin before shutting the door and circling around to the driver's side.

A white bag and two large coffees were nestled into the console. Samantha hungrily yanked out a kolache and took a big bite, savoring the warm bread and spicy sausage. Around her chewing, she said, "Gawd, I love you."

Jeff grinned at her words as he drove up the street. "I aim to please."

"You always think of everything. It's like you're magic or something." She hesitated, gave him a thoughtful look, and said, "*Are* you magic or something?"

"Ordinary human. Boringly so," Jeff assured her.

"Not a secret elf, or fairy, or something?"

"Nope. Human as can be. I promise."

"I wonder what I am now," Samantha said with a sigh.

"A fabulous and very pretty human woman with a little extra flair." Jeff lightly touched her hand.

Unexpected tears glimmered in her eyes as she took another quick bite of her breakfast. Jeff had a wonderful way of making her feel good even when things were going horribly wrong.

Traffic was light and they made decent time driving past downtown to the walking trail encircling Lady Bird Lake. The parking lot was fairly empty near the Lamar Boulevard Bridge. They didn't talk much as they both munched on the warm kolaches and chased the tasty breakfast down with sweet, milky coffee. Samantha enjoyed the camaraderie and her high anxiety mellowed out to a low ping in the back of her mind.

As they climbed out of the SUV, Jeff snagged two sweating water bottles from a cooler tucked behind his seat and shoved them into his messenger bag. Again, he had anticipated their needs, and Samantha was grateful. It was already humid and sticky, the bugs in the trees lining the lake humming loudly. Samantha smiled as Jeff reached for her hand when they strolled onto the path. While they waded through the humid air and enjoyed the beauty of the mid-morning sun glinting off the waves, she tried to pretend this was just a nice day out together instead of a ghost hunt.

Rubbing her lips together, she tried not to ruin the moment by saying anything about their true purpose for strolling along the trail. The tree boughs creaked above as the wind played in the leaves. Glancing upward, she saw a squirrel watching them pass with a thoughtful look in its beady eyes. She stuck her tongue out at it.

Jeff must have seen her because he laughed. His fingers tightened on her hand and he gave her a furtive look.

"What?"

"Nothing."

CHAPTER FIFTEEN

Samantha rolled her eyes. "Sure."

"I just think you're adorable," Jeff confessed.

"Really?" Samantha nudged him with her shoulder. "I thought I was an annoying cartoon character."

"Oh, you heard Eduardo say that, huh?"

"On more than one occasion."

"He's a coyote. They're mischievous and moody. Just ignore him." Jeff nudged her back.

Turning her attention forward, Samantha could see the Mopac Bridge looming ahead. Little flutters of anxiety in her tummy made her wish now that she hadn't eaten. Beside her, Jeff seemed unaware of her sudden nervousness as he dug around in his bag.

"When we get to the walkway, I need you to wait until I take care of a few precautions."

"Like what?"

Jeff pulled out a plastic bag with a cloth bag tucked into it. "I had this spell sent to me from a witch in Georgia awhile back. It's a ward. It will throw up a barrier for about ten minutes."

"Huh?"

"It will make anyone coming close to it have the sudden desire to go somewhere else. If I estimated this correctly, the area of effect should cover the entire bridge."

"What about the cars?"

"It won't affect them. It specifically sends away people on foot. At least that's what the directions say." Jeff gave her a sheepish grin. "I have been dying to use one. I saw one in action a few years a back and..."

Samantha's eyebrows couldn't crawl up any higher on her brow. At her expression, Jeff finally seemed to understand this was not fun in her book.

He cleared his throat. "So, anyway, I'll set this down, activate it, then we need to hurry up and find the ghost." Jeff gave her a worried little smile. "You are ready to do this, right?"

Shrugging, Samantha stared straight ahead. No one was really out this morning, which was a relief. But it felt odd dealing with ghosts during the day, not that she would have preferred the night or early morning. It was creepy enough dealing with someone who was dead.

The warm air stirred the dry, dead leaves bordering the walk. The sound was usually soothing, but now it made her uneasy. Maybe she was just being paranoid now that she was mentally preparing herself to see the ghost again, but she was feeling watched.

"Samantha, I know this is hard for you, but we have to start figuring out exactly what you can do with your abilities."

"I know."

"And I'll be here for you."

"I know."

"And nothing will hurt you. Ghosts can't hurt you. You have to remember that."

"Okay."

"Is anything I'm saying helping?"

"Nope."

Samantha couldn't tear her eyes away from the footbridge sprawling across the lake tucked into the shadows of the Mopac Bridge above.

Jeff took hold of her hand again and stopped her in her tracks. Pulling her about to face him, Jeff looked down into her eyes. The warmth in them made her slightly smile. He really did care about her.

"You're going to be okay. I will not let anything bad happen to you. I promise. A ghost can't hurt you. They're just a remnant of someone died. Okay?"

"Okay." Samantha swallowed and tried to believe him.

Pressing a kiss to her temple, Jeff looped his arm around her shoulders and held her close. Lowering his chin, he rested his forehead against hers. Samantha raised her lips slightly to kiss the tip of his chin. A shiver slithered through her body, making her blush. With a little giggle, she looked away as he grinned down at her. Kissing her cheek, he cuddled her against him. He was warm, sweaty, and smelled like coffee, soap, and cologne. It was the closest she had ever allowed herself be to him and she was surprised at how comforting it was to be in his arms. Cian's body had been cold, hard, and unrelenting in her embrace, but Jeff molded against her and she could feel his heart beating. Sudden tears filled her eyes and she drew away.

Fucking Cian. Why couldn't she just enjoy being with Jeff without comparing him to the vampire?

Jeff started to let her slide out of his arms, but then changed his mind. He dragged her back and kissed her.

It was the sweetest kiss she had ever experienced. His fingers cradled her face as his lips pressed lightly to hers for a few tender moments. Gently releasing her mouth, his eyes peered into hers. "No more. Don't let him stand between us anymore. Time is too short and too much could go wrong."

Samantha nodded, her heart beating hard inside of her chest. "You're right." Her lips tingled from the kiss. Tiny tremors of delight were spiraling through her and her spirit felt lighter, happier.

Jeff's solemn expression disappeared into a bright smile. "Good."

Tilting her head, Samantha gazed into his warm eyes and touched his cheek before kissing him tenderly. It deepened gradually into a more intense kiss than before. Jeff enfolded her in his arms as she buried her hand in his hair. Slowly, they both became aware of their very public display and drew away reluctantly. She giggled as she wiped her pink lipstick off his lips and he kissed her fingers. Exchanging smiles, they held hands as they continued to the footpath.

It didn't seem as ominous as before, much to Samantha's relief. Jeff drew her

CHAPTER FIFTEEN

to the side of the path to watch the few people under the footbridge make their way to the other side. There wasn't anyone following close behind, so he waited until the last person left the bridge before opening the plastic bag and dumping the spell bag onto the ground.

"Oh, God! Are you sure it's not the smell that keeps them away?" Samantha gasped, her nose on fire.

Jeff pulled a small bottle from his bag. Wincing, he was obviously trying not to smell, or breathe in the noxious fumes from the woven bag. Unstopping the bottle, he motioned to Samantha to move past the spell as he also stepped back.

"We want to be inside the radius when it pops," Jeff informed her.

Once they were in position, he poured three drops of brown liquid onto the bag.

Samantha jolted when an audible bang went off and the air shimmered around her.

"Whoa! That was hardcore. Aimee really knows her shit," Jeff said in awe.

"That was kinda scary," Samantha admitted.

A jogger was coming up the path swiftly, but within fifteen feet of the footbridge, he stumbled to a stop. Looking warily at the bridge, he started jogging back in the direction he had come.

"It's working! We got ten minutes!" Jeff grabbed Samantha's hand and drew her along the footbridge.

The long expanse was empty now that the spell was in effect. The long walkway lined with metal railings appeared normal and not at all daunting now that Samantha was actually there. The dark water lapped up against the concrete pylons as the sounds of the city created a soft soundscape to the scene. It was peaceful and Samantha began to wonder if she had even seen the ghost of Cassidy Longoria.

"Do you sense anything?" Jeff asked. He had pulled a small device from his pack and was staring at it intently.

"What's that?" Samantha pointed at what looked like an archaic cellphone.

"EVP. It reads cold spots and stuff like that," Jeff answered, sweeping it back and forth. "Why don't you start walking down the path?"

Samantha sighed. "Okay."

"Try to relax, I guess. She contacted you once, she'll do it again."

"Are you sure?"

"No, but I'm hoping." Jeff gave his watch a wary glance. "And hopefully in the next nine minutes."

"No pressure at all there, Jeff," Samantha said under her breath.

Slowly, she walked forward. She took small steps, her hands slightly held out from her sides, palms outward, trying to feel for any cold spots. If her memory was correct, she had been near the center of the walkway when she had first heard Cassidy calling out to her. With the sun shining brightly and the sounds of the traffic rumbling overhead, she wondered if the ghost would actually appear.

The previous morning a thick mist had provided enough of a spooky element to compel a ghost to reveal itself.

"Samantha."

"Yeah, Jeff?" she answered.

"I didn't say anything," Jeff responded.

Samantha flung a startled look over her shoulder toward Jeff just as she felt a cold wisp encircle her ankle. "I think I found her." Swiftly kneeling, Samantha held out her hands, skimming them over the cement. There was a distinctly cold area in just one spot and it seemed to be growing in size.

"It's a cold spot," Jeff said excitedly, joining her. He waved his EVP back and forth, watching the results excitedly. "It's growing, too."

"Cassidy?" Samantha called out. "You there?"

The coldness wrapped around her turned to ice, forcing a startled gasp from Samantha's lips. Cassidy's dead face emerged from the concrete as though rising out of water. Once her body was clearly visible, the dead woman's eyes opened.

"Samantha," Cassidy said, her fingers tight around Samantha's leg.

"She's here now," Samantha informed Jeff, tossing a quick glance in his direction.

His widened eyes and open mouth said it all. He could see her, too.

"Jeff?"

"Sam, I see her. I can see her!" Jeff exclaimed.

"Stop geeking out. Help me! What do I do?"

Snatching up his bag, Jeff rummaged through it excitedly. "Talk to her."

"Samantha, he hurt me," Cassidy cried out. Her grievous wounds looked garish in the sunlight. Her flesh, tanned in life, was now gray and bloodless. "He hurt me so much. He wouldn't stop."

"I'm so sorry, Cassidy. I am," Samantha answered. She tentatively forced her quivering fingers toward the woman's wrist. The grip on her ankle was pretty tight, but didn't feel like anything more than icy air. Curious if she could feel the ghost, Samantha laid her hand on the specter's arm. To her shock, she felt substance. It didn't feel like flesh, but it was almost solid. Wrapping her fingers around the dead woman's wrist, she felt it gaining mass.

"Okay, let me snap a few pictures," Jeff was muttering, raising his digital camera.

"No!" Cassidy lashed out at him, her hand impacting with the camera. It flew through the air, hit the cement walkway, skittered, then tumbled into the lake.

"What the hell?" Jeff gasped.

"No! Not like this!" Cassidy wailed. She continued to lash out at Jeff, flailing in anger.

"Cassidy, he's not the one who hurt you!" Samantha grabbed onto the woman's shoulders and tried to wrestle her back.

Jeff fell back as the ghost clawed at him. Intestines spilled out of her nearly empty torso to lie wetly on the ground as she crawled closer to Jeff, trying to

CHAPTER FIFTEEN

gain purchase.

"You let him do this to me!" Cassidy wailed. "You didn't protect me!"

Samantha tried to haul the dead woman back, but she was growing heavier and stronger with every second.

With a yelp, Jeff grabbed one of the ghost's hands, trying to keep it from his face. Red scratch marks already marred his arms and his left cheek. "Samantha, let go of her!"

"She'll hurt you!"

"Let go!"

Samantha let out a cry of frustration, releasing Cassidy. "Cassidy, stop hurting him!"

Cassidy wailed, striking out at Jeff angrily, but her body lost cohesion, misted, and sank away into the cold cement. Gasping, Jeff and Samantha stared at each other in shock.

"What was that?" Jeff cried out.

"Why are you asking me?" Samantha rubbed her arms vigorously. Holding Cassidy had felt like holding a block of ice. She was still shivering.

Gingerly touching his bleeding cheek, Jeff said in an awed voice, "She was tangible, Samantha! That never happens. She even scratched me!"

Samantha sat on her heels and tried to stop her teeth from chattering as she spoke. "It's not my fault!"

"I mean sometimes entities manage to knock something over, maybe scratch you a little, but I felt her nails. I felt her body!" Jeff stared at the scratches on his body in amazement. "When you touched her, she became solid."

Shaking her head vigorously, Samantha didn't want to acknowledge that what he was saying was true. "No, no. No, that isn't it."

"Yes, it is. When you stepped into the area that she haunts, that gave her enough energy to call out to you. When you touched her, she gained substance. *You* did that! Holy shit, Samantha, you did that!"

Trying not to cry, Samantha whispered, "What does that mean?"

"You're a phasmagnus!" Jeff stared at her in awe. "One of the most rare supernatural abilities around. You can call the specters of the dead, make them real, have them do your bidding."

Wiping away a tear, Samantha continued to shiver. She felt a bit sick to her stomach and overwhelmed by what he was saying. But wasn't it true? When she let go of Cassidy and ordered her to leave Jeff alone, Cassidy had stopped her attack, lost form, and vanished.

Realizing her distress, Jeff moved to enfold her in his arms. "It's okay, Samantha. It's okay. Now that we know what you are, we can deal with this better. I promise."

Samantha leaned against him, staring at the spot where Cassidy had disappeared. The thump of feet against the concrete drew her attention. Joggers were once more running along the footbridge. The spell was over.

"Everything okay?" a runner asked as he ran toward them. His tan skin was covered in sweat and he was rippling with lean muscle.

Dimly, Samantha wondered if he was a ghost, too.

"Yeah. We had a little tumble. All good now," Jeff answered quickly.

The jogger nodded and kept going.

"Samantha," Jeff whispered. "We need to get up and go now. Okay?"

"I'm a phasmagnus," Samantha answered, the word sounding odd coming from her lips.

"I know, honey." He helped her to her feet and gathered his stuff, shoving it into his bag.

Standing in the center of the footbridge, Samantha stared at the towering buildings of downtown Austin looming over the glittering lake. Colorful kayaks and canoes were gliding over the water. Runners and walkers dotted the winding pathway as far as her eyes could see and cars glinted in the sunlight as they passed over the Lamar Boulevard Bridge in the distance. It all looked so normal.

"I'm not normal anymore," Samantha said at last when Jeff took her hand. "I don't belong to that world anymore."

Jeff surveyed the scene she was gazing at and sighed. "Neither one of us does. Not now."

Looking at him, Samantha said, "I'm afraid." Her lips felt numb and her throat was tight.

"I know. So am I," Jeff confessed. "But I am here for you. And this power can help us, Samantha. It can."

Nodding, she let him guide her back the way they had come. Her fingers clutched his tightly and she was still shivering. "Jeff?"

"Yeah, Sam?"

"Take me home."

"Okay," he said, nodding.

"And when we get there, I want you to go to bed with me," she said, boldly meeting his eyes.

He lifted an eyebrow slowly. "You sure?"

Samantha nodded vehemently. "Oh, yeah. I'm not wasting any more of my life being afraid of stupid shit."

With a slight smile, Jeff said, "Okay."

Lifting her chin, Samantha gripped his hand with both of hers. "Time to move on and then kick some monster ass."

Laughing, Jeff walked with her out from beneath the shadows of the bridge and into the bright Texas sunlight.

Chapter Sixteen

Innocente was exhausted. Every cell in her body seemed to be complaining as she scooted out of bed. Joints protesting, she slid her feet into her slippers and reached for her pale blue housecoat with daisies decorating it. After the ghostly visitation and her call to Amaliya she had fallen into a deep, dreamless sleep. It had been a relief not to have any nightmares, but now her brain felt muddled. Shrugging on her housecoat over her pajamas and snapping the top four buttons together, she peered into the mirror above her vanity. She winced at the sign of her pale pallor and the bags under her hazel eyes. Running her hands through her wavy salt and pepper hair, she sighed. The image in the mirror never matched the internal one she had of herself at a much younger age, but she was usually pleased with the lack of wrinkles or lines in her face. Today she looked every minute of her age and she hated it.

Opening up her container of face cream, she rubbed it gently into her cheeks, forehead, and chin hoping it would help perk up her complexion. She did not want Sergio worrying about her. The smell of chorizo and coffee wafted under the door into her room making her stomach rumble. She screwed the lid back onto the pink jar and glanced one more time into the mirror. Her cheeks were a little rosier from her rubbing them and her eyes were now more alert and looking more gold than hazel.

Innocente opened the door and trudged down the dimly-lit hallway. From the quiet coming from the other rooms in the house it was clear that the kids were already outside playing. Innocente hated that they all had missed church, but it had been a rough night; she was sure God would understand.

She wished she could call Amaliya and check on her, but knew that her granddaughter was already asleep. It bothered her greatly that Amaliya was a vampire. It broke her heart into a million pieces, yet she never allowed her granddaughter to see her inner turmoil. Amaliya may now live in darkness, but Innocente fervently believed in her inherent goodness. It had hurt to see her granddaughter growing up in a broken home and poisonous environment. Life had been cruel to Amaliya, yet now she appeared to be happy with Cian. Innocente wondered, however, what life would have been like for Amaliya if Samuel Vezorak had been a better man. She hoped Cian would never hurt Amaliya like so many of the men in her life had in the past.

Entering the kitchen, it took Innocente a few moments to take in the scene. Two men sat at the table eating breakfast tacos as Cynthia and Sergio were serving themselves. The sight of one of the men made Innocente's blood boil with anger. Uttering "*Dios mio*," Innocente took a step forward.

"You!"

Both men started in their chairs, looking at her in surprise.

"How dare you come into my house after what you did!" Innocente shouted. Losing her temper, she descended on the table and started smacking the man who had hurt her granddaughter.

"Hey! Stop!" Pete cried out as she slapped at him.

"Grandmama!" Sergio immediately tried to stop her, pushing his big body between her and Pete.

Innocente would have none of it and slapped him, too.

"Innocente, please, stop!" Cynthia cried out, grabbing at her hand. "The kids might come in. Calm down!"

"What did I do?" Pete said, trying to shield himself as Innocente managed to get a few whacks past Sergio.

His words made her stop as she realized she couldn't reveal why she was angry at him. Everyone in the kitchen was staring at her in shock and she couldn't explain herself. The stranger looked amused by the whole episode while Pete looked more than a little hurt.

"I can't talk about it," Innocente finally said.

"Well, something pissed you off." Sergio kept between her and Pete.

Innocente sniffed and walked over to the stove to serve herself breakfast. She wanted to go hit Pete again, but it wouldn't do any good. She really couldn't explain why she was angry at Pete in front of the gathered company.

"Whatever I did, I'm sorry," Pete said, sounding properly meek.

"Grandmama, Pete and his friend here, Ethan, dropped by to say hello and you beating on Pete really isn't the way to go about greeting a friend."

Innocente turned and pinned Sergio with her fiercest look. He looked away, cowed, but Cynthia was immune to her scathing look.

"Do you want them to leave?" Cynthia asked pointedly. "Because you're obviously not in a good way right now."

"We can't leave," Pete protested. "We have something really important to discuss with y'all."

Ethan nodded solemnly, his gaze unwavering as he regarded Innocente. She

CHAPTER SIXTEEN

met his gaze curiously. He didn't flinch, but slightly smiled.

Her anger was still smoldering, but Innocente was at a loss as to how to explain her outburst or deal with the unexpected company. She was tempted to grab a taco and retreat to her bedroom until they left. The feeling of surliness was not leaving her system and her restless night wasn't helping. If only she could pick up the phone and talk to Amaliya, but that wasn't even an option anymore.

"If my grandmother isn't up for company, maybe you could come by some other time, or call," Sergio suggested.

"No, this is really important," Pete insisted.

Ethan finished eating his taco as Innocente set a serving on a plate and stared at it.

"What is it about?" Innocente asked.

Pete hesitated, then said, "Amaliya."

"She's dead," Sergio said quickly and nervously.

Innocente caught the exchange of looks between Pete and Ethan. Curiosity gripped her and she said, "What about Amaliya?"

Pete cleared his throat and again looked to Ethan for guidance.

"We know she's not dead and buried," Ethan said at last. "That why we're here."

"No, you got that wrong. She is dead. She was murdered," Sergio said in a tumble of words.

"She was dead. And buried. But she got out, didn't she?" Ethan asked. He pushed back his plate and settled back in his chair.

Cynthia swept Anna Belle into her arms before looking out the window to check on her kids, all the while backing up to where Sergio kept the revolver tucked into a cranny behind the refrigerator. Innocente could see the fear in her daughter-in-law's eyes. Innocente wasn't afraid, but she was very curious.

"Why would you say that?" Innocente asked, a challenge in her voice.

Pete shifted in his chair, clearly uncomfortable. "I saw her Easter night. After she was supposed to be dead."

"You *puto*! You do remember!" Innocente exclaimed.

The recollection of Amaliya whispering to her all that she had endured after rising was vivid in Innocente's mind. It was during one of her visits to Austin to see her granddaughter that Amaliya had laid with her head on Innocente's lap and told her all the terrible things that happened before she had finally made her way to her grandmother's house. Pete's terrible rejection of Amaliya in the hotel room had infuriated Innocente. Though Amaliya had not gone into great details about what had occurred, she had cried bloody tears when recounting how Pete had panicked and tried to flee from her presence. Maybe she was being unreasonable, but the thought of anyone hurting her granddaughter infuriated her.

Pete visibly paled. "Not right away. Just recently!"

"You hurt her! You made her cry! You abandoned her when she needed you most!" Innocente shouted at him, snatching up a frying pan and heading in his direction.

"Whoa! Whoa! Whoa!" Sergio dove across the kitchen and wrestled it from her grip. "Grandmama, calm down!"

"He abandoned your cousin when she needed him most! How can you forgive him?"

"I don't even know what you're talking about!" Sergio protested.

The man called Ethan stood up and the action drew all eyes to him. "The fact of the matter is that Amaliya is a vampire. We all know it. Let's just cut to the chase. I am trying to find her because I can turn her back to human. Pete's helping me."

Silence filled the room as shock registered across the faces of Sergio and Cynthia. Anna Belle gnawed on her fingers thoughtfully as she stared at the adults. Innocente felt the room tipping as her vision narrowed. It was Sergio's big arms that slid around her and lifted her up. The world dimmed while worried voices echoed around her. Innocente faded into a strange waking dream where her long dead husband kept whispering everything was going to be all right.

When the world came clearly back into focus again and the words spoken to her once more made sense, Innocente found herself sitting in her living room clutching a glass of cold water. Sergio and Cynthia sat on either side of her, the baby cooing on Cynthia's lap. Ethan and Pete sat across from them in the two recliners. Everyone wore a look of concern, but Innocente felt the pulse of urgency just under the surface.

"You can make her mortal again?" she asked, her voice slightly cracking.

Ethan nodded. "I need to know where her master is. The one who made her. Once I kill him, I will use his ashes to bring her back."

"He's dead," Innocente answered. She set the glass on a coaster on her coffee table. Her hand was trembling.

"We killed him," Sergio added.

Pete glanced worriedly at Ethan. "What does that mean?"

"What did you do with the body?" Ethan asked, ignoring Pete.

"He was torn apart...by...zombies," Sergio said, obviously not sure what he should, or shouldn't say.

"He's in tiny pieces. When they went back to the grave, they took him with them." Innocente hesitated, then said, "Why should I tell you any more?"

"I'm a vampire hunter, ma'am. I track down the old ones and kill them. I find the young ones and turn them back to mortals. My family has done this for centuries. I have a ritual from the Catholic Church that allows me to return young vampires to their human selves by using the ashes of their makers. If you can take me to where this vampire died, maybe I can dig up his remains and get what I need."

"He was in really small pieces," Sergio said, wincing.

"Very small pieces," Innocente agreed.

CHAPTER SIXTEEN

Ethan shrugged. "I just need a small piece for the ritual to work."

Innocente was surprised at how desperately she wanted to believe the stranger. The thought of Amaliya regaining her life was almost too precious to grab onto in fear of it being an illusion. "Are you sure you can do this?"

"Oh, I'm more than certain," Ethan responded with confidence.

As the man launched into a detailed explanation of his investigation into Amaliya's death and her body's disappearance, Innocente gripped Sergio's hand tightly. Even though she was still angry at Pete, she could see that the young man was desperate to believe Ethan, too. His expression was almost heartbreaking. Maybe he was an idiot, but Innocente realized he was an idiot who loved her granddaughter.

"So if we can go to where this vampire died and I can find a piece of him, even a fragment of bone, I can perform a ritual that will make her human again," Ethan finished.

"We need to tell Amaliya," Cynthia said in an awestruck, but elated voice. "We have to tell her!"

"She's asleep right now," Sergio reminded his wife.

"Where is Amaliya?" Pete asked.

Innocente gave both Sergio and Cynthia a warning look, but they had both already clamped their mouths shut.

"Well?" Ethan asked.

"Somewhere safe," Innocente finally said. "We will help you get what you need for the ritual, but I'm not going to tell you where Amaliya is yet."

Ethan raised his eyebrows, then nodded. "Fair enough. You don't know me. I get that. But I am your best shot at getting your granddaughter back."

"If there is any chance she can come back to us, you have to help him," Pete urged.

"I agree," Innocente said shortly. "But she's my granddaughter and I won't do anything until I can talk to her. And that won't be until tonight."

"But we can go out to the graveyard now," Sergio suggested. "We can drive down there during the day and get this rolling, right?"

"That we can," Ethan agreed.

Cynthia nodded her head. "I'll watch the kids. You can go with them Sergio."

"It will take us a few hours to get there," Innocente said thoughtfully.

"You should stay here, Grandmama," Sergio suggested.

"No," Innocente snapped, "I shouldn't."

"Okay, okay." Sergio surrendered immediately, knowing better than to rile her up again.

"I know I hurt Amaliya, Innocente, but I promise I just want to save her and make it up to her now," Pete promised.

The sweetness on his face almost made her feel bad for him, but Innocente shoved the thought away. There was much to think about and the long drive would give her time to do so. With Bianca calling for help, she wasn't too sure now was the best time to restore Amaliya. But then again, maybe if she was just human again the forces conspiring against her would leave her be.

"I'm going to eat, then get ready," Innocente announced.

"We should leave soon," Ethan suggested.

"We'll leave when I'm ready," Innocente informed him. She wasn't about to let anyone tell her what to do when it came to her granddaughter.

If only she could call Amaliya...

Chapter Seventeen

Jeff awoke to see Beatrice staring at him from her perch on the headboard of Samantha's bed. The tabby narrowed her green eyes at him.

"Uh, hi?" he whispered, reaching up slowly, offering to scratch her behind the ears.

The cat deftly avoided his hand, leaped past it, and landed heavily on Jeff's stomach. He was positive the cat had increased her mass somehow. When she landed she felt like she weighed a ton, not a few pounds. Flicking her tail, Beatrice settled into the curve of Samantha's back and began to delicately lick one paw.

"Okay, I get it. She's yours and I'm in your spot," Jeff grunted.

Beatrice regarded him for a long moment as if to say, 'Yes, stupid human.'

The bedroom was freezing cold. The air unit in the window was gusting air, making the flimsy curtains holding back the sunlight billow outward like dancing ghosts. Rubbing his face, he slowly sat up and glanced over at Samantha. She was deeply asleep, curled on her side, her hand tucked under her chin, breathing deeply. The sight of her made him smile and he gently touched her naked hip.

Outside the window, the huge oak tree threw dark shadows over the house and the insects were buzzing contentedly. It sounded like a lazy Sunday afternoon and he was tempted to lie back down and continue his nap. Sadly, there was much work to do before night fell.

Snagging his cellphone off the bed stand, he quickly scrolled through his messages. There were numerous ones from Benchley and Alexia. Surrendering to the inevitable, he swung his legs out from the silky rose colored sheets and winced as the frosty air washed over his flesh. He fumbled for his boxers, shimmied into them, then reached for his prosthetic leg.

Looking over his shoulder, he wondered if he could love Samantha any more than he already did. She had been completely undaunted by the fact one of his legs ended in a stump just below the knee. Other women had responded not too well to that revelation, but Samantha had acted as though it was completely natural for someone to have to remove a limb before making love. Tenderly, he trailed his fingers through her blond hair, cherishing the feel of it against his skin.

The phone vibrated in his other hand, summoning his attention. It was yet another message from Benchley. Shivering, Jeff abandoned the bed and made his way to Samantha's kitchen. The sunlight was hitting this side of the house and it was substantially warmer. Beatrice breezed past him, sauntering forward with a haughty air. It was obvious that his presence was an intrusion as far as Samantha's cat was concerned.

Dialing Benchley, Jeff poured himself a glass of orange juice from the refrigerator.

"Dude, where have you been?"

"I'm with Sam. I told you that," Jeff answered.

"You text me she's a phasmagnus and to research it then don't answer your phone. Not cool at all," Benchley protested.

"We were...uh...busy."

The silence on the other end drew on a little too long.

"Bench?"

"You're getting laid while my sister and I are busting our asses to get ready? Really? *Really?*"

Jeff winced. "Well, uh, you know...the whole 'we may die soon' argument sealed the deal."

"I think I kinda hate you right now."

"What's up, Benchley? You weren't texting me every few minutes for nothing." Jeff dropped his friendly voice and opted for his more authoritative one which he rarely used.

"Fine. I did some digging while Alexia was fixing up the van. Phasmagnus are super-rare. Vampires did a great job whacking nearly all of them. Phasmagnus can summon ghosts and have them do their bidding. Phasmagnus could get them to spy, to steal stuff, and could also make them corporeal enough to do damage or kill. The more the phasmagnus uses their power, the stronger they get. If this is what Samantha is...Jeff, seriously, every vampire in the world will be gunning for her."

"I saw her make a ghost solid." Jeff's happiness was dissolving into dread. "Samantha touched the ghost and within seconds it was solid enough to scratch me, knock me back, and draw blood."

"Fuck me, dude."

"I know." Jeff rubbed his brow, wishing away his sudden headache.

"All from drinking Amaliya's blood just once..."

CHAPTER SEVENTEEN

"Samantha was close to death. That has to be why."

"Okay, well, we've got to keep this on the lowdown. We've got to. Because if the vampires find out, it's going to be bad. It's bad enough Cian knows."

"Cian won't let any harm come to Samantha. They may have broken up, but he does care for her. I've seen it." Jeff freshened Beatrice's water bowl and searched the cabinets for her cat food as the cat stared forlornly into her nearly empty food dish.

"Everything is happening too fast," Benchley's voice protested. "How can we handle all of this?"

"Look at it this way. It's good to know we have another weapon in our arsenal that no one else knows about."

"What weapon?" Samantha's voice asked from behind him.

Turning, he saw her standing in the kitchen doorway blinking. Her blond hair was mussed and the strap of her tank top was sliding off one shoulder. She had pulled on matching pajama shorts and looked insanely sexy in Jeff's eyes.

"You, babe," he answered honestly.

"Fuck," Samantha answered with a sigh, sitting down heavily at the kitchen table.

"Also, Jeff, if Bianca Leduc has any of her mom's powers, we're in trouble. Not only could Josephine astral project, she could summon the dead at will, move objects with her mind, read minds, and was said to be able to appear from one place to another, over great distances, in a very short period of time. We need this chick on our side, or we need to...uh..."

"Gotcha, Benchley. I get it."

"Anyway, I'll leave you two lovebirds alone, but you better get your ass over here soon. Alexia wants you to check out the van and she's foaming at the mouth."

"Okay. We'll be over in an hour," Jeff answered, then clicked off the call.

"So I'm a bad ass weapon?" Samantha asked.

"Yeah. You are." Jeff gave her the details as he poured her a glass of juice and joined her at the table.

"So Amaliya gets zombies. I get ghosts." Samantha stared at him sadly.

"Yeah."

"And no way to get out of it?"

"No."

"Is there at least an instruction manual?"

Jeff shook his head. "We have some information about the phasmagnus, but nothing in depth."

"Why not?"

"The vampires killed all of them a long time ago." Jeff winced.

Samantha shaped her hand into a gun and pretended to shoot herself.

"Sorry."

With a shrug, she leaned over and gripped his hand. "I love you. I trust you to get me through this."

"I love you and I promise I will do everything I can to help you." Jeff kissed her fingers and Samantha gave him a wan smile.

The phone hummed beside him and he sighed as he picked it up. It was an unknown number and he almost sent it to voicemail until he realized it was an area code in Texas. "Hello?"

"Jeff?"

"Yeah?" Jeff didn't recognize the woman's voice on the other end and shifted uncomfortably in his chair. "Can I help you?"

"Jeff, this is Cynthia Guerra. Sergio's wife." She sounded rather excited, but nervous.

"Hello, Cynthia. What can I do for you?"

Samantha tilted her head, curiosity etched into her features. She snagged the pad and pencil she used to build her grocery lists from the counter nearby and shoved it toward him.

"Jeff, I don't know why we didn't think of calling you earlier, but I tried calling my husband a little while ago and he didn't answer his phone. He may be having bad reception, but I got a little nervous. So I thought about calling you."

Jeff scribbled the woman's name onto the pad. "Call me about what?"

Samantha raised her eyebrows after she read it was Cynthia Guerra on the phone.

"Pete Talbert came by this morning with a man named Ethan Logan. Do you know him?"

"Damn," Jeff muttered. He added another notation.

Samantha tilted her head, her brow furrowed as she saw him underline the man's name.

"Jeff?" Cynthia's voice asked after he was silent for a little too long.

"Yeah, I know him." Jeff sighed, rubbing his chin.

"So he *is* a paranormal investigator," Cynthia said with relief.

"No, he's actually a supernatural bounty hunter. He tracks down monsters of all kinds for various employers for a ton of money," Jeff answered.

"Oh, God, Jeff." Cynthia sounded suddenly terrified.

Beside him, Samantha's eyes visibly widened.

"Ethan came to your house for what reason?"

"We should have called you!"

"Cynthia, talk to me. Why was he at your house?"

"He said he has the cure to vampirism. That he could turn Amaliya back to human, but that he needed the ashes of the vampire who made her."

Jeff scribbled down everything she was saying, the sick feeling in his stomach growing. "And he was with Pete Talbert. The guy Amaliya admitted to feeding off of and wiping his memory?"

"Pete remembered her again. He knows she's a vampire. That's why he was helping Ethan. Pete wants to help her become human again. Can Ethan do that?"

CHAPTER SEVENTEEN

Or is he trying to track her down to kill her?"

"I can't say for sure, but if he's after The Summoner's ashes this may have nothing to do with Amaliya at all. Or at least, not directly. I'm not sure. Dammit. Why didn't Sergio or Innocente call me?" Jeff lifted his eyes to see Samantha biting her bottom lip. Fear and horror tangled in her gaze.

"I don't know! We were all so excited about being able to save Amaliya we didn't even think about it! Jeff, they went to the cemetery where The Summoner died! They left three hours ago and I can't reach Sergio!" Cynthia sounded close to hysterics.

"Cynthia, we'll deal with this. I swear it!" Jeff gripped Samantha's hand tightly. "I just need to talk to my team and make a plan, okay?"

"Jeff, should I call the police?"

"No! It will make it even more dangerous for all of them. Hopefully, Ethan will get what he wants and move on without causing an issue. We'll deal with this, I promise. I will call you as soon as I know something."

The woman's sobs from the other end of the call made Jeff's chest hurt.

"Cynthia, I promise. We'll take care of this. It's what we do."

"Jackie kept telling me that Ethan was a liar. She said she could see it in his mind," Cynthia wailed. "I should have called you sooner!"

"Jackie reads minds?" Jeff was flabbergasted.

"We think she got it from Innocente. Plus, I'm Irish you know. Could be from my side, too." Cynthia regained control of her voice, but she was obviously scared. "I should have listened to her."

"Cynthia, you can't blame yourself. Ethan is very, very good at his job. Trust me. I've heard what he is capable of. I want you to make sure to call me if you hear from Sergio. Okay?"

"Okay...okay...I trust you," Cynthia whispered. "And call me if you hear anything."

"I will, Cynthia. I promise."

There was a soft click when she hung up.

"Shit!"

"What are we going to do?" Samantha asked, her face pale and her lips trembling.

"Get to the shop, organize, and plan. We've got four hours before Cian and Amaliya are awake. We're on our own," Jeff answered.

"Do you think he really just wants The Summoner's ashes?"

"Maybe. But for what?" Jeff hurried to Samantha's bedroom and began to gather his clothes.

"Maybe he really does have the cure for Amaliya?" Samantha's voice was full of doubt, but he could see she was struggling not to be terrified by the turn of events.

"I doubt that he was hired to save Amaliya. It's just a convenient lie. One that Pete, Sergio, and Innocente all fell for." Jerking on his clothes, Jeff struggled not to be ragingly pissed at Sergio and Innocente for not contacting him. Love made fools out of everyone.

On the other side of the room Samantha dressed in black jeans, cowboy boots and a silky black tank. Tugging her hair back into a short ponytail, she glanced over at him when she realized he was watching her.

"What?"

"You look amazing," he said bashfully.

"This is my badass outfit," she informed him, holding out her arms and rotating. "If I am this phasmagnus thing, then I'm going to look uber-cool kicking bad guy butt."

Catching her about the waist, Jeff drew her to him and kissed her ardently. The love he felt for her was overwhelming and he couldn't endure the thought of anything bad happening to her. When his lips reluctantly left hers, Samantha's eyelashes fluttered as she moaned.

"Dammit! I want more sex!"

"Later," Jeff promised, grabbing her hand and rushing her out the door. He hoped there would be a later.

The long highway weaving through the hills was nearly empty of traffic. The sun had burned away all the lush greenery of the spring, leaving a dry, yet lovely tapestry of the Texas Hill Country.

Pete took a long sip of the lukewarm soda he'd bought at a small gas station when they had filled up the gas tank again and wondered how much longer they had to drive. Sergio's huge navy-blue Ford truck sped along in front of them, the shadowy outlines of the big guy and the diminutive old woman barely visible through the tinted rear window.

Ethan had lapsed into silence. The tall man wasn't particularly talkative when driving. He didn't even like to listen to music while they traveled, so Pete listened to music on his phone by streaming it through his Bluetooth. Johnny Cash was his fallback when he was nervous and the Man in Black was crooning in his ear. He still remembered Amaliya as a child dancing in her backyard to her little radio as it played her favorite Johnny Cash song, singing along loudly as the sun played in her blond hair.

Rubbing his goatee, Pete wondered if Amaliya would return to her golden locks once she was mortal again. He kind of missed them, but he didn't really care in the end. As long as he could ask for her forgiveness and start again. His heart longed for her and he couldn't wait to hold her in his arms again. She had to forgive him. He would find a way to make it up to her. Never again would he reject her or hurt her. He had been a fool to spurn her.

A strange beeping noise sounded in the console. Ethan flipped it open to retract a rather large phone with a long antenna sticking out of the side.

CHAPTER SEVENTEEN

"Hello," Ethan said briskly, inclining his head slightly in Pete's direction.

Pete pretended to look out the side window, ignoring Ethan. He made a bit of a show tapping his fingers on his knee to the music. His cellphone didn't have any bars at all and he wondered if the phone Ethan was using was one of the special ones that had access to satellites.

"Yes, I have located the master vampire. Apparently he was killed in a small ghost town called Fenton. Sergio Guerra and his grandmother are taking me there now. By tonight I should have all the ingredients for the ritual to restore Amaliya. So, yes, everything is fine. Nothing to worry about." Ethan's voice was calm, measured, and a somehow reassuring. "Okay. Talk to you later." Once the phone was stored away, Ethan said to Pete, "That was my employer. They're pleased with how things are progressing. If not for you, I'm not sure I could have gotten this far."

"I want to help Amaliya," Pete answered. "Who does your employer want to help?"

Ethan cast a shadow of a smile in Pete's direction. "Believe it or not... Amaliya."

"Oh, yeah?"

"Yeah."

"You don't find that strange? That someone that's not her family is trying to make her human again?" Pete lifted his eyebrows, turning to view the driver."

"The world is a lot more complicated than you realize, Pete. It's not all nice and tidy like most of humanity thinks it is. Those who become aware of the truth, that the monsters really are lurking in the dark, either go crazy or adapt. I have adapted. My employer has as well."

"That's not answering my question."

"Maybe not. Besides, you're going to get what you want. Amaliya human again." Ethan said pointedly. "Am I right?"

Pete frowned as he stared at Sergio's truck speeding along before them. "Yeah, but I don't get why you were hired."

"Maybe my employer just wants one less vampire in the world." Ethan shrugged slightly. "Did that occur to you?"

"So someone hired you, a vampire hunter, to go and kill Amaliya's creator and then make her human just because they want one less vampire?" Pete pondered on his own words, mulling them over. Could it be that simple? Maybe it was. Why couldn't it be possible that someone out there was so afraid of vampires they wanted them dead or turned back to mortals?

"Again, does it really matter what the motives of my employer are? I'm a vampire hunter. People hire me to eliminate vampires one way or the other. I'm good at it. It's what I do. Be happy that I've been hired to make her mortal, not stake her through the heart and chop off her head."

"You'd do that?" Pete gulped, the mere thought making him a bit sick to his stomach.

"It's the only way to make sure they don't come back." Ethan shrugged slightly. "But your girlfriend is lucky. She's young enough for the ritual to work. She can go home, say she was in hiding, and start her life all over again."

"Yeah," Pete said thoughtfully, picturing it all in his mind. A smile tugged on his lips and he glanced out the window at the hills streaming past him.

"It's a second chance. Most people don't get those, do they?"

Pete shook his head. "No they don't."

"So stop worrying and relax. We'll find a few bits of that bastard's body, burn it, and prepare the ritual. Easy as that."

"Easy," Pete said, his voice full of wonder, hope, and a little fear. "Can it really be that easy?"

"Why not?" Ethan asked.

"Yeah, why not?" Grinning, Pete settled in his seat. Maybe this was God's way of working it all out and he just had to accept it. He was helping rescue the woman he loved and it was a good and noble thing.

CHAPTER EIGHTEEN

Samantha stared out the passenger window of Jeff's battered Land Rover at the crowded sidewalks lining Congress Avenue. Even though the thermometer had tipped over the 100 degree mark, there were plenty of people out and about. Dogs trotted in front of owners while babies in strollers stared out at the world through tiny sunglasses.

The food trailers clustered in a lot were under siege by hungry shoppers. Women in filmy summer dresses and sandals and men in shorts and t-shirts huddled in the shade sipping water and eating delicious entrees or sweet desserts.

It made Samantha want to cry. It was all so beautiful and normal. Families, young couples, old couples, friends, siblings, pets with their owners, all living their lives without the knowledge that the world was not as it seemed.

Among them, Samantha could now clearly see the specters of those who had passed on. They wandered amidst the crowds, unseen and unnoticed. A few of the dead looked confused by the chaos around them, but others tilted their heads to gaze at her when the SUV drove past. A male ghost in a pink thong, boa, and big sunglasses stood on a corner and waved to her as she passed. Samantha returned his smile and blew him a kiss.

Jeff turned down a residential street and the shade of the trees was a welcome relief from the blazing sunlight.

"Are you okay?" Jeff asked, reaching out to touch her hand.

"There are so many ghosts," Samantha answered. "I never realized."

"You're growing stronger, aren't you?"

"I think so." Samantha tore her gaze away from the hazy figure of an old woman sitting on the porch of a house. She looked straight ahead and curled her hands into fists. "It feels weird not being human anymore."

"You're still human," Jeff assured her. "Just with extra powers."

"Like a superhero," Samantha said, flashing a smile in his direction.

"Absolutely."

"It's kind of a relief. Seeing all of them makes me not so afraid of dying. Not that I want to die. I really don't want to experience the pain of it."

"Let's not talk about dying."

"But it could happen," Samantha said sadly.

Jeff lapsed into silence at her words. She felt a little bitchy for speaking the truth, but she was tired of hiding from it. For the last year she had lived a life of half-truths that had done nothing more than slowly wreck her life. Now she recognized she couldn't allow herself to lie about the reality of her life. She was a phasmagnus and there was no going back. Even though her heart was still bruised from her relationship with Cian, she was beginning to love Jeff. He was sweet, kind, and goofy just like her. She loved his soulful eyes and floppy brown hair. When his thick brows arched upward, he looked so cute she wanted to smother him with kisses. The last few months while she had come to terms with her heartache over Cian, she had probably taken advantage of Jeff's kind nature. She wouldn't do that again. She was done pining over a lost fantasy.

The Land Rover pulled into the alley that led to the parking lot of the bookstore. A hunter-green van was tucked under the big cedar tree that shaded the rear entrance. The door was open and Alexia and Benchley were carrying boxes to the van. Jeff pulled up beside the van and parked.

"Sam?"

"Yeah?" Unbuckling her seatbelt, she twisted in her seat toward him.

"I don't know what's going to happen tonight, but I want you to know that I have no regrets. Even if things go really wrong tonight, I'm glad that I met you that day at the Spiderhouse."

The earnest expression coupled with his sincere gaze melted Samantha's heart just that much more. Gripping his hand, she leaned over and kissed him. His lips were soft against hers and she marveled at how much she loved his kisses already.

Sharing smiles, they parted and slid out of the SUV.

"About damn time," Benchley called out to them from where he stood next to the open side doors of the van.

Alexia leaned her head out to glare at them before ducking back inside.

"We agreed to meet at four o'clock today. We're not late," Jeff pointed out as he greeted Benchley. They clasped hands and briefly embraced even though Benchley looked decidedly grumpy.

"Yeah, dude, but we were busting our asses while you were..." Benchley trailed off as he caught Samantha's expression.

"Just shut up, Shark Boy," Samantha said, playfully punching his shoulder. "If you could spend the afternoon getting laid, you would have done exactly that."

CHAPTER EIGHTEEN

"Yeah..." Benchley admitted. His crush on her was sweet, but she could see he was a little hurt by the reality that Jeff and Samantha really were together at last.

Samantha peered into the van. "Whoa. All FBI-ish and stuff."

Alexia was tucked under a console messing with wires. Monitors and computers were tucked into a custom-built workstation that could seat two. A bench lined the opposite side, complete with seatbelts. The seat was open to reveal weapons arranged carefully, cushioned by black foam. A thick black curtain separated the two front seats from the rest of the area.

"Still have more work to do on it," Alexia admitted. She grunted as she crawled out from under the console. She was dressed in dark shorts, purple Converse sneakers, a purple tank top, and a lightweight sleeveless hoodie. Her short hair was messy and her glasses were crooked. "But it'll do for tonight."

Jeff leaned against the doorway. "Looks good, Alexia. Got all the cameras set up?"

"Got it done this morning before sunrise. I have them set to start transmitting at ten when they meet with Rachoń. I have four set up so we can see what is going on clearly. We can get the van a little closer than I thought because of a service road. We'll have to off-road it a little, but Benchley assures me that his mods on the van will hold up."

"I know what I'm doing. Games and cars, those are my things," Benchley said confidently.

"But what's going on with Ethan Logan? That dude is fucking scary bad news," Alexia asked worriedly.

"We don't know," Jeff admitted, "which is why I'm considering driving out there."

Samantha gave him a sharp look. "Huh?"

"I want to know what he's up to. And if Innocente and Sergio are with him, I feel an obligation to go make sure they're okay." Jeff met her gaze steadily. There was unexpected steel in his eyes.

Her stomach knotted. He was right. Though Sergio and Innocente didn't live in Austin, they were a part of their crew.

"I've tried calling both of them after you told me what's up. No answer. I tried finding out Ethan's cell number by calling his 'work number', but his answering service just took a message." Benchley stood with his arms folded across his wide chest. His dour expression spoke loudly.

"You think he'll do something to them?" Samantha asked.

"Ethan's a dick," Alexia said grumpily. "He'll fuck over anyone to get his job done."

"So you've met him?" Samantha tilted her head to study Jeff's tense face. "Jeff?"

He shook his head. "No. We've only heard stories. He's a bit of a legend."

"He's ruthless. And he has money to back him up." Benchley climbed into the van and sat on one of the chairs bolted to the floor next to the console. "Word is he killed some cops in Chicago. They arrested him, but he was out the next morning with no charges. Some other guy ended up going to trial and got convicted. They even kept Ethan's name out of the news. That's what kind of clout he has."

The mildew smell of the creek that ran behind the store mingled with the fresh aroma of cupcakes emanating from the bakery on the other side of Jeff's store. The fresh breeze was warm against her skin and the heat coming off the van burned her arm as she leaned against it. With a sigh, Samantha lifted her eyes to gaze at the blue sky through the canopy of the pecan tree.

"We should go," she said at last.

"We've got to cover Amaliya and Cian tonight," Benchley pointed out.

"No, me and Jeff should go. It's a graveyard, right? Ghosts will be there. I can do my ghost magic if we run into trouble."

"You really think you can use it?" Alexia said, looking impressed. "Already?"

Samantha shrugged. "Sure, why not?"

Jeff scrutinized her, and she met his gaze steadily.

"We can leave Shark Boy, Alexia, and Eduardo to help Amaliya and Cian. We can go check out this Ethan guy," Samantha insisted, ready for a fight. There was no way in hell Jeff was going alone.

"Okay," Jeff said.

"Okay?" Samantha was ready for an argument, so her surprise made her voice squeak.

"Yep. Okay. Let's go. Benchley and Alexia know what they're doing. So does Eduardo. We'll haul ass out of town and get to the graveyard." Jeff climbed into the van and leaned over the weapons in the bench.

"We can handle Rachon and Prosper," Benchley said confidently. "Two vampires, a shifter, and me and my mean sister are more than enough to handle those two."

Alexia rolled her eyes. "Take silver and blessed bullets just in case, Jeff."

"We're going to shoot Ethan?" Samantha asked incredulously.

"Not if we can help it," Jeff answered. He tucked a pistol into a holster and handed it to Sam. "Not quite your pretty pink Glock, but this will do."

Samantha gave him a small smile as she started to fasten the holster to her belt. "I can shoot the wings off flies."

"Really?" Benchley asked, impressed.

"She's a fierce shot," Jeff admitted.

"A woman of many talents," Benchley mused.

Alexia made gagging noises.

On more than one occasion, Jeff had joined her and her family at the firing range. Samantha prided herself on her ability to outshoot everyone in her family except her mother. Jeff had been startled by her accuracy.

Finishing with the holster, Samantha tugged her shirt down over it. The gun

CHAPTER EIGHTEEN

felt good and solid against her back. Jeff crammed extra ammunition into his shorts before sliding out of the van. His gun had disappeared under the hem of his shirt.

"Alexia, can we take the Little Bitch?" Jeff asked. "The Land Rover has been temperamental."

Tossing him the keys, Alexia gave him a stern look. "No dents. No scratches. No guts. No blood."

Jeff looked hurt. "Like I would do that."

Samantha glanced over at Alexia's white Jeep. It was an exact replica of Cher's 1994 Jeep Wrangler in the movie *Clueless*. It was pretty cute. Samantha respected Alexia's devotion to such a great movie. Samantha had considered herself a bit of a Cher when she was younger.

Alexia narrowed her eyes slightly. "Any scratch and I will cut you."

"She will. She's vicious. Those nails." Benchley shuddered.

Alexia hissed like a cat and bared her sharp little nails.

"We'll try to keep in touch, but it seems everyone is having bad cell service out there," Jeff said as he snagged Samantha's hand.

"We meet up here, right? After it all goes down?" Benchley asked.

"Yep. See you later. And good luck," Jeff said solemnly, then began walking toward the Jeep, pulling Samantha behind him.

Samantha waved at the siblings. The matching somber looks on their faces reflected her own.

"We'll see them again, right?" Samantha said softly when they were a few feet away.

Jeff glanced over his shoulder at his friends before returning his attention to her. She could see the worry in his eyes and willed him to lie to her. "I don't know."

Samantha sighed, then nodded. The truth was better to deal with than lies. Holding tight to his slightly sweaty hand, she let him guide her to the Jeep.

It was late afternoon when Sergio pulled his truck over to the side of the road near the edge of the ghost town of Fenton. In the rearview mirror he could see the hotel where The Summoner had taken refuge just a few months before. The sight sent a sliver of fear through him and made him shiver. Before the truck was a thick copse of trees that shielded a dilapidated farmhouse and overgrown cemetery from the eyes of any travelers on the narrow country road. The memory of the life and death struggle he had experienced there not too long ago caused his chest to tighten.

Shooting a worried look at his grandmother, he saw that she, too, was staring over the field with a fearful but determined expression on her face. Her tiny hands gripped her big purse crammed with holy relics. Twisting her lips from side to side, the older woman appeared to be concentrating.

"Grandmama?"

"It feels wrong," she said, obviously apprehensive.

"What do you mean?"

"The cemetery. It feels wrong. It feels...empty."

"But that's good, right?" Sergio shifted in his seat uncomfortably.

"I don't know," Innocente confessed. "I can usually feel something of the dead when I'm near a graveyard. This one just feels like a void."

Nervously, Sergio picked his phone up off the dashboard and checked the bars again. Now he was wishing he had brought a weapon. With no coverage, he couldn't call for help if something went wrong. At a few stops, he had tried to use the convenience store business phones, but he had been rebuffed every time. They had stopped at a little barbecue place and he had tried to bribe the owner, but had met with resistance. It was annoying when all he wanted to do was check in with Cynthia and see how the kids were doing.

The rumble of another engine drew his attention to his side mirror. The big dark truck pulling the camper stopped alongside them. Pete rolled down the window and leaned out.

"Where is it?"

"Across the field. There's a dirt driveway, but it's mostly overgrown. I don't know if you can get the camper up close," Sergio answered.

Ethan's face was shrouded in shadow, hidden by his sunglasses and his cowboy hat. "Then we'll park at that hotel and drive up with you. Okay?"

Sergio nodded. "Okay." Shifting gears, he backed up the road a little, then u-turned. Behind him, Ethan followed suit. He noticed Innocente's deepening frown and reached over to squeeze her hand. "We're doing the right thing. If there is the slightest possibility of bringing her back to life, we have to do it. We both know it."

"I know, Sergio. I thought that maybe I would feel him in the cemetery... since he died there. But it's so...empty," Innocente sighed, then forced a smile. "Which is a good thing, I guess. I like the idea of him burning in hell."

Cracking a grin and chuckling, Sergio agreed heartily. "Absolutely. That's a great place for that bastard."

The big truck drove up to the front of the old rundown hotel. The thick weeds and creeping vines were slowly tearing the building apart. Across the street, the remains of a gas station sat in the center of a weed-choked concrete pad. The cracked and broken asphalt made for a bumpy parking job, but Sergio was more unsettled by the hotel. It looked like something out of a horror movie.

"It feels empty here, too," Innocente complained.

"But isn't that a good thing?"

She shrugged, appearing unsettled. "I always feel *something*."

Ethan and Pete climbed out of the now parked vehicle and strolled across the lot to the truck.

CHAPTER EIGHTEEN

"What about him? Do you feel anything about him?" Sergio asked.

Innocente again wagged her head. "No, no. He just feels like another person. Nothing special. I don't think he's anything more than a man."

"Then we probably shouldn't worry," Sergio suggested.

"You think I'm a paranoid old woman," Innocente huffed.

"I think you're a worried grandmother that wants to save her granddaughter."

"Eh, true."

Sergio unlocked the doors so Ethan and Pete could climb in. Watching them over his shoulder, he noted that Pete appeared just as uneasy as his grandmother. The thought of restoring his cousin to a mere mortal made Sergio very happy, but he, too, was plagued by niggling worries. Maybe it was because Ethan was so imposing with his dark sunglasses and rugged appearance. He reminded Sergio of a gunslinger from the Old West. His presence wasn't comforting, but it wasn't uncomfortable either. At times, he didn't seem quite real to Sergio. No, that wasn't right. It felt as though Ethan was somehow standing outside of the world, watching them all. Yeah, that's what it was. It was a little creepy now that he put his finger on it.

"Drive up to the old house and park behind it. I don't want to tip off any passing locals that we're digging up their cemetery," Ethan instructed.

"Gotcha."

Sergio drove the truck in a circle and headed up the road toward the turnoff. It was hard to see with the thick golden-brown wild grass drowning the fence, but he managed to see it in time. Turning sharply, he grunted as the truck bounced up the deeply rutted drive. His grandmother grumbled in Spanish as she clung to the dashboard with both hands. A few groans issued from the backseat. He tried to drive slow enough so they wouldn't be tossed around inside the truck, but he had to go fast enough to not get stuck in either the deep ruts or the pasty mud at the bottom of some of the deeper holes made by a recent rain.

Finally he drove up to the old farmhouse where Amaliya and Cian had taken refuge from The Summoner. It was also the house where Sergio, Innocente, Samantha, and Jeff had been trapped by an army of the dead. The sight of it gave him the willies. The house was listing a bit more to one side than he remembered and a good chunk of the roof had caved in. Sergio wondered if it was the result of the battle that had happened there, or a recent storm. He couldn't remember how the house had looked the night they had survived The Summoner's attack.

"Park up behind those bushes." Ethan leaned forward to point at one heavily overgrown area next to the house.

Sergio complied without answering. Now that they were at the spot where Amaliya had destroyed The Summoner, he was feeling more than a little spooked. His grandmother sat beside him, her rosary clutched in her fingers, her lips soundlessly moving in prayer.

"So this is where it went down?" Pete said, awe in his voice.

"Yeah, Amaliya killed him and saved Cian," Sergio said, then realized he had inadvertently let a valuable bit of information slip out. He shot a look at Ethan and saw a flash of a slight smile.

"So she's in Austin, huh?" Ethan shoved open the truck door, slipped out, and reached into the bed of the truck to grab the shovels.

"Austin?" Pete's voice was thoughtful. "She always loved Austin. I should have known she'd go there. I hope she's not alone."

Innocente gave Sergio a warning look. They'd both agreed to keep quiet about Amaliya's new life in Austin and about Cian. It was obvious that Pete was pining hard for her and neither one of them really knew what Amaliya would do once she had the cure. Would she try to stay with Cian? Or would she try to find happiness in a mortal life? Sergio knew what he was hoping for. It would be nice to see his cousin married with kids living a nice normal life. It would suck for Cian, but Sergio was never too sure about the vampire anyway.

Pete climbed out of the car and Sergio followed, pocketing his keys. Both of them snagged shovels and waded into the thick grass behind Ethan to where the mottled gray gravestones stuck out of the weeds. Sergio twisted about to give his grandmother a slight wave. She sat with the truck door open, clutching her rosary, observing their progress with a solemn expression on her face.

"So we dig up the bits of the big bad vampire, burn it, then find Amaliya and turn her mortal, huh?" Pete's voice was full of hope and desire.

"Yep," Ethan answered.

"Just like that?" Sergio asked.

"Just like that." Ethan climbed over the remains of a wrought-iron fence and dropped into the graveyard.

"Seems so easy," Pete remarked, wonder in his voice.

"Yep. Which is how I like things. Easy. No fuss, no muss," Ethan answered. Walking through the dead grass, he searched for a gravestone. "Let's start near the fence and hope we hit pay dirt." Lifting the shovel, he slammed it hard into the packed earth. "Got a few more hours until sundown. Let's make it count."

Sergio already felt the sunlight pricking along his skin and the heat sucking the energy out of him. "For Amaliya," he said, and broke ground with his shovel.

"For Amaliya," Pete said in a prayerful tone.

Together, the three men began to dig.

Chapter Nineteen

Amaliya tossed her waist-length hair over one shoulder and leaned forward on her elbows. The table wobbled slightly, sloshing the chai latte in her cup over the edge.

"Crap!" Amaliya exclaimed, fumbling for her napkin.

With smooth elegance, Professor Sumner blotted the spill with a few extra napkins. "There you go."

"Thanks," Amaliya said, embarrassed by her blunder.

She was trying so hard to be seductive and failing. It was the third time she had managed to spill her drink while trying to be coy. PJ Harvey's deep voice was singing mournfully over the coffee shop's sound system and the clank of dishes being washed were the only sounds other than their conversation. The coffee shop was nearly empty, its mismatched chairs and leaning tables devoid of the usual students cramming for their latest exam, or writing a paper.

"We all make mistakes, don't we?" Professor Sumner said with a charming smile and a wink.

"And sometimes they're enjoyable." Flirtatiously, her eyes lingered on his handsome face as she took a sip.

With the Easter break underway, most of the students were out of town visiting with family. Amaliya had just finished doing laundry so she could pack and head home when Professor Sumner had knocked on her dorm door. She had been surprised to open the door and find the tall man with the keen blue eyes and long blond hair standing in the hallway.

"Care for a coffee?" he had asked in his refined English accent.

Amaliya knew she was foolish to go anywhere with one of her professors, but she hadn't thought twice before saying yes. Now sitting across from him, she wondered how long it would take for her to get him into bed. There was something intensely magnetic about the man. He was not her type in any way, but there was something about him that made her want to crawl over the table and ravish him. Though he was dressed simply in black trousers and a blue shirt under a soft leather coat, he exuded raw power and sensuality. She watched his fingers caress the mug filled with steaming black coffee that he'd barely sipped from.

"So why are you taking Psychology?" he asked, picking up the conversation again.

"I guess I want to know why my family is so fucked up," Amaliya answered, shrugging.

"Are you thinking about pursuing a career in the field?" He tilted his head as he set his hand on the table a scant inch from her own. His nails were immaculately groomed and a thick antique gold ring glimmered on his ring finger. The blue of the sparkling stone matched his eyes.

Glancing at her fingernails, Amaliya wished she had touched up the polish. "I'm not sure yet. I'm still not sure what I want to do. I thought about maybe going into counseling and helping kids who are grieving, but I don't know." She rubbed her arm, caressing her tattoo under her thin black sweater. It was her tribute to her mother, long gone, long dead.

"You went through a loss at a young age?" His intense blue eyes never strayed from her face and she felt her cheeks flushing despite the serious topic.

"Yes, my mother. A little later on, my little sister. I lost them both to cancer." Amaliya sipped her drink, trying to ignore the pain inside of her. It was hard to think of her deceased loved ones and not feel lost and alone in the world. Her family had never recovered from the death of her mother and it had fallen apart completely at the death of her sister.

"Death changes everything, doesn't it?" Professor Sumner said, his fingers lightly stroking her fingertips.

She raised her eyes to see that he was gazing at her contemplatively. "Yes, it does."

The sound of a cup falling drew Amaliya's attention across the room. Bianca Leduc was on her hands and knees carefully picking up the shattered remains of her cup. The girl lifted her blue eyes and met Amaliya's gaze.

Panicky to be spotted with their professor, Amaliya quickly looked away.

Professor Sumner fully took her hand in his and his thumb gently rubbed her palm. "Have you feared death since then?"

Nodding, Amaliya swept her hair over one shoulder to hide her face from Bianca. "It just seemed so cruel for them to die so young."

"Die young and make a good looking corpse," Bianca said in a low voice, walking past their table.

Amaliya twisted in her chair to retort, but the professor yanked on her hand, pulling her attention back to him.

CHAPTER NINETEEN

"Are you afraid to die young?"

Uncomfortable, Amaliya squirmed in her rickety wooden chair. "I don't want to talk about this."

"Why?"

"It's morbid," she said crossly. She didn't want to think about her mother and sister dying. She didn't want to think about death. The purpose of this date was to finally get her hot professor into bed.

"Ah, but it's the inevitable end that we all fight against, but never can escape... not fully."

Amaliya stared down into her drink, her image reflected in the milky brown surface. "No, no, we can't."

"You will be so pretty when you die," Professor Sumner said, his hand stroking her cheek.

Amaliya lifted her head to find herself standing in the shadow of the dorm building. The light of the moon filtering through the treetops illuminated the professor's hair into a halo. His face was in shadow as he loomed over her.

"Your whole life you've been fleeing death even while you courted self-destruction," his melodic, seductive voice whispered as his long, tall body pinned her to the cool concrete wall.

Amaliya's lips trembled as she tried to find the words to defend herself, but he was speaking the truth. His slender, silky fingers slid over skin as he traced her collarbone.

"Always living dangerously, dating all the wrong men, always taking the unnecessary risks, then running away when you realize you've gone too far. Isn't that the truth of your life?" His voice mesmerized her as he inclined his head toward her.

"Yes," she answered in a hushed voice.

"Even tonight you came with me instead of packing your bags and going home. Why, Amaliya?"

"Because you're dangerous," she answered, her heart thudding in her chest.

"Yes, I am."

His kiss was searing, terrifying, and consuming. She panted into his mouth as his lips and tongue danced with her own. Clinging to him, she moaned. His hands slid under her shirt and over her pierced nipples, making her whimper. The thrill of possibly being discovered and the subsequent scandal made his intense kisses and skilled caresses even more arousing. When he slid his hand into her jeans, she ground herself against his seeking fingers. Fingers gripping his jacket, she wanted him more than she had ever wanted anyone. His mouth, wet and warm, slid over her cheek to her throat while his hand stroked her aching sex.

The bite came savagely, the pain instantly unbearable. Overcome in agony, her mouth parted in a silent scream. Her lover held her against his body, and she heard him gulping her blood as he ravaged her neck. The excruciating hurt was too much to endure and her vision grew hazy, her hands flailing against him.

Dropping her to the ground, the vampire watched as she trembled in agony. Her hands slid over her torn neck, the wound gaping and pumping blood.

"Yes, so very pretty as you die," his proper British voice said with pleasure.

A whimper drew Amaliya's attention away from the vampire. Beside her Bianca lay staring at Amaliya with large beautiful eyes. Her hand strained toward Amaliya, seeking comfort. Bianca's pale throat was gashed open and blood poured onto the ground. Amaliya struggled to touch the girl, wanting to console her even as she felt her own life fading.

"Do you really believe I would let you fade away forever? My beautiful, beautiful creations," The Summoner's voice whispered.

Amaliya almost reached Bianca's trembling hand when The Summoner lifted her up and flung her.

Amaliya landed on a bed, gouts of blood bubbling up around her body. The bed was saturated with the blood and it was warm and sticky against her naked flesh. She was in the room where the secret orgy had been held. All around her were the dead of her first feast.

Gasping, she was overwhelmed with the smell and taste of blood. Her power surged while her hunger begged to be sated. Rolling onto her back, she lifted her hands to find them slathered in blood. Violently hungry, she licked her fingers, her body trembling with need.

Then The Summoner was there with her, his naked body pressing her into the blood-soaked linens. His white blond hair tumbled over her face as he kissed her bloody lips. Sharp teeth pulled at her tongue and lips, drawing blood, and she moaned with pleasure.

"All your life you played with the darkness and now it has consumed you," The Summoner whispered tugging on the bar bells adorning her erect nipples. "Is it all you hoped for?"

Amaliya tangled her fingers in his hair, kissing him fervently. He was everything she had ever desired, everything she had ever wanted. He was her liberator from fear and pain. From death. Her bloody fingers slid down his firm stomach to find his hard cock and stroke it while her legs wrapped around him.

"We are death," a young woman's voice whispered in her ear. "We are the consumers of life. We bring pain and terror to all who stand before us."

The Summoner's erection found her sex and plunged into her. His mouth ravaged hers, the taste of his powerful blood sending shivers of pleasure through her.

"We are the monsters in the dark," the feminine voice continued to utter in her ear. "We are everything that humanity fears."

Amaliya's eyelids fluttered, her body shuddering. Her power grew, building inside of her, matching the pleasure filling her body. She was gloriously dead and alive. Her hips lifted to meet the fierce, possessive thrusts of her vampire creator.

CHAPTER NINETEEN

"We belong to him because he made us. No one will ever be able to take us from him." The velvety lips of the whisperer caressed her ear.

The Summoner slid his mouth over her cheek to nuzzle her ear. "Forever joined in darkness." He bit her earlobe lightly, then lowered his head to bite into her throat.

Amaliya cried out in pleasure.

"His bite was our awakening, Amaliya." Bloody fingers traced the edges of her sharp teeth.

Opening her eyes, Amaliya saw Bianca lying next to her. The pale blond hair of the girl was drenched in blood and her nude body was splattered with it. The young woman's eyes were no longer blue, but pure white and slightly glowing. Her sharp little teeth were visible between her pink lips as she lightly caressed Amaliya's mouth with her fingertips. "We can never escape. We are part of him and part of each other."

"Bianca," Amaliya whispered, her hand caressing the younger woman's cheek. "Where are you?"

"Forever with you," Bianca answered before her supple lips covered Amaliya's.

The Summoner arms enfolded both of them. Bodies writhing together on the bloody bed, Amaliya was lost to all but the pleasure of the bite, the kiss, and sex...

Waking, gasping, trembling, Amaliya thrashed about before realizing she was safely ensconced in the secret bed chamber Cian had built in the apartment. The man she loved remained blissfully asleep beside her, one hand resting on his chest and the other lightly touching her leg. The peacefulness on his face was a stark contrast to the turmoil within her.

Sitting up, Amaliya wrapped her arms around her knees and gritted her teeth against the piercing throb between her thighs. Her body screamed for The Summoner's touch and her power lashed around her, seeking him out. Concentrating, she gathered the tendrils of her power about her and dragged them firmly within her. Panting, she struggled to regain control while her body continued to yearn for the man who had killed her and created her in his own image. Wiping away a bloody tear, she focused on retaining the sliver of control she still had over her own body and power.

Rubbing her lips furiously, she tried to remove the memory of Bianca's kiss. The softness of the other woman's lips haunted her. Amaliya's traitorous mind had somehow interwoven Bianca into her memories. Amaliya had died alone and killed alone. Though Amaliya had seen Bianca virtually every day in class, she had never spoken to her. Yet, Bianca's words haunted her. What did the dream mean? Had Bianca been trying to warn her somehow? Or was it just her own fears manifesting in a nightmare?

Amaliya rocked back and forth, trying to ignore the throbbing of her sex. She felt swollen, violated, and unsatisfied. Pressing the heel of her hand against her eyes, she tried to block the memory of the one time she had sex with The Summoner. It felt like a betrayal of Cian to remember. It hurt to admit that she had felt acute pleasure and utter fulfillment when The Summoner had taken her.

Bianca's words returned to her thoughts.

"We belong to him because he made us. No one will ever be able to take us from him."

Amaliya swept her hair back from her face as she stared at the clock on the headboard of the bed. Only another hour until sunset.

The Summoner was dead. Long gone. Buried in tiny pieces all over a remote country graveyard. She didn't belong to him anymore, but to herself.

Tears slid down her cheeks. The memory of The Summoner's cruelty and his touch tormented her.

She couldn't wait for the night to fall so she could escape the bed chamber.

The heat of the day had dulled as the sun set, but the air was still warm and thick against Innocente's skin. Sitting in the cab of her grandson's truck fanning herself with a piece of paper while watching the men work, she once again said a silent prayer for guidance. Ethan had set lanterns around the grave the men were digging up and the light wavered as it cast eerie shadows over their faces.

Closing her eyes, she reached out with the invisible tendrils of her gift. There was no answer. The dead were truly silent in their graves. Not even a whisper of memory remained. She had never experienced anything quite like it. Usually when she entered a graveyard she could feel the wispy remnants of spirits, fragments of the person who had died, painful memories that lingered long after life had departed. She wondered if this particular graveyard had always been this way. She was uncertain since she had not actually entered the graveyard the night they had confronted Amaliya's creator. When Amaliya had faced The Summoner, she had done it alone. Innocente had escaped with the others and had not actually stepped into the graveyard.

Sergio trudged over to the truck, dragging his shovel behind him. "How are you doing, Grandmama?"

"I'm okay. Anything yet?"

Leaning into the truck, Sergio popped open the Styrofoam ice chest he had purchased earlier in the day and filled with ice and water bottles. He grabbed two and shoved the lid back in place. "Not yet. Kinda hard to figure out which grave might have a piece of him. Could be a really long night." He twisted the cap off of one of the bottles and drank it in four large gulps.

"It doesn't feel right," Innocente said. She knew she sounded like a looped recording, but she couldn't help it. Something was wrong and it was niggling at her.

"I won't lie, Grandmama. I would rather be anywhere but in a cemetery at

CHAPTER NINETEEN

night. But we have to try to save Amal, right?"

Moved by his love for his cousin, Innocente touched his muscular arm lightly. "You're a good boy, Sergio." His skin was very warm under her fingers and she felt the beads of sweat dotting his upper lip when he kissed her cheek.

"We're family, Grandmama. We take care of each other. Besides, after all the shit Amal has been through she deserves a happy ending, right?"

Innocente inclined her head solemnly. "Yes, she does."

Finishing off the second bottle of water, Sergio threw the empty containers into a plastic bag and wiped his mouth. "I better get back to it. Let me know if you get any bars on the phone. Maybe we'll get lucky."

"I will."

Innocente sighed, watching Sergio return to his task. She was tired and her back ached, but she didn't dare take a nap. She felt she had to stay alert and be aware of all that was happening around them.

Clutching her rosary tight in one hand, she continued to pray silently.

CHAPTER TWENTY

The water in the shower ran hot against Amaliya's revitalized flesh, warming her, cleansing her, and grounding her. As soon as the sun had set, she had escaped the sleeping chamber she shared with Cian just as he was stirring. She had felt crazed in her own skin, terrified of her dream, and didn't want to deal with the man she loved until she could gather her wits about her.

It had taken all her willpower to banish the nightmare from her thoughts. The need to flee had been almost unbearable. It had taken all her willpower not to grab a bag, her car keys, and head out of town. The instinct to run was so deeply ingrained in her it felt like an addiction. She had literally felt her body craving the feel of speed as she put the city of Austin behind her.

Instead of running away from the life she had built with Cian, she'd slipped silently in and out of the apartments of the people who lived in the building. She had often teased Cian about living above his pantry, but it wasn't far from the truth. Since Cian owned the building, both he and Amaliya could enter the apartments of the tenants without an invitation. It made hunting so much easier. Because it was early in the evening, Amaliya only visited the single people living on the floors below them. She never drank from children, but occasionally fed from their parents if there was a lack of people in the building when she needed to sate her hunger.

The intimacy of feeding always enthralled her. It made her feel painfully dead and wholly alive at the same time as she felt the fresh blood rushing through her veins returning life to a body that should be long dead. Arms wrapped around people who didn't even know her name; she fed from their throats in an almost sacred act of rebirth. Of all the new aspects of her life, this was the one thing she loved most. Feeding was exquisite and fulfilling. It calmed the hunger and restored her sanity.

The blood she consumed was transformed by her nature, not only renewing her body, but her power. She could feel her necromantic nature slithering through her like silken batwings, expanding and contracting. Its icy tendrils flexed and coiled inside of her, craving to touch the dead and commune with them.

Her vampire nature summoned her to drink the blood of humans, but her necromancer nature beckoned to her to raise the dead. She wanted to walk among them, feel them touching her, drawing life from her, loving her as she restored them.

This was the blessing and the curse that The Summoner had inflicted upon her. It angered her that her nightmare tainted her usual pleasure in her new nature. She loved being a vampire and had grown to embrace her necromancer power. Yet, Bianca's words now haunted her.

When she was done, she'd drunkenly returned to the apartment she shared with Cian. He was gone, feeding somewhere in the building. The space felt empty without him. She felt empty without him. She didn't care what Bianca had whispered in her dream. Amaliya was her own person. She made her own decisions and she chose to be with Cian.

Almost feeling feverishly delirious, Amaliya took refuge in the shower. The water flowing over her helped her subdue the call of the graveyards. The warm water formed a barrier over her skin, calming the need to call the dead.

"Something's wrong," Amaliya whispered.

Ever since she had consumed the witch's spell, she could feel it inside of her, twisted into her own magic. It felt intrusive, but it was now a part of her. Just like Samantha was trapped by magic she didn't understand, so was she. They were tangled in the web of magicks neither one of them fully understood. Even though Jeff and Cian were trying to help them, in reality no one really had any idea of what was truly happening to them. The Summoner had been no ordinary vampire and in the end, he had created three beings of unusual and unknown powers. Maybe Bianca was right in that context. They could never truly be free of The Summoner because it was his power that was infused into their very essence.

Resting her forehead against the cool tiles, she sighed. In a very short time she would be facing Rachoń and her people. Though Amaliya believed in her powers, she was afraid of the unknown. Would Bianca obey Rachoń? Would she be stronger than Amaliya? A piece of Amaliya was terrified to rescue Bianca. What if the girl looked to Amaliya to guide her? In her dream Bianca had been reaching for her. What did that mean? Amaliya didn't even know what *she* was doing half the time. How was she supposed to help another necro-vamp?

The warm water sluiced over her long black hair, flattening it to her flesh. Running a hand down her arm, Amaliya caressed the scar that was once a tattooed rosary. She had fallen so far from grace. Was there any salvation for her

CHAPTER TWENTY

and Cian? What would she find beyond the veil of death?

A gust of cold air and the sound of the shower door popping open announced Cian's arrival. She could smell fresh blood on his breath and his familiar scent. Remaining under the stream of water, she was reluctant to acknowledge his presence. Wallowing in her fears and anxieties, she found it difficult to let him into her thoughts.

The presence of the master vampire made her skin tingle. The shower was quite large and his body didn't touch hers as his hand reached past her to make the water hotter. Closing her eyes, her fingers continued to stroke the roughened scar at the center of her tattoo. What would her mother think of her? What would she tell her if she were still alive?

"Don't be afraid," Cian said, as if answering her question.

She opened her eyes and shifted her stance so she could see him. His hair was longer and his cheeks and chin scruffy. The heavy fringe of his lashes made his hazel eyes even more beautiful.

"Aren't you?" she asked. Though she loved him, he was still a mystery at times. There was a hardness to him that lurked under his pretty smile and calm demeanor.

With a slight shrug, he said, "What's the point?"

Amaliya twisted around so she could rest her back against the wall, just on the other side of the water spray. "Uh, we might die."

"We already did die."

"True," Amaliya conceded. "You were afraid of The Summoner."

"Because he would do much worse than kill us," Cian reminded her. "Honestly, death in comparison to the things he could have done to us would have been a welcome relief."

"Are you afraid of what's on the other side?"

Cian picked up a loofah and some soap, his brown hair darkened by the water. "Of course. Who isn't?"

Frowning, Amaliya rested her hand over her scar. "I don't want to die. I want to live, you know." The conversation she had with The Summoner in her dream reared its head and she shuddered. "I don't want to deal with all this bullshit. I just want to live our lives without this crap from the others."

The soap trailed over Cian's lean, muscular form as he bathed. He drew closer to her so he could peer into her eyes. "I did that for almost three decades. It can be rather boring."

A burst of laughter erupting from her lips surprised Amaliya. "I've never been accused of that!"

Cian appeared amused. "No, you're not. And our lives are not ever going to be simple. I hid myself in the shadow of The Summoner for a very long time. Vampires did not dare come against me while he lived. Now we will have to deal with them and perhaps other creatures now that he is gone. He was a curse and a blessing. In many ways, he was my salvation when he was alive. His mere existence kept me safe."

Amaliya narrowed her eyes. "Oh, my God! This is such a guy thing! You're wanting to show everyone you can stand on your own two feet, aren't you? Prove that you're a badass without Daddy watching over you!"

Amaliya knew she was onto the truth when Cian averted his face and studiously scrubbed his chest.

"You're such a fuckin' man!" Amaliya shook her head, her wet hair sliding over her skin.

"If we prove ourselves to the others, they will think twice before coming against us. Let Rachoń come. I'm older and stronger than she is."

"But she controls Louisiana," Amaliya said. "Doesn't that make her stronger?"

"She has many minions under her. That is where I failed." Cian frowned as he ducked his head under the water again.

"You didn't build a cabal."

"And she did. But I am stronger than she is. She knows it. I suspect that's why she has Bianca now, to strengthen her base of power."

"Like you're using me to strengthen yours," Amaliya said with a tiny bit of bitterness. She knew her presence at Cian's side strengthened his status in the world of the vampires. It annoyed her.

Cian plucked at her bottom lip with one finger. "You know you're more than that."

Quirking an eyebrow, Amaliya cocked her head. "Oh, yeah?"

Resting his hands against the wall just over her shoulders, he leaned toward her. His eyes were so intense she had to force herself to stare into them. Sometimes it was difficult to meet his gaze. Maybe it was his vampiric power, but whenever he looked into her eyes, she felt as though she was connected to the very core of his being, drowning in him.

"What's the point of living forever if you have no one to share it with? What's the point of fighting to survive against all sorts of monsters if you're alone? Life is not worth living when you have none to love. I have lived so many different lives since the night I died. I lived for vengeance, for power, for money, for lust. When all those grew stale and empty, I tried to be human again and failed."

Overwhelmed by the emotion in his words and the intensity of his eyes, Amaliya averted her eyes. He caught her chin, lifting it. Unsteady, she met his gaze.

"You restored me, Amaliya," Cian said, his voice thick with his accent and emotion. "I'll fight to protect what we have."

The love she saw in his eyes banished all thoughts of The Summoner and his cruelty. Sliding her arms around his waist, she pressed her body against him, her mouth catching his in a searing kiss. The coppery taste of blood was on his tongue and lips and it made her hungrier for him. Pressing her against the cold tiles, Cian met her passionate kiss with equal desire. His sharp teeth grazed her

CHAPTER TWENTY

tongue and fresh blood spilled into their kiss.

All thoughts of death washed away in the flood of her love for him. Tangling her fingers in his wet hair, she drew his head back to bite into his throat. Simultaneously, he pushed her thighs apart and slid into her. His blood filled her mouth and tangled her even deeper into his fiery power. It was flooding her, filling her, strengthening her, and binding her to him.

Gasping, her fangs released the hold on his flesh. Cian gripped her hair and bit into her neck. Her power swirled out to meet his when their blood mingled together in his vampire kiss. Her lover's fingers slid over her wet skin as he lifted one of her legs, thrusting harder into her.

Pleasure and pain built inside of her as their power continued to burn over her flesh. She could almost see the swirling colors of their power against the backdrop of her closed eyes. The blackness of her power mingled with his fiery aura when they reached the peak of their pleasure. Cian ground himself into her while she scored his back with her nails, eliciting a low moan from him. His tongue trailed over her lips and she shuddered with pleasure. The pulse of his cock inside of her as he orgasmed forced a growl out of him that sent a shiver through her.

"Fuck," she whispered against his lips.

Kissing her, he slid his fingers between them. "Come for me."

"You're an asshole," Amaliya gasped.

Cian chuckled and pinned her to the wall, relentlessly stroking her.

The doorbell rang.

Amaliya gripped Cian's wrist. "Eduardo is here."

"Let him wait," Cian ordered watching her face.

With a gasp, she felt her climax wash over her, rippling like a great wave as their combined power slammed into her. Her eyes rolled as she collapsed against Cian. Unexpectedly, he was inside of her not only physically, but supernaturally. She could feel his overwhelming love and desire for her, his strength, his determination, and his need. It was almost too much to bear on top of the powerful jolts of her orgasm.

Kissing her deeply, Cian held her until the wave of power ebbed away leaving her trembling in its wake.

"What did you do?" Amaliya gasped.

"Claimed you," Cian answered. "I made you mine. And I am yours. Bound by more than The Summoner's blood, but by our power."

A touch of anger mingled with her awe. "Why didn't you ask me?"

Tenderly touching her cheek, Cian ignored the insistent ringing of the doorbell. "Because you already said yes. You didn't flee tonight."

Punching him in the shoulder, Amaliya frowned at him. "Oh, fuck you."

"You just did," Cian smirked.

"Are we married or something now?" Amaliya clenched him inside of her, eliciting a tortured moan from him.

"Or something," Cian answered, nuzzling her neck.

"Dickhead."

"I love you, too."

The doorbell continued to ring tenaciously.

"I'll get it," Amaliya reluctantly said. "Before he thinks we're already dead."

As their bodies parted, Amaliya felt a pang of remorse at their separation, yet she still felt an invisible cord connecting them. She rinsed off under the water and slipped out of the glass box to snag her robe.

"Don't let him see you naked," Cian called out.

"Yeah, yeah, whatever," Amaliya answered.

The robe was black silk and fell to her feet. It was Cian's originally, but she had claimed it as her own. She nabbed a towel off the counter and rushed out to answer the door. Wrapping her soaking wet hair in the towel, she checked the security feed before heading down the front hall.

The doorbell buzzed over and over again.

Opening the door, she set a hand on her hip and arched an eyebrow. "No patience, eh?"

Eduardo grinned, a feral expression. "Not at all." The short man was clad in tight blue jeans, a form-fitting black silk T-shirt, and cowboy boots. He smelled of the earth and death. Handing over a red thermos, he said, "So when does the fun start?"

Amaliya ignored the way his eyes lingered on her breasts. "We're getting ready. Rachoń isn't due at Zilker Park for another hour." She unscrewed the thermos lid and glanced inside, sniffing loudly. Her blood still coated the interior and top. "Didn't clean it out, eh?"

"I was tempted to lick it clean."

"What stopped you?"

"I don't really want to end up like Sam. Ghosts freak me out." Eduardo shrugged, shut the door, and followed her to the kitchen.

The comment smarted more than it should have, but Amaliya simply shrugged her shoulders, dismissing it.

"I hit every cemetery in Austin." Eduardo leaned against the bar and raked his gaze over body again.

Amaliya rinsed out the thermos thoroughly, the bloody water swirling down the drain. "And you made sure to pour it onto a grave right? The blood has to be on a grave."

"Yep. And I waited until the sun was under the horizon. So it's all good." Eduardo scrutinized the apartment, taking in the brick walls, cement floors, and modern furniture. "Boring place."

"I had nothing to do with it. This is all Cian's Ikea fetish."

"Speaking of the devil..." Eduardo gave Cian a slight salute as the vampire strode toward them.

Amaliya felt her nipples harden and her sex tingle at the sight of her lover. He

CHAPTER TWENTY

was dressed all in black from his jeans to his western style shirt. The tips of his black cowboy boots were edged in silver and he wore a silver buckle that could be used as a weapon. His hair was longer and shaggier and his beard made him look a little dangerous.

"We're set up I take it?" Cian asked.

"Cameras are in the park. The whole thing will be under surveillance, and your fearless vampire hunters are armed to the teeth," Eduardo replied. "And you have me."

Cian regarded Eduardo thoughtfully. "Don't start shit just to have a fight."

"Would I do that?" Eduardo feigned hurt.

"You're a coyote."

Eduardo flared a grin.

"I'm going to get ready," Amaliya said. "The male posturing and testosterone is just a little too much. Isn't it enough we have a vicious vampire and a necro-vamp to deal with?" She strode past them, rolling her eyes.

"Just keeping it interesting," Eduardo called after her. "Because life is too short to be boring."

"Or too long to be too exciting," Amaliya said over her shoulder, then slipped upstairs to change.

Part Five

Sunday Night

CHAPTER TWENTY-ONE

T he sun had set in a blaze of glory that had given way to deep and darkest night. It was a new moon and the blackness of the evening was absolute. Only the stars glittering above and the headlights of the Jeep issued any light in the darkness.

Samantha sighed, twisting one of her silver rings around her index finger nervously. She had loaded her digits and limbs with silver jewelry at the last moment before leaving the house when she remembered the pain it caused vampires. While with Cian, she had stopped wearing it. Now she felt a little safer with the silver bands glittering on her fingers and around her wrists.

"It's so dark," she muttered.

"There should be a flashlight in the glove compartment. Alexia is always well prepared," Jeff answered, his fingers flexing on the steering wheel.

The drive had been uncomfortable since they left Austin. Listening to music had only set their nerves on edge and conversation had drifted off into silence. Samantha sighed. She didn't really want to talk about how her intestines were cramping uncomfortably anyway. She had already thrown up when they made a restroom stop at a small convenience store. Every instinct, supernatural and otherwise, was screaming inside her head that something was terribly wrong. The further the Jeep traveled down the empty country road, the more unnerved she became.

It wasn't that long ago that she had nearly died after traveling this exact same road to rescue Cian from The Summoner. She had been fearless in her determination, but after nearly dying and all that had ensued, she had a healthy appreciation for the supernatural world and all the dangers it contained.

Continuing to spin the ring around her finger, she pressed her lips tightly together as the edge of the ghost town was caught in the headlights of the vehicle. A familiar faded and rotting sign that read "Fenton, TX. Best Homemade Peach Cobbler in Texas!" flashed past her window, then the rotting facades of long abandoned buildings loomed in dark shapes near the narrow road. Ahead was the "Y" in the road that cradled the dilapidated hotel where The Summoner had taken refuge and the gas station where Amaliya had fought constructs made out of her victims' bodies. Samantha was grateful she hadn't seen those things. Amaliya's description alone had grossed her out.

The Jeep slowed. A big black truck attached to a camper was parked in front of the hotel. Jeff tapped his fingers on the steering wheel nervously. "They're definitely here." Jeff snagged his cellphone off the dashboard and checked for bars. "And we have no service."

A hard lump formed in Samantha's throat and threatened to choke her as a familiar figure stepped into the headlights and waved them down.

"So we're in the same boat they are. No service. Out in the middle of no—"

"Stop!" Samantha screamed, finding her voice.

Jeff pounded down on the brakes and they were both pitched forward as the tires squealed. The seatbelt snapped taunt against Samantha's torso in a painful vise. She gasped, clutching the buckle tightly.

Roberto stood in the headlights, arms folded across his chest, his head tilted to one side. His raven black hair and dark fringed green eyes were exactly as she remembered him. So was the condescending smile on his face.

"What the hell, Sam?" Jeff asked, twisting around in his seat trying to figure out what was wrong.

"It's Roberto," Samantha gasped.

"Cian's dead minion?" Jeff lifted his eyebrows. "Seriously?"

Roberto's smile grew as he casually walked over to the passenger door. His black suit and white shirt were immaculate. Gesturing for her to lower the window, he rested one hand on the roof of the car. Samantha stared at him through the glass, her hands trembling.

"Lower the window, Sam," Roberto said, sounding slightly annoyed.

"You're dead," Sam informed him.

"I am aware of that," Roberto said, his smile tightening. "Now, lower the window."

"You're talking to him?" Jeff asked, staring past her. "He's there?"

"Yeah," Samantha grumbled, lowering the window. "And being a bossy ass as usual." She had never gotten along particularly well with Cian's long time mortal companion. Roberto and Cian had met in Mexico over a hundred years before and had forged a strong friendship that had been destroyed by Roberto's betrayal. Roberto had chosen to become a vampire and serve The Summoner instead of standing at Cian's side. Samantha was sure Amaliya had pushed Roberto over the edge, but that didn't take away from the fact that Roberto was a Class-A asshole.

CHAPTER TWENTY-ONE

Once the window lowered, Roberto leaned his elbows on the window sill and stared at her for a long moment. "So you're finally useful."

"Fuck you."

"And still charming."

Samantha swallowed hard, leaning away from him. She remembered too vividly what happened when she had touched Cassidy. The last thing she wanted was Roberto gaining the ability to hurt them. "What do you want, Roberto?"

"Death does something to you..." Roberto mused, his fingers playing along the edge of the open window. "Not being able to affect the world around you and wandering in circles, trapped. It's not the most pleasant of experiences."

"Why didn't you move on? You know, go into the light? Or was that light all flamey and fiery?" Samantha arched her brows.

Only Jeff's steady breathing indicated he was leaning toward her. He was utterly still, waiting to see what would happen. She appreciated him letting her deal with the testy ghost.

Roberto grinned, laughed, and shook his head. "There was nothing. Just darkness and the knowledge that I am tethered here." Casting a sorrowful look at the hotel, he said, "I'm stuck in this hell hole."

"Why?" Samantha tried to stealthily unbuckle her seatbelt, but the click gave her away.

The ghost's intense green eyes flicked toward her, his hand flexing slightly on the window sill. "I'm not sure, honestly. The night The Summoner died there were many of us here, trapped by his power. When he died, I fled. I ran down the road. I'm not sure if I even realized I was dead, I just wanted to escape. I got as far as the city limits and was tossed all the way back to the hotel." Roberto cast a wary look at the structure.

"And?" Samantha prompted, sensing he was scared and uncertain. She almost felt bad for him, but then she remembered he was a dick.

"The other ghosts were gone," he said after a beat. "I was alone." The lines in his face seemed to deepen as his eyes darkened.

"What do you mean alone?"

"The other ghosts were gone. Some were barely there to begin with. Faded memories, but others were very vivid. Including the girl who shot me. She wouldn't stop crying. When The Summoner died, I..." He seemed to fade just a little, his form dissolving into the darkness that barely relented to the headlights of the Jeep. Appearing distracted, he stared into the night, toward the graveyard. "Even the graveyard was empty."

The sense of being surrounded by the menacing unknown intensified. Of course, she was also speaking to a ghost, so that had her nerves a bit frayed.

Her hands quivered as she twisted in her seat to stare at the phantom. His form was blurring. It was as if she couldn't focus her eyes upon him. She needed him to talk to her. There was only one way to keep him from slipping away.

Timidly, she touched his hand. For a second she felt nothing, then his flesh became tangible, cold and hard like a corpse.

Roberto sighed with relief and returned his attention to her. "I'm sorry. It is hard to...hold on."

"Why did you stop the Jeep?" Samantha queried, curious.

"I felt you coming."

"How?"

"I don't know. I just...knew." He shrugged his shoulders slightly. "I felt you..."

"I can see him," Jeff whispered in her ear.

Samantha kept her hand pressed to Roberto's even though it was disconcerting to feel the icy flesh beneath her fingers. "Roberto, why did you stop the car? You don't like me. If you felt me, why would you stop us?"

"Because of what you are." Roberto attempted to give her a condescending smile, but it failed. He looked more afraid than any other emotion. It was disturbing to witness. "I somehow knew you would be able to see me, to help me."

Samantha shook her head. "I can't help you, Roberto. I don't even know what I'm doing! This is all new to me."

The ghost gripped her hand tightly, startling her. Leaning through the open window, his face was illuminated by the glow of the dashboard. "They're in the graveyard. Something is wrong there. It has been wrong since he died. They're going to..." Roberto struggled to speak, his tightening grip eliciting a cry of pain from her. "He died there. Do you understand? He died there!"

"You're hurting me!" Samantha cried out, rotating her hand in a futile attempt to wrest free.

"He died there!" Roberto screamed in her face. "He died there! And the ghosts are gone!"

"Let her go!" Jeff exclaimed, lunging over Samantha to wrestle her hand free.

"You have to stop them!"

Prying Roberto's frigid fingers from her wrist, Jeff leaned his shoulder into the ghost, pressing him out the window. "Let go of her!"

Samantha twisted her wrist back and forth in the ghost's grip trying to break free. She could feel the specter drawing power out of her. Through his touch, Samantha sensed his terrible fear and frustration. He was increasingly agitated, his thoughts flitting incoherently from fear to raw anger.

"I shouldn't be dead," Roberto shouted. "I was supposed to live forever!"

Jeff finally got Samantha's wrist free. Using his body as wedge, the vampire hunter shielded her as she scrambled into the driver's seat and hit the button to raise the window.

"Roberto, back off!" Jeff ordered.

"No, no! You have to stop them!" Roberto cried out, trying to reach past Jeff and snag Samantha.

The window slid up, cutting off the grasping ghost. With the last of his remaining energy, he beat against the window. Samantha stared at him, tears in her

CHAPTER TWENTY-ONE

eyes, sorrow filling her. What little connection remained between them dissipated like a wisp of smoke. Sapped of her energy, Roberto wailed and vanished.

"He can't reform unless you will it," Jeff said in a tight, scared voice. He collapsed into the passenger seat, his hands resting on the dashboard. "Next time you need to tell him to let you go!"

"I...I..." She realized she hadn't told Roberto to let go and felt like a fool. Closing her eyes, she saw something, faintly, tying her to the ghost—a silver thread writhing in the darkness. She imagined it snapping and suddenly felt Roberto fade from the grip of her power. "I cut off whatever it was connecting us," Samantha whispered. Now it was gone and she felt strangely alone. Yet, if she concentrated just a little, she could sense the lost ghost circling the car in confusion. She immediately withdrew any thought of him, trying to raise a barrier between herself and the phantom.

"What did he tell you?" Jeff asked, breathing a little heavier than normal. He appeared shaken and his eyes darted back and forth, searching the illuminated road.

Samantha inhaled deeply, then told him. "Why would all the ghosts be gone?"

"You can't feel any?"

Shaking her head, she said, "No, just Roberto and he's, like, totally wispy."

Frowning, Jeff dragged his fingers through his floppy brown hair. "I'm not sure. But they're definitely out in that graveyard doing something that's..."

"This Ethan guy is trying to bring him back, isn't he?" Samantha's voice quivered and she hated the fear that laced her words.

"I'm pretty sure that's not possible," Jeff said vehemently.

"But you're not sure, are you?"

Jeff stared out at the bleak darkness, before reluctantly shaking his head. "No."

Settling into the driver's seat, Samantha pouted. "Okay, that's not good. So we can't just drive out to the cemetery and say hello, can we?"

"I think we should. I think we should just go out there and say hello to Sergio and Innocente. If Ethan's up to no good, we'll stop him...somehow. But hanging back here isn't going to help anyone. Maybe when he sees we're here and realizes that our crew back in Austin knows we're here, he'll think twice about doing anything, you know, dangerous."

"Like bringing back the asshole?" Samantha lifted her eyebrows.

"Exactly," Jeff shifted in the passenger seat. "Can we trust Roberto?"

"He's a dick, but he was really seriously scared. And mad. And lost. I think he got stuck here because something went wrong that night. He probably wants to move on. Though I totally think he's going to the burning place."

"If it exists."

Samantha rolled her eyes. "So we just drive out there and go, 'Oh, hi! Just passing through?' and act like nothing is up?"

"I think we should totally go out there and say the truth, but avoid talking

PRETTY WHEN SHE KILLS

about Roberto or bringing back The Summoner. Talk about the whole bringing Amaliya back to mortal status thing."

"She'd never do that, you know," Samantha said confidently. "She likes being a vampire."

"We can't—and shouldn't—speak for her though. So we'll just go out there and be all friendly. Think you can do that?"

Samantha flashed her widest, most sarcastic grin.

"Well, that's not comforting."

"Because you're wrong," Samantha answered. "If we go out there after Roberto warned us, we're as stupid as people in horror movies."

Jeff let out an explosive breath, then his shoulders sagged. "Fine. So what do we do?"

"I think we should park the car and sneak around. Sneaking seriously appeals to me. I don't want to just pop up and get my ass shot or something. I think we should do the sneaking thing, like Buffy."

Jeff chuckled. "The Buffy approach, huh?"

"Sneaking is totally a good idea and you know it." Samantha shifted the gears and the Jeep rolled forward before she looped it around.

"Okay, we'll sneak around. I'll trust you on this."

"Good, because I'm not a total ditz," Samantha assured him.

Jeff touched her cheek affectionately. "I've never thought that."

Samantha parked the Jeep behind the gas station, lodging it between the building and a dense thicket of overgrown bushes and grass. Popping out of the driver's side, she checked to make sure she had the ammunition she had brought along tucked into one pocket. Her hands had stopped shaking now that she had decided how to deal with the situation. Jeff rummaged around under his seat before yanking out a small bag. Opening it, he pulled out two sheathed daggers. He handed Samantha one, then strapped the other onto his belt.

"Silver?" Samantha asked.

"Yep. Aim for eyes and throats...if it comes to that." Jeff shut his door and Samantha locked the vehicle.

"Ready to go kick some ass...if we have to?" Samantha tried to put on her best tough girl pose.

Jeff leaned over and kissed her on the lips. "Be careful. You're not Buffy."

Rubbing her fingertips lightly across his chin, she said, "Good, because then I'd be totally doing my Giles."

Hand in hand, they headed toward the cemetery behind the old farmhouse.

Rachoń was annoyed. Prosper's pop star crush was singing about the joys of S & M, the music blasting out of the car speakers as his Cadillac sailed along the highway. No matter how many times Rachoń told him to turn down the noise,

CHAPTER TWENTY-ONE

it seemed to creep steadily back up. Sitting in the back seat, she glowered at the back of his bald head. He ignored her, his fingers tapping on the steering wheel.

They had spent the day in a hotel in San Marcos, south of Austin, watched over by their human minions while they slept. Rachoń hated being out of her state and had slept clutching a dagger. She had kept Bianca at her side, her other hand holding the girl's wrist. She was paranoid, but with good reason. She was so close to fulfilling her duty to The Summoner she couldn't allow any possibility of failure to creep into her dealings.

Upon awakening, the vampires had feasted on a few students from the nearby university. Prosper had left their human minions behind to clean up the mess. The vampires had overindulged in anticipation of the night's events. Rachoń still felt her body transforming the blood she had consumed into power and life.

Rachoń was in high spirits, but that didn't mean her temper was in check. She was anxious to deal with the situation and move on to her greater plans. Lounging comfortably in the backseat of the Cadillac, she busily texted on her phone.

Next to her, Bianca stared out the car window at dark terrain. As always, she was silent, her huge blue eyes vacant. Rachoń lifted one hand and gently stroked the silky white-blond hair.

"We're almost there, pretty girl," Rachoń said over the pounding music.

Bianca didn't blink, didn't move, didn't acknowledge her in the slightest.

Gently, Rachoń placed her dark fingers under the white chin of the delicate face and turned it toward her. Bianca's lovely face was devoid of thought or emotion. "When we get there, you must do what I say, my little darling. Can you do that?"

The blue eyes shifted toward her slightly.

"Do you understand me, Bianca? You must do as I tell you."

Very slowly, the girl blinked, her blue eyes resting on Rachoń's face, but not seeming to really see her.

"You do understand, don't you?" Rachoń grinned, rubbing the girl's pink cheek with the back of her hand. "I think you're somewhere in there, listening to me."

"Almost there!" Prosper shouted over the music.

Cradling Bianca's face between her hands, Rachoń gently kissed her forehead, then rubbed her lips on the girl's silky hair. "Oh, my sweet little thing. We're about to rain hell down on our enemies. And it will be glorious."

Bianca did not answer. She simply stared.

CHAPTER TWENTY-TWO

The night wind tossed the limbs of the trees into a wild dance while the bats darted through the sky chasing succulent insects. Cian crouched in the clearing in the middle of Zilker Park near downtown Austin, his head craned, listening to the sounds of the city just beyond the belt of thick foliage spreading out along the river.

It was well past the appointed time of Rachon's arrival. She was not answering her cellphone and her absence was disturbing. Resting his elbow on his knees, Cian's fingers raked the coarse grass.

Amaliya stood next to him, arms folded over her breasts, her bleeding wrists dripping cold blood onto the ground. She'd be able to call the dead from the cemeteries scattered around Austin thanks to Eduardo pouring her blood onto a grave in each one. They had come prepared for a battle, but all was silent in the park. The scent of Amaliya's blood was intoxicating. It blotted out the musty smell of the detritus putrefying after a recent rain and the mold growing over the rocks tucked into the edge of the river. It almost overwhelmed Eduardo's cologne, but not quite.

Tucked behind the tree line, Cian could barely make out the hulking shape of the hunters' van. It had been there when the three supernaturals had arrived at the park. It was just like mortals to believe they were concealed when they actually weren't. He could even spot the cameras in the trees. Jeff's people were not quite as good as they thought they were.

Eduardo yawned, sounding more animal than human.

Cian drew himself up. Amaliya glanced at him briefly, then returned her gaze to some distant point in the trees. She was dressed in tight black jeans, thick combat boots, and a black tank top with a middle finger emblazoned on it. It had amused Cian when he had seen it. Amaliya didn't seem to quite grasp the concept of diplomacy.

"They're not coming," Amaliya said.

"Maybe they're delayed," Cian mused.

"Nah, she's right. They're not coming." Eduardo shrugged his wide shoulders. "You got power-played, man."

Casting a sharp look at the coyote, Cian said, "Do you know something?"

"No, I'm just taking a guess here, but I think your sister got you all riled up just so she could stand you up and show you who's da boss."

"I'm bleeding all over the place for no damn good reason," Amaliya grumbled.

Cian hated admitting it to himself, but Eduardo had a good point. Rachoń was temperamental and prone to unusual stunts. He hadn't anticipated that she simply wouldn't show up.

"Maybe we were lured out here for Santos to attack us," Amaliya offered.

Eduardo inhaled deeply through his nose, then shook his head. "Except that there aren't any vampires around but you two."

Amaliya grimaced and lifted her wrists. Cian saw the weeping wounds gradually heal as her eyes glowed. With a growl of frustration, he kicked the ground, striking a divot into the dirt.

"She's playing games," Cian uttered through clenched teeth.

"Well, she's his favorite kid," Amaliya reminded him.

He bobbed his head in terse agreement, stalking about the other two. "What purpose does it serve to lure us out here? What does she gain from this?"

Amaliya shrugged. "It pisses you off."

"Which is actually kind of funny," Eduardo added.

The wind swirled around him, ruffling his hair and bringing with it the scents of humanity, not the supernaturals. Cian shook his head in anger.

"No, no. It's something else. She does nothing lightly. There is a purpose to all she does, even if she is temperamental. What is Rachoń up to?" Cian ran a hand through his long hair, letting it fall through his fingers to rest against his shoulders.

"What does she want?" Amaliya asked. "That's what we have to figure out."

Cian peered upward at the cloudless sky and pondered the question. Rachoń had loved The Summoner. They had fought at times, but Cian knew that she would come to their creator's side to defend him despite the distance. He remembered Rachoń's glee as she had tortured Cian in the ruins of a pyramid in Mexico while The Summoner calmly killed Cian's mortal minions and stitched them back together as grotesque creatures. Maybe he had underestimated her devotion to The Summoner. If Rachoń was out for revenge, she would have to find a way to destroy Cian and Amaliya. Possessing Bianca definitely evened the odds, but Rachoń had not shown up with her own powerhouse of necromantic magic.

"It's a distraction," Cian decided, stopping in his stride, frowning. "She drew

CHAPTER TWENTY-TWO

us here to distract us from something else."

"If she wants Austin doesn't she have to kill us?" Amaliya asked.

"Yep, but she's not here," Eduardo said and yawned again. "Fucking boring night. Thought I'd have a nice little fight to enjoy."

"What else would Rachoń want?" Cian paced, agitated. "This makes no sense. We're missing something."

"We don't know something," Amaliya corrected him.

Eduardo's head jerked swiftly to one side and he inhaled deeply. "We have company and it's not vampires."

A scream rent the air.

"The van!" Amaliya shouted, breaking into a run.

Cian sprinted after her, Eduardo on his heels. Through the trees the van was hidden behind, he saw the flash of a light. The scream sounded male and raised voices competed with it. Amaliya plunged into the trees, eyes flashing white. Cian followed in her wake and barely caught sight of a woman shouting into the van just before Amaliya grabbed her and tossed her away.

"Back off, bitch!" another woman shouted, raised one hand, and swept it toward Amaliya.

Amaliya flew backward into the trees, branches snapping and cracking as she vanished into the gloom.

Alexia and Benchley shouted incoherently at Cian and Eduardo, but both men ignored them as they lunged toward the woman with long bronze hair and blue eyes. Jaw set and eyes blazing, she thrust her hands outward. Cian was hit with the force of a truck and knocked through the foliage. His body hit a tree trunk, snapping bones.

"Fuck!" Cian roared, healing instantly.

Recovering, he leaped to his feet and hurtled back into the fray. He was almost to the witch when the first woman he had seen appeared before him and slammed her fist into his face. He staggered, then seized her arm. She instantly raised her other hand, a silver tipped dagger in it.

"Get the fuck away from us!" The light from the open van spilled over her features. She had heavily-fringed blue eyes and chestnut-brown hair that fell in silky waves to her chin.

"Galina?" Cian gasped.

The young woman hesitated, her full lips parting slightly. After a second, she said, "No, that's my mother."

Cian let go of her abruptly. Staring at the defiant woman before him, he rubbed his chin as it healed. She wasn't a vampire, but...

"Stupid bitches!" Eduardo howled, his mouth full of teeth that were not human as he lunged forward out of the darkness. He had obviously been cast away, too. Bits of twigs and leaves clung to his hair.

Cian caught Eduardo by the back of the neck and hauled him to his side. "Stand down!"

"They're friends!" Alexia's words finally registered over Benchley's incoherent shouting.

Behind the woman who had slugged him and held him hostage at the end of her stake, the witch lowered her hands, though her body was still tensed for battle.

Amaliya surged out of the trees, eyes glowing bright white. One of her arms was broken, the bone protruding just below her elbow. As she stomped forward, she popped it back into place.

"Fucking cunt!" Amaliya screamed, slashing one wrist with her nails.

"Amaliya, stop!" Cian ordered. He held out a hand to ward her off.

"Don't make me give you flying lessons again," the witch threatened.

"They're friends!" Alexia shouted again. "Amaliya, don't do anything!"

Amaliya's eyes continued to glow as her blood dripped onto the ground. "Cian, what's going on?"

"I'm not certain yet." Cian couldn't tear his eyes from the face of the young woman standing before him. She strongly resembled Galina, the human lover of the former Master of the Austin cabal, the woman Cian had spared from the massacre because he had loved her. But there was a hint of another familiar face in her features. He could barely comprehend what he was seeing. "Who are you?"

The woman slowly lowered the stake and stood before him with a defiant tilt to her head. "My name is Cassandra. This is my girlfriend Aimee. We're here to find Jeff."

Both of the women were in jeans. Cassandra was wearing a form-fitting t-shirt with the Batman logo on it while Aimee wore a frothy white blouse over a tank top. He noted Cassandra's combat boots and Aimee's cowboy boots. They both looked like any of the young women in Austin, but he knew they were not.

Cian found it difficult to speak for a moment. "You're a dhampir and she's a witch."

"Yeah," Cassandra answered.

Aimee smiled slightly. "Surprise."

Cassandra warily returned to her girlfriend's side, taking on a protective stance. "We're friends of Jeff. We're tracking someone and you're in our way."

"Do you know who I am?" Cian asked, his voice a bit harsher than he liked.

Cassandra smiled widely. "Oh, yeah. Cian Lynch, Master Vampire of Austin, Texas." Cassandra paused, then leaned toward him, her eyes sparkling with mischief. "Howya doing, Dad?"

Sweat poured down Pete's face as he trod carefully through the graveyard in the direction of Sergio's truck. The muscles in his back and arms screamed in pain, but he ignored the discomfort. He was absolutely sure that what he was

CHAPTER TWENTY-TWO

doing was the right thing. Restoring Amaliya to life was all that mattered. His aching joints and sore muscles would have to endure until the task was done.

He passed Ethan huddled over one of the graves they had uncovered sorting through the remains in the rotting coffin. Pete assumed the hunter was looking for bits of The Summoner again. It disturbed Pete to unearth the old bodies, but most were nothing more than bones. So far they hadn't found what Ethan was searching for. Pete wasn't sure how Ethan could tell the difference between a human dead body and that of a vampire, but he supposed there were some sort of telltale signs.

Wiping his forehead with the back of his hand, he exhaled with frustration. The night was oppressively warm and the darkest black he had ever seen. A thick cloud cover obscured the cold light of the stars and he wished they had brought more lights with them.

Innocente stared past him toward the graveyard when he approached the truck. He had expected to find her napping, but her eyes were alert and her posture tense.

"Need to grab some water," he said, stopping before her.

"Do you ever feel like you're doing the right thing, but that it will not end well?" Innocente asked.

"All the time," Pete admitted. Opening the back door, he leaned in and opened the cooler. He scrounged around in the frigid water created by the melting ice and jerked out a water bottle. "That's why they gave me Prozac for a while."

Innocente frowned at him. "You know what I mean."

"It's just the graveyard. We wouldn't be human if we didn't get the willies being around the dead," Pete assured her.

"It's not the true dead I worry about. It's the others. The ones who are dead, but still moving around." Innocente took the water he offered her. "Thank you."

"Look, the way I see it, all of us out here are doing the best we can for Amaliya. It doesn't help that we now all recognize that all those scary stories we thought weren't real apparently are very real. You've seen Amaliya since she came back. So have I." Pete gulped the water, trying to forget the image of Amaliya's bloody tears and sharp teeth. "It changes everything once you realize that vampires are real."

Innocente lifted her shoulders in a shrug. "I always knew ghosts were real. Vampires aren't so surprising. I just don't like my granddaughter being one. It makes her life so much harder."

"I want to make her life easier," Pete said in a timid voice. He was certain that his intentions toward Amaliya were pretty clear, but it was embarrassing to know that Innocente was aware of how he had rejected Amaliya and the circumstances around it.

Sighing, the old woman took another gulp of water.

"I know I hurt her. I was just afraid. Weren't you afraid when you first saw her?" Pete leaned against the truck, staring at the woman, willing her to understand."

Shoulders slumping, Innocente nodded. "Yes, I was afraid. But then I realized that she was still my granddaughter and she needed my help." Her voice was barbed with her anger.

"But you already knew about ghosts. I'm just a good Baptist. I don't believe in that stuff. I mean, I didn't. Now my eyes are open, and I won't hurt her again. I promise."

Innocente's eyes flicked toward him, her mouth pursing. She appeared to be pondering something. "It's not me you need to talk to. It's her."

"I plan to. I want to make right by her. Once we restore her to human, I plan to take her far away from all this bullshit. I don't care how far we have to go; I will find a safe place for her." Pete touched Innocente's shoulder and she glanced at him again. "I promise, Innocente."

"She's not the same," Innocente said sadly.

"I love her. I don't care what has happened since she died. If she killed people, I know it's because she didn't have a choice. When she's human again, she'll never have to live through that nightmare again."

Wiping a tear away, Innocente aimed her focus toward the graveyard. "She's a good girl. She's just always so lost..."

Pete's heart sped up at the thought of the pain he had caused Amaliya. He wanted to find her and make her safe again. He didn't want her to ever feel lost again. Together, they could help each other create a home and a life. His arms craved to feel her nestled in them again. Even though his memories of their last night together were horrible, they were also wonderful. They had shared incredible moments of passion when they had made love. Pete had never been so happy. If only he hadn't recoiled from her.

"Pete, things may not be as easy as you hope they will be," Innocente said, her words careful.

"I know that. But I will find a way to make amends." It was a vow he was taking very seriously.

The wind rustled through the tall grasses around them, cooling off his overheated skin. Pete closed the rear door of the truck and rested against it. He would give himself a few more minutes before rejoining Sergio and Ethan. The sweat between his shoulder blades was trickling down his back and his skin itched fiercely under its coating of sweat and dirt.

Innocente finished her water and tucked the empty bottle away in a plastic bag. Pawing through her big purse, she pulled out two fruit bars. Silently, she handed him one. Pete took it gratefully. Unwrapping it, he bit into the apple and whole wheat bar. It was the best thing he had ever tasted, or else he was just that hungry.

Sergio's big shoulders were illuminated by the lanterns as he tossed great gouts dirt off to one side while he dug into a grave he was standing in. Amaliya's cousin was a big guy and his muscles glistened in the lamplight. Pete was

CHAPTER TWENTY-TWO

embarrassed by how much more Sergio had done throughout the night. It was obvious that Sergio was just as determined as Pete was to restore Amaliya.

Pete and Innocente watched Ethan stride toward Sergio, gingerly maneuvering around the heaps of dirt. In one hand he was cradling something. Reaching downward with his other hand, Ethan stilled Sergio's movements with a touch to his shoulder. Motioning for the shovel, Ethan stood on the other side of the open grave. Sergio handed up the tool and craned his head to see what Ethan was holding in his hand. Pete took a few steps forward, excitement filling him.

"I think Ethan found something!"

"Oh, thank God. I'm so ready to leave," Innocente said with relief.

Pete started toward Ethan and Sergio, thrilled that they had finally accomplished the first step in returning Amaliya to mortal. He was only a few feet from the fence lining the graveyard when Ethan flung whatever was in his hand in Sergio's face. Motes of a powdery substance danced in the light cast by the lantern as Sergio was engulfed in a small cloud. Sergio gasped, swayed, then collapsed, falling out of sight.

"Sergio!" Innocente cried out.

"Ethan!" Pete shouted at the same time, darting forward.

Standing, Ethan yanked off a glove Pete hadn't realized he was wearing and tossed it aside. At the same exact moment a woman stepped into the light. Her skin was glossy dark and her hair was twisted into spirals around her head. Clad in jeans, a maroon blouse, and a lightweight leather jacket, she was an imposing figure. Pete stumbled to a halt as her eyes flashed in the light, red fires in their depths. Out of the darkness, a massive man with a shaved head wearing an immaculate gray suit escorted a delicate young woman with white blond hair clad in a white lace dress.

"Pete, Pete," Innocente hissed from the truck.

Pete backed away from the trio that he knew instinctively were not human.

The woman's eyes darted toward Pete and her shapely dark lips smirked. "I see you have brought what I requested."

It took a second for Pete to realize she was talking to Ethan.

"Yep." Ethan motioned toward the truck. "The blood of a mother, and the heart of a lover. Easy as pie."

"And the ritual will restore her to mortal, correct?" the woman asked.

"Absolutely," Ethan assured the woman.

"And once she's mortal, we can kill her." The woman laughed with delight. Directing her gaze toward Pete, she said, "How does that sound to you, lover boy?"

Pete shifted around on his heel and raced toward the truck. Innocente had already shut her door and was waiting for him. Sprinting around the front of the pickup, Pete's heart thudded in his chest with sheer terror. His hand snagged the latch and yanked the door open. He scrambled into the thick darkness of the cab and slammed the door shut.

"Where are the keys?" he asked, grabbing at the ignition and finding it empty.

"I..." Innocente faltered. "They were there!"

Ducking down, Pete felt around on the floor.

Beside him, Innocente clasped a handful of rosaries.

A loud bang on the hood made Pete start, hitting his head on the steering wheel. Clutching the back of his head, he sat up to see Ethan standing in front of the vehicle. The keys to the truck dangled in his fingers.

"Shit," Pete gasped.

"This is not good," Innocente whispered, clutching her rosaries to her chest.

Ethan flicked back his duster and drew a wicked-looking silver revolver. "Now, I suggest the both of you get out of the truck."

CHAPTER TWENTY-THREE

"Fuck me," Amaliya whispered in disbelief.

"Oh, shit," Eduardo said, then roared with laughter.

"I think you may want to sit down," Benchley advised Cian.

Instead, Cian took a step toward Cassandra, studying every feature of her face. It was undeniable that she was the perfect mix of her mother and himself. "You're mine."

"That's why I'm a dhampir," Cassandra agreed. "The whole half-vampire, half-mortal thing."

The emotions churning inside of Cian were difficult to separate and he had trouble focusing. A part of his nature hissed at him to kill the dhampir, one of the most dangerous enemies of the vampires. Yet another part of him wanted to enfold the woman in his arms. Standing near her, he could feel that she was his, her blood answering his power. Even her penetrating gaze echoed his own. Slowly, he extended his hand to her.

"A pleasure to meet you," he said at last.

Cassandra made a show of sheathing the stake in her boot before taking his hand. Her grip was firm and strong. "This really wasn't the way I planned to meet you. I had no intention of showing up all, 'Hi, Dad, I'm a dhampir and a lesbian, howya doin'.'"

Cian's eyes flicked to Aimee, then back to Cassandra. The defiant looks on their faces and stiff posture was a clear indication that they were ready for a fight with him. He deliberately took a step backward and lowered his hands.

"I'm glad you're not alone," he said at last, and meant it.

Cassandra lifted an eyebrow and exchanged a quick glance with her girl-friend. "Not that I need your approval for my existence…"

"Of course, not."

"You have a kid, Cian," Amaliya said at last, interrupting. Her grin was a mixture of surprise and amusement. "How can you have a kid?"

"Dhampirs are rare, but they sometimes happen," Cian answered. "No one knows why they are sometimes conceived."

Cassandra shrugged slightly. "But I'm here."

"Yes, you are," Cian said, still trying to comprehend that reality.

"You can call me Cass. You're the necropire, right?"

"Necro-vamp," Benchley corrected while awkwardly climbing out of the van.

Amaliya slightly nodded. "Yeah. How do you know about us?"

"They're hunters like we are," Alexia explained, joining the gathering.

"How did you find us?" Benchley asked.

"Tracking spell," Aimee answered. "I went off the aura remains on the back door of the bookstore. I thought it would be Jeff when he locked up."

"It was me," Benchley admitted.

"Which is why we found you," Cass said, then smirked. "And got to hear you scream like a little girl."

"Hey! You scared the shit out of us! We were waiting for vampires and the side door goes sliding open and—" Benchley trailed off. "Yeah...I screamed like a girl."

"Next time, lock the damn door," Cass said.

Alexia elbowed her brother. "What she said."

"Why do you need Jeff?" Cian asked, his Irish accent more pronounced than usual. It irked him that he couldn't stop staring at his daughter's face. Her subtle expressions ghosted his own.

"Shit is going down in an epic way and we need Jeff. He's not at the shop and he's not answering his phone. We're tracking someone and we need information from Jeff."

"Who are you tracking?"

"His name is Ethan Logan. He's a bounty hunter," Cass answered. "He's been hired by some vampires to recover an item of great occult power."

Aimee yanked a photo out of her pocket and handed it to Cian. It was the shot of a ring resting on a velvet pad. Amaliya leaned forward to see it as the others gathered around, too.

"The Summoner wore a ring just like that," Amaliya said in a strangled voice. Her eyes had returned to normal and Cian saw the fear blooming in them.

"Recognize it, Dad?" Cassandra was obviously needling Cian.

"No, I don't. He didn't wear a ring like this when I was with him," Cian said somberly.

"We're not sure how many there are, but these rings are bad news," Aimee explained. "We were hired to lift one off a vampire in Dallas a month ago. It got messy."

"He bled a lot," Cassandra admitted.

CHAPTER TWENTY-THREE

"You're thieves?" Cian flicked his gaze back and forth between the two women. The night was full of surprises.

"I only rob the bad guys," Cassandra said defensively.

"They're thieves and vampire hunters," Benchley explained.

Aimee leaned against Cassandra, who wrapped a protective arm around her waist. "We do what we have to."

"So it got messy…" Amaliya prompted.

"Yeah, it got really bloody. And the ring…" Cass took a deep breath. "The ring touched the blood of a mortal who was in the room when I kind of took the head off the vampire Master of Dallas."

"So you killed him. Not Courtney who took his place." Eduardo looked impressed.

"Yep. And his stupid blood minion got in the way. When the human's blood touched the ring…weird shit started to happen." Cass shifted on her feet uncomfortably. "It started tearing the veil between our world and the other one. I snagged the ring and threw it into an ice bucket to get the blood off. Once it was clean, the rip healed. But something big and nasty came through."

"It took a whole lot of firepower and magic to take it down," Aimee added.

"We escaped in the chaos. We didn't turn the ring over to the person who hired us. A ring like this in the hands of the wrong person is bad news. So we bailed and went into hiding," Cassandra admitted. "A few days later the guy who hired us was dead."

"So we investigated it and figured out that the guy who hired us had been a front for another vampire." Aimee's eyes swept over the faces of those gathered around them. "It took some time, but we found out that guy was hired by a Professor Sumner. Which is weird, because he died four months ago after the satanic killings in East Texas."

"Jeff told us about you, Amaliya. We knew that The Summoner made you and used that poor sap as a cover. Just like him to play off the similarity in the names." Cass tilted her head and regarded Amaliya thoughtfully. "We found one of The Summoner's peeps and after a few hours of me beating on him, he admitted that The Summoner had one ring already and was looking for more."

"So there are more than the two rings?" Cian arched his eyebrows at the same time his daughter did.

Cassandra took the picture of the ring from Cian and handed it back to Aimee. "Yep. We were shocked to find out about ring number two, though Amaliya here just confirmed its existence. We were coming here to talk to Jeff about the ring when one of our people got a lead about the ring and Ethan Logan. They said he was tracking down Amaliya and that there had been the mention of a ring."

"How do you know we don't have the ring?" Cian asked.

"Neither one of you is wearing it," Cass answered. "And if you possessed this ring, you'd be wearing it. Its power is addicting. When I held it in my hand…" She shivered. "Aimee felt it, too. That ring has some major mojo infused into it."

"The Summoner is dead. I killed him. The ring is somewhere in a graveyard, buried forever," Amaliya said confidently.

"Oh, fuck," Alexia gasped. "That's why they're digging up his remains! To get the ring! Not to turn Amaliya back to mortal!"

"This isn't good," Benchley said nervously. "This isn't good at all."

"What the hell are you talking about?" Amaliya said sharply.

"Ethan Logan is with Pete Talbert, Sergio, and Innocente out in Fenton digging up the pieces of The Summoner," Benchley blurted out. "Cynthia called Jeff today when she couldn't get a hold of Sergio. Jeff and Samantha drove out there earlier to see what was really going on. Ethan told all of them he has a ritual to restore Amaliya to mortal, but that he needed The Summoner's remains!"

"The distraction!" Cian roared the words, anger flooding him. "Rachoń is after the ring! She hired Ethan Logan! She never wanted us to begin with. She just wanted us distracted while they used Amaliya's family to get to the ring!"

Amaliya shoved past the group and broke into a sprint.

"Amaliya!" Cian called after her.

"I have to get to my family!" Amaliya disappeared into the trees.

"They're in Fenton! You can't run there!" Benchley shouted after her.

"Who does she think she is? Wonder Woman?" Cass scoffed.

"If they're in the cemetery right now digging up his remains, they'll have the ring soon, if they don't already. Those rings are dangerous," Aimee exclaimed, gripping Cassandra's arm.

"It'll take a couple of hours to get there," Benchley said.

"So why don't you fly!" Cassandra flung up her hands at Cian.

"I can fly, but not that far," he answered defensively.

"I can get us there," Aimee said in somber tone.

"Babe," Cass said, worried.

"I can do it. It'll severely drain me, but I can do it." The witch raised her chin confidently.

"We need to get Amaliya back here." Cian wondered how far she had gotten and just what she was planning on doing. Running there? Stealing a car?

"I'll go get her," Eduardo volunteered.

"Do it," Cian ordered.

The coyote dashed after the female vampire, looking a little too gleeful.

"Get my stuff, Cass" Aimee said to Cassandra.

Cass squeezed her hand, then dashed off.

"We are parked near here," Aimee explained. She rubbed her hands together nervously.

"What happened to the ring you stole?" Cian asked.

"We hid it when we realized what it could do. We didn't want to hold onto it any longer than we had to." Aimee pulled her bronze colored hair back from her face, wrapping it into a bun and tucking the ends under to secure it. "A ring that can rip the veil is dangerous, but now there appears to be more than one."

CHAPTER TWENTY-THREE

Cassandra rushed up with two big bags and handed one off to the witch. "I got the energy bars, too."

"I'll need them," Aimee said glumly. "Sorry I won't be much help when we get there."

"Just do it. We'll handle the rest," Cass assured her.

Aimee smiled as Cass kissed her lips lightly, then stepped away to let her do her task. The witch immediately started digging through her bag for the items she needed. "I'll open a portal between here and the cemetery. I'll need someone to help me focus the spell. Someone who has been there."

"I can do it," Cian assured her, squatting down to watch her work.

"Once the portal opens, everyone needs to get through as fast as possible. Cass, you need to drag my ass through. I'll only be able to stay conscious around five seconds," Aimee instructed.

"I'll get you through," Cassandra promised.

"I think we shouldn't go straight to the cemetery, but the hotel nearby," Cian suggested. "They probably shouldn't see us coming."

"Agreed." Cass opened up the second bag and started to strap on weapons. "Need some, Dad?"

Cian narrowed his eyes at her and she gave him a delighted grin. "I have what I need, Cassandra."

"He already sounds like a dad," Aimee noted with a slight smile.

Cassandra lifted her eyes. "Great."

"Got her!" Eduardo said triumphantly, dragging Amaliya behind him.

"I need to get a car and get out there!" Amaliya protested angrily. "Cian, I have to go!"

"We have it covered, Amaliya. The witch—"

"Aimee," Cassandra cut in tersely.

"—will open a portal directly to the cemetery," Cian explained.

"Very World of Warcraft," Benchley said, grinning.

Alexia knelt next to Aimee helping her sort her magical items. "Shut up, Benchley."

"Are you sure?" Amaliya asked, worried.

Aimee lifted her head, gave her a lopsided grin. "Oh, yeah. I'm sure. I'm pretty impressive, if I say so myself."

Cian wrapped his arm around Amaliya's waist and gazed into her frightened eyes. "It'll be fine."

"My grandmother..." Amaliya whispered. "My cousin...Pete...they could die."

"We'll get there soon," Cian promised. "We'll stop whatever Rachon is planning."

Cian pulled Amaliya away from where Aimee began to draw a large circle using a bag of white salt. His gaze met Cassandra's for a moment and the sardonic expression that lingered in her eyes since they met was now gone. He promised himself that once they survived whatever the night would bring he would find the right time to speak with Cassandra. His vampire nature and human nature battled within him, one side demanding her death, another thrilled at the prospect of fatherhood. As if sensing his internal war, Cassandra lightly tapped her stake and smiled at him.

Holding Amaliya close, Cian comforted her as they waited for the witch to weave her magic.

Samantha and Jeff crouched down, making their way through the overgrown field toward the old farmhouse and the graveyard. They had seen a car park alongside the road and then its headlights had flicked off just as the back doors opened. Jeff had hit the ground, hauling Samantha down with him, and they had waited in silence for the occupants to pass by. Curled up together, they had listened to the grass rustle around them, but never sensed the passing of the newcomers.

After ten minutes, they had risen and started toward the graveyard again. Lights flickered and danced in the old weedy cemetery. There were several people silhouetted against the lantern illumination. Samantha counted five people, but it was difficult to discern who they were.

Samantha eyed Jeff and he motioned for her to remain silent. He scrounged around in his messenger bag and pulled out a small pair of binoculars. Raising them to his face, he studied the scene before them.

Scratching her arm, Samantha cursed not wearing a long sleeved shirt. The wild grass and weeds were making her skin itch. The air smelled oddly stale and the warmth of the night was uncomfortable.

Jeff handed her the binoculars and gestured for her to take a peek. Lifting them, she peered at the people. A tall man in a cowboy hat and duster held Innocente and another man at gunpoint. There was no sign of Sergio. A beautiful woman and an imposing man with a bald head stood over a slim young woman with whitish hair dressed in an old-fashioned ivory dress. Samantha knew instantly who they were. Rachoń was here—not in Austin—and Bianca was with her.

Scribbling on a pad of paper, Jeff's mouth was tightened into a harsh line. Samantha poked his side to get his attention and emphatically motioned at the scene. If he couldn't understand her urging him into action, he was an idiot.

Jeff grabbed her wildly-gesturing hands and leaned toward her. His voice was barely audible. "We need to be careful not to lose the element of surprise." He then pointed to a copse of trees near the cemetery and pantomimed them crawling.

Samantha nodded her head.

Jeff stroked her cheek. She ran her fingers lightly over his features and kissed

CHAPTER TWENTY-THREE

him. Not needing words, they shared a moment before they both sighed. Together, they crept slowly forward.

When Ethan dragged her out of the truck and ripped her purse from her hands, Innocente had promptly kicked him in the shins. He instantly shoved her off her feet and onto the hard soil.

"Hey!" Pete protested from where he sat on the ground nursing a bloody nose. He had tried to disarm Ethan and failed miserably.

"You don't need this anymore. We don't want to insult our guests, do we?" Ethan threw her purse into the brush and, gripping her arm, yanked her to her feet. "Get up, lover boy. Let's not waste her time."

Innocente tried to wrench free, but she was no match for Ethan. He easily dragged her along behind him as he aimed his gun at Pete's head.

"Get up," Ethan ordered.

Looking a bit woozy, Pete clambered to his feet. He stood on wobbly legs as he wiped the blood from his face. "So it was all a lie."

Ethan shrugged. "A bit of a lie, a bit of truth. They are going to turn her human, strip her of her powers, and then kill her. Sorry, Pete, no happy ending for you."

Innocente observed Bianca staring at her. Tired and angry, Innocente summoned her power. It boiled up inside of her and swirled out into the night, seeking the remnants of the dead. None answered her. She wasn't sure how they could help her, but she was desperate. Her gaze shifted from Bianca to the grave where Sergio now lay. She wasn't certain if he was even alive and her anger and frustration grew.

Beside her, Pete looked crushed and just as furious as she was. They were both in a terrible position and they knew it. There appeared to be little or no hope of escaping whatever the ebony-skinned woman had planned for them. The vampire stood confidently next to Bianca and the tall handsome man loomed over both of them. The female vampire's large maroon eyes rested on Innocente, a satisfied smile on her face.

Ethan kicked Pete's ass to get him moving forward. Pete cast an angry look over one shoulder, but marched forward. Ethan shoved Innocente before him, gripping her upper arm tightly. The gun Ethan had aimed at her head was enough to keep Pete under control. Innocente knew that Pete wouldn't dare do anything if he thought they would hurt her

"I have to say I'm not disappointed at all in your services, Mr. Logan. All that I heard about you is absolutely true. You certainly do get the job done," Rachoń said, laughter in her voice.

"I aim to please, ma'am, especially when the wire transfer has so many zeros." Ethan hauled Innocente over the broken wrought-iron fence. Stumbling, she fell to her hands and knees.

"You could be a bit nicer to an old woman," the big black man protested.

"I thought mortals didn't matter to your kind," Ethan answered, dragging Innocente to her feet.

"It doesn't hurt to be respectful to the elderly," the man answered.

"Prosper is a stickler for manners," Rachoń explained.

Beside her, Bianca gaped openly at Innocente.

Innocente returned her gaze. On impulse, she silently reached out to the girl on the wings of her power. Her power allowed her to speak to the dead and technically Bianca was dead. Innocente felt a shiver of a link.

Bianca blinked.

Bianca, help us.

The girl's eyes slightly shifted toward Rachoń and Prosper.

You're more powerful than they are. Help us, Bianca, and we'll help you.

Bianca's eyelids slightly lowered, then Innocente thought she may have given the barest of nods.

"So, you have all the ingredients for your ritual now," Ethan said. He gruffly forced Innocente to sit on a gravestone. He kicked Pete's feet out from under him and the younger man fell with a thud to the ground. "Mother's blood and lover's heart. Just call up the dead and you can claim the bones of Amaliya's creator."

"You won't get final payment until Amaliya is mortal, understood?" Rachoń said firmly.

"By tomorrow night, she'll have a pulse and you can do whatever you want with her," Ethan said confidently.

"You're evil," Innocente spat at Ethan.

Ethan shrugged. "I like to consider myself amoral."

Rachoń turned to take Bianca's hand. Tenderly, the woman guided Bianca toward the center of the graveyard. "Time to bring forth the dead, my little one."

Don't do this, Innocente urged the girl. She felt her power pulsing between them.

Bianca shifted her eyes again toward Innocente, confirming that she could hear her.

Rachoń ran her long fingers through the young woman's hair and ducked her head to gaze into her face. "Bianca, raise the graveyard. We need my master's bones. Do you understand?"

Gradually, the girl lifted her eyes to regard Rachoń.

"Bianca, raise the graveyard," Rachoń urged again, her voice soft, but firm.

Tilting her head toward Innocente, Bianca's eyes flashed to white.

Don't do this, Bianca. Don't let them kill us.

Help me, Innocente.

Innocente blinked in surprise, then relief filled her. Bianca could hear her and was crying out for help. "Please, don't make her do this!" she cried out, hoping to distract her enemies from the young woman.

CHAPTER TWENTY-THREE

"Shut up!" Ethan ordered, shaking her gruffly.

"Hey, I told you to treat her with respect," Prosper said tersely.

"Bianca, are you listening to me?" Rachoń's voice was taking on a sharp quality.

Innocente, help me! the girl's voice cried out in the old woman's mind.

Twisting away from Ethan's grasp, Innocente boldly stood and glared at him. "Stop touching me!"

"Old woman, I've about had enough of you." Ethan lunged to grip her arm.

Prosper marched toward Ethan. "She's an old lady with not much time to live. Let her be!"

Innocente's eyes met Bianca's glowing ones.

Come to me, Bianca.

Rachoń cupped the young woman's face between her hands, trying to make eye contact with her. "Bianca, why aren't you obeying me? Do as I say!"

The young woman abruptly shoved Rachoń away, sending her sprawling among the graves. With a soundless cry, she ran to Innocente.

"What the hell?" Ethan gasped.

"Innocente, watch out!" Pete cried out in terror.

Stumbling forward, Innocente met the girl in the midst of the broken tombstones and dry grass. The slender young thing fell into her embrace, clutching her tightly. Enclosing Bianca in her arms, Innocente felt the vampire trembling.

"It's okay. Just help us escape now..." Innocente whispered in her ear. "Bring the dead up, but have them protect us!"

"Bianca!" Rachoń roared in anger. "Bianca, come here!"

Prosper was closer, so he stomped toward them. "I told you she wasn't right in the head, Rachoń."

Bianca twisted in Innocente's arms and flung up one hand. The dead shot out of the ground, cutting off Prosper. Gasping, he stumbled back, surprised by the turn of events.

"Good girl!" Innocente said with delight.

Bianca raised another hand and more dead sprung up between them and Rachoń. The vampires stared in surprise at the young woman.

"Bianca, obey me!" Rachoń said, moving to rip the dead apart and descend on them.

"Pete, come here," Innocente said. "Hurry!"

Ethan moved to cut him off, but more dead burst forth from the ground. The dead creatures grappled with Ethan, allowing Pete to slip past them.

"Good girl, Bianca," Innocente said proudly. "We need to get Sergio, then we can go."

"I'll get him!" Pete dropped into the grave where Sergio had collapsed earlier. "He's still alive!"

"Hurry, Pete!" Innocente cried out.

Rachoń lunged forward, her hands shredding the corpses, but more sprang up to block her way. This time they attacked her, wrestling with her.

"Rachoń!" Prosper leaped past the dead impeding him to rush to her defense. Nearby, Ethan struggled with the corpses trying to wrest his gun from him.

Pete dragged Sergio out of the grave, grunting. "I need help."

The power around Bianca was growing. Innocente could feel it swelling as the girl faced the people who had kept her trapped for so long.

"Bianca, raise the graveyard," Innocente instructed. "They will be too busy with the zombies to come after us. We have to help Pete with Sergio."

Pivoting toward Innocente, the glowing white eyes of the young woman seemed to grow brighter. Innocente felt her own power mingling with that of the necromancer vampire. Bianca's appearance was deceiving, for Innocente sensed the great dark majesty of the girl's power expanding over the graveyard like a great cloak. Her appearance spoke of fragility and innocence, but her power was vast, great, and...

Innocente gasped.

...evil.

Bianca smiled.

"You!"

Bianca tilted her head, her fingers grazing Innocente's cheek. "No one defeats me. No one lives who defies me."

Innocente tried to jerk away, tried to scream a warning to Pete who was still grappling with her unconscious grandson, then she felt the delicate fingers of the girl's hand grip her arm. A gasp erupted from her lips seconds before she was tossed through the air, her body suddenly weightless. The world whirled around her, the cloudy sky tumbling about with the earth. Then she was falling, her body crashing through branches, her body spinning about. As the ground rushed up to meet her, she saw her husband standing in the darkness below her.

"Everything is going to be all right," he said.

The earth met her with an agonizing embrace that devoured her last thoughts and extinguished her life.

CHAPTER TWENTY-FOUR

Jeff barely grabbed hold of Samantha before she could plunge into the terrible scene before them. His hand clamped over her mouth to keep her from crying out while they watched Innocente's body vanish into the woods beyond the graveyard. The young woman with the glowing white eyes stood with a triumphant smile upon her face as the vampires gawked at her in shock.

Pete hadn't seen what occurred and continued to struggle with Sergio's unconscious form.

"Bianca?" Rachoń's voice was rough with emotion.

The towering man who had come to her defense against the zombies positioned himself between the pale young woman and his mistress. The risen dead shambled away from the vampires, moving toward Pete and the other struggling man.

Samantha twisted in Jeff's arms, her eyes wide with anger and fear. He felt her bite down on his fingers and he gasped. She frantically motioned toward the area where Innocente had fallen.

Sighing, he nodded. He had misjudged Samantha, assuming she wanted to challenge the vampires. He motioned for her to go without him and was a little surprised when she quickly agreed. Feeling a little abandoned, he watched her scramble away into the darkness.

"Bianca?" Rachoń's voice repeated, pulling Jeff's attention to the scene in the graveyard.

"Are you afraid, Rachoń?" Bianca answered, tilting her head. Her glowing eyes were eerie.

"Why is she talking? She wasn't talking before!" Prosper exclaimed. He kept Rachoń firmly behind him, a silver knife glittering in his hand.

Jeff could see that Rachoń was startled and a little afraid.

Pete and Ethan finally became aware of the dead encircling them.

"Innocente?" Pete called out, his head whipping back and forth trying to find her.

"She's dead," Bianca answered. "Fucking bitch deserved it after what she did to me."

"She never did nothing to you! Who are you?" Pete said, his voice quavering.

Scooting forward, Jeff ignored the protest in his thighs and his calf. His back was spasming from crouching for so long, but he gritted his teeth. Drawing his pistol, he studied the standoff before him, trying to ascertain how he could intercede and protect Pete.

Ethan finally broke free from the dead and stumbled to Pete's side. Crouching, he drew a smaller firearm from his boot. "Rachoń, what's going on?"

"I don't know," she answered. "Bianca, you're not making sense."

Walking at a leisurely pace toward Rachoń and Prosper, Bianca touched the desiccated forms of the zombies around her. They shuddered at her touch, as though in pain, but then visibly took on a more human form, becoming stronger.

"I have to admit it's been fascinating watching all your little plots unfurling. I thought more highly of you when I didn't realize how mired in the human world you remain. I knew your family was your minions, but you actually retain human attachments to them," Bianca said, her tone mocking. "Where is my bloodthirsty love? Oh, yes. Living a cozy life with her mother."

Jeff froze as he listened to the words of the young woman. Closing his eyes, he felt his breath leave him. The world was tilting around him and fear clamped tightly around his chest.

"You..." Rachoń managed to say, aghast. "You..."

Opening his eyes, Jeff saw that Bianca was almost to the two vampires, her zombies crowding in behind her.

"Rachoń, what's happening?" Prosper demanded.

"Are you afraid of a pasty little white thing like me?" Bianca taunted.

"Fuck me," Prosper gasped. "Fuck me! It's *him*!"

"Did you really think I would die so easily?" Bianca asked, then her form was a blur of white.

Rachoń screamed, blood splattering her face. Prosper grunted once, then tumbled to the ground. Bianca stood over his fallen form clutching his heart. His dark vampire blood spotted her white dress and pale skin.

"No!" Rachoń cried out, falling to her knees.

Tossing the heart over her shoulder, Bianca stood over Rachoń. "You disappoint me, Rachoń."

Skirting the edge of the graveyard, Jeff headed toward the part of the fence that had fallen down. Pete and Sergio were near that area. Ethan was already on the move, using the confrontation between the vampires to make his escape. The zombies that had been keeping him trapped paid him no heed, their attention on

CHAPTER TWENTY-FOUR

their mistress.

Rachoń's terrified protests and Bianca's mocking responses filled the night air. Jeff watched Ethan jump the fence and dart across the field toward the hotel where his truck was parked. Jeff was glad to see him go. One less bad guy to worry about.

Taking a deep breath, Jeff went in the opposite direction, scrambling over the fallen fence, trying to avoid catching his prosthetic leg. Pete tugged on Sergio, trying to drag him away, but Amaliya's cousin was too big for him to handle alone. Jeff ran to his side, crouched over, and gripped Sergio's other arm.

Pete looked at him in surprise.

"I'm a friend," Jeff whispered.

Together, they dragged Sergio past the motionless zombies and toward the truck.

With the sky overcast and the darkness of the night swallowing the terrain completely, Ethan stumbled a few times as he dashed toward the hotel where his truck waited for him. The small LED penlight he kept on his key ring barely penetrated the gloom, but it was enough to keep him from a bad fall.

The dilapidated hotel enshrouded in thick foliage loomed before him, foreboding in its appearance. Though Ethan had seen plenty of bizarre and downright creepy things in his life, he had never seen anything quite as terrifying as Bianca. Necromancers were rare and he had heard stories of their nightmarish powers his whole life, but had never witnessed their raw power. He could still feel the ragged hands of the dead scrabbling at his flesh. The mere memory sent shivers down his spine.

Clutching his pistol, he climbed over the fence lining the road and scurried onto the pavement. The road was empty, devoid of any traffic at such a late hour. Tossing a fearful look over his shoulder, he was relieved to see none of the zombies trailing him. He couldn't even see the farmhouse and graveyard beyond the line of trees.

Relieved, he fell to a swift walk toward the hotel. He should have known better than to take any job offered by one of The Summoner's offspring, but he had thought with the old necromancer dead there shouldn't be any major problems. He had been horribly wrong.

Ethan's duster fluttered around him, tossed by the wind whistling through the swaying trees. As he neared the hotel, he felt his spine stiffen. It was a small roadside hotel, but it still reminded him of other haunted hotels he had encountered on his job. He could imagine all manner of ghosts staring out at him from the hollowed out windows.

Nearing the parking lot, he felt the knot in his shoulders begin to relax. He was almost to his truck. In a matter of minutes he would be safely on the road and away from this disaster. He would never again risk his life for an obscene paycheck if it was in any way connected to The Summoner.

Ethan rounded the corner of the building and felt relief fill him as his truck and camper came into view. Breaking into a run again, he headed toward the driver's side.

The bounty hunter never saw what hit him. One second he was almost to his truck, the next he was slammed into the side of the hotel. His nose burst on impact and his lips split against the hard surface. Crumpling to the ground, he let out a moan. He had lost his weapon in the assault, but he fumbled for his last gun tucked into his shoulder holster.

Something seized his head in a vice-like grip and he grunted, drawing his weapon. It clattered to the ground as his head was twisted brutally about, nearly tearing off his shoulders.

As Ethan died, his last thought was of the glowing eyes of The Summoner.

Amaliya thought stepping through the portal would be like stepping through a doorway. She was wrong. It felt like she was plunged into icy cold water, unable to determine which way was up or down, lost in an endless ocean of blackness, then her foot set down on the other side and she found herself facing the old hotel.

Remembering Aimee's instructions, she ducked away from the spot she had appeared just seconds before Cian appeared out of thin air. She was surprised to see no sign of the glowing blue oval doorway that had appeared in Zilker Park at Aimee's summoning.

Darting to one side, Cian barely avoided Eduardo. The coyote whirled around once, sniffing loudly, then jogged to Amaliya's side.

"That was a helluva ride," he said, shivering.

Benchley appeared next and promptly threw up. His sister banged into him as she appeared, knocking him out of her way.

"Oh, fucking gross!" Alexia cried out as she stepped in the vomit.

Cian gripped her arm and swiftly yanked her aside as Benchley crawled away on all fours.

"That was not pleasant," Eduardo said, his usual smirk nowhere to be seen.

Cian cast a glare at the man just seconds before Cassandra stumbled out of the empty air, clutching Aimee in her arms. They both fell to pavement, pulled down by Aimee's dead weight. They both narrowly avoided the puddle of Benchley's last meal.

Aimee had warned them that she would be completely drained after raising the portal. The young woman who looked strikingly similar to Cian anxiously checked the witch's pulse.

"She's okay....just knocked out," Cassandra said in relief.

CHAPTER TWENTY-FOUR

"Let me get her," Cian said, and easily lifted Aimee into his arms.

"She needs water and protein," Alexia said.

"Aimee, baby, wake up," Cassandra called out, keeping pace with Cian as he carried Aimee to the gas station across the street.

"That's Ethan's," Benchley said, pointing to the truck parked in front of the hotel.

"A reason to avoid it," Eduardo decided.

Cian kicked open the door to the gas station and carried Aimee inside. Alexia scrambled ahead, clutching the bag Cassandra had given her earlier. Benchley, looking a bit green still, stood near the doorway, his pistol in his hands.

"I smell vampires," Eduardo informed them, squatting before the door.

Amaliya pointed at her and Cian.

"No, other ones. And they smell worse than you two."

Rolling her eyes, Amaliya rushed to help Alexia. The hunter removed a yoga mat from the bag that would have to do for a bed while Amaliya cleared some space on the floor. Once it was unrolled, Cian gently laid Aimee upon it.

Cassandra hovered over them, watching fretfully. Amaliya felt bad for her. She knew how she'd felt when she had witnessed Cian in a helpless state. Alexia patted the witch's cheeks, trying to rouse her.

"Wake up, babe," Cass called out not too loudly.

Cian rose to his feet and headed toward the door. "We need to go, Cassandra."

"I got her," Alexia assured Cassandra. "I will take care of her." The bag next to her was filled with protein bars, water, and weapons. Aimee set a shotgun at her side. "I've got blessed bullets."

"I will keep them covered," Benchley promised from his location near the door.

Cassandra nodded mutely, then scooted past Cian to fall to her knees beside Aimee. Stroking her girlfriend's hair, she leaned over to kiss her on the lips. "I'll be back, Aims."

Amaliya looked away, feeling like she was intruding on the moment. She saw Cian also direct his attention elsewhere.

"She reminds me of you," Amaliya confessed.

"Me too." Cian gave her a slight smile.

Cassandra pushed past them. "Let's go." Blades of silver glittered in her hands.

They were halfway across the street when Eduardo sniffed loudly, obviously catching a scent. Falling to his hands, he loped across the street reminding Amaliya of a dog. They tailed the coyote to the hotel. The old building held many bad memories for Amaliya, but she trusted Eduardo not to place them in a bad situation.

"Fresh kill," Eduardo said around the many sharp teeth in his mouth as he looked back at them.

They found the body shoved into the bushes. It was a tall muscular man clad in a long duster. His head was nearly twisted off his body.

Cassandra drew in a sharp breath through her teeth. "Ethan," she said.

Amaliya observed the truck for a second, then averted her gaze. Silver crosses imbedded into the rims and the doors pulsed in the darkness, hurting her eyes. "He almost made it."

"This is what happens when you play with the wrong people," Cass decided.

"We need to get to the graveyard," Amaliya said urgently. The thought of her cousin or her grandmother suffering such a fate made her sick.

"Agreed." Cian's hand brushed hers lightly, his eyes locking with hers. "But we need to be cautious."

Amaliya couldn't help but look at the broken body of Ethan Logan one last time. "I can't make any promises if they've hurt my family."

Cian nodded in understanding.

The four of them broke into a run.

Samantha found it hard to walk through the thick woods behind the cemetery. The dry grass hid gnarled roots, deep dips in the forest floor, and broken branches. Without a flashlight or moonlight to brighten her path, she had to feel her way through the darkness.

Even though she was determined to be a bad ass vampire-kicking chick, tears were streaming down her face. She knew that Innocente was most likely dead, but she couldn't just let the older woman die alone if she was gravely injured.

Scratches covered her hands and face. She was also limping, since a root had sent her tumbling earlier. It was increasingly difficult to see the deeper into the woods she wandered. She wasn't even certain if she was headed in the right direction anymore.

A branch snapped against her shin and she strangled a cry in her throat. She didn't want any of the dangerous creatures in the graveyard to hear her. Whimpering, she leaned against a tree.

If only she could see...

Samantha widened her eyes.

Wasn't she a phasmagnus? Maybe someone could guide her. Mentally dropping her defenses, she gingerly searched for a ghost with her newfound powers. In her mind, she saw it like a controlled wave, weaving in and out around the tree trunks seeking out any spectral remains.

"Here I am," a voice said.

The gentle touch of a hand rested on her shoulder. Samantha shot a frightened look over her shoulder. To her relief a tall, kindly-looking man with blond hair and blue eyes was gazing at her. He seemed untouched by the night, standing out sharply against the darkness.

"I'm trying to find Innocente," she told him.

CHAPTER TWENTY-FOUR

"I'll show you where she is," the ghost answered.

Timidly, Samantha held out her hand to him. The ghost smiled, taking it gently in his own. Walking ahead of her, his ghostly form illuminated her path.

CHAPTER TWENTY-FIVE

Jeff and Pete dragged Sergio through the high grass, grunting and panting with exertion. The big man was still out cold and was a dead weight. Jeff's arms felt like they were about to pop out of their sockets and the muscles in his thighs burned. Keeping his eyes on the swaying zombies, he hoped that Samantha had found Innocente and was able to help her.

"Who are you?" Pete asked in a hushed voice.

"A friend of Amaliya. My name is Jeff."

"Where's Ethan?"

"He ran off. Now, we better keep quiet." Jeff jerked his head toward the sound of the two vampire women arguing loudly.

"Lover's spat," Pete decided.

Jeff shushed him again.

It did sound like a lover's argument. Both of the vampires were shouting at each other. Rachoń's voice was both pleading and furious; Bianca's was mocking, yet angry.

"I did everything you asked! I was even going to avenge your death!" Rachoń cried out.

"Yet you allowed your pathetic minion to mock me!"

The men reached the truck and Pete tugged the back door of the cab open. Together, they pulled and shoved Sergio's limp mass into the backseat. When they finally settled the man onto the seat, they shut the door, then scurried around to the other side of the truck to hide.

"Where are the keys?" Jeff asked.

"Ethan had them," Pete answered.

Jeff groaned and leaned his head against the side of the pickup. "Great, just great."

Peeking around the front of the truck, Pete whispered, "The zombies still ain't moving. That's good, right?"

"It's because The Summoner is too busy being angry at Rachoń to send them after us. Or maybe he just doesn't care," Jeff answered.

"I thought that bastard was dead." Pete's brow furrowed.

Jeff shrugged. "He was. Is. Something. I'm pretty sure that the pretty girl out there is him. He must have somehow transferred to her body."

"Gimme your gun," Pete abruptly ordered.

"What?"

"Does it have bullets that can kill a vampire?"

"If you hit it in the heart," Jeff admitted.

"Then give it to me. I'll kill that son of a bitch so he can't ever hurt Amaliya again." Pete held out his hand, waiting.

"We can't attack them. If we draw attention to ourselves, we won't be able to fight off all those zombies. Do you understand?"

"I'm a fuckin' great shot. I can take out The Summoner before she knows, or he knows, what hits her...uh...him." Pete insistently held out his hand.

"Rachoń will probably come after us then." Jeff felt sick to his stomach at the thought. They were damned either way.

"You got other weapons?"

"Yeah."

"Then after I shoot The Summoner, you best be ready to help me take out the other one. At least we won't have to deal with those damn zombies once the bastard is down, right?"

Jeff nodded.

"So give me the damn gun." Pete's blue eyes were determined and merciless.

Not sure if he was doing the right thing, Jeff handed over his weapon.

Pete gave him a solemn nod. "Now back into the graveyard so I can get a good shot. You with me?"

Rubbing his aching knee, Jeff nodded in the affirmative. He hadn't come this far to give up so easily. At least Sergio was safely tucked away and Sam was far away from the confrontation. The sick feeling in his gut made him want to puke, but he knew that he couldn't allow The Summoner to live.

"Let's go," Pete said.

Together, they ducked down and headed back in the direction of the quarreling vampires.

To Amaliya's surprise, Eduardo and Cassandra were just as swift as she and Cian when they sprinted across the overgrown field toward the graveyard. The world was a blur around her, but she could see the dhampir and coyote out of

CHAPTER TWENTY-FIVE

her peripheral vision keeping pace. Cian led their pack of supernaturals, his hair rippling in the wind.

Raised voices carried on the wind. The risen dead called out to Amaliya, her necromancy burning in her veins, crying for release. As they closed in on the graveyard, Amaliya saw the clusters of undead among the fallen headstones. They were wizened and barely more than skeletons. A few stronger ones, more fully-formed, were near the center of the pack near the necromancer who had raised them. Amaliya could feel Bianca's power woven among the zombies, holding them up, keeping them alive.

The scents of the grave, fresh blood, and earth filled her nostrils as they leaped over the low lying wrought-iron fence and landed inside the graveyard where Amaliya had defeated The Summoner. A stab of fear and a thrill of excitement tangled together inside of her. She had struck down her creator and embraced her power in this very place. Now she would face Rachoń and her minions, and she would not allow them to defeat her.

Cian moved in front of her, casting away the zombies that blocked his path. They shattered against headstones and fell to pieces as they tumbled away. The sight upset Amaliya, but she said nothing. The angry voices were just ahead, beyond the dead.

"They haven't all risen," she whispered to Cassandra.

"The zombies?" Cassandra asked warily.

Amaliya nodded.

Behind Cassandra an enormous beast that was part coyote and part man prowled in their wake. Eduardo flashed his fangs. Amaliya ignored him. Slicing open her wrists with her nails, she let her cold blood drop onto the graves while she walked.

"I should have no mercy on you!"

"I did all you asked!"

Cian thrust aside a few more zombies and the two arguing vampires came into view. Rachoń was on her knees before Bianca. The sight startled Amaliya. She had not expected this at all. Cian's darting look in Amaliya's direction said he was surprised as well.

Bianca's glowing white eyes flicked in their direction. Rachoń shot to her feet and stumbled back a few steps to the side of the rapidly-dissolving body of a massive vampire.

"We have company, Rachoń," Bianca said. "Hello, Cian."

"Bianca..." Cian said warily. "We're here to rescue you and stop Rachoń..." His voice trailed off as Rachoń vehemently shook her head at him.

Amaliya stepped around Cian to gaze at the young woman in her blood-splattered dress. Bianca appeared exactly how Amaliya had viewed her in her dream: glowing white, beautiful, stained in blood.

The power of the girl before her was chilling in its intensity. Amaliya felt it slithering over her, touching her, exploring the edges of Amaliya's own abilities.

The silken touch of the dark necromancy elicited a shudder of arousal as it caressed her body. Amaliya gasped.

Disregarding Rachoń, Bianca gazed at the interlopers thoughtfully.

"What is going on?" Cassandra dared to ask.

"Well, Rachoń's plan was to collect the ingredients for a ritual that would have rendered Amaliya human so she could kill her to avenge The Summoner's death," Bianca said.

Her voice was slightly different from her dream, Amaliya realized.

"Is that possible?" Cian asked warily.

Bianca nodded once. "Yes."

"But you stopped her?" Cian tilted his head, scrutinizing the girl.

"Yes."

Amaliya trembled in the wash of Bianca's necromantic power. It wrapped her in great dark, icy waves. It lapped against her, seeking a way in, trying to overcome her defenses. A hollow ache opened up within Amaliya, the power calling to her. She wanted to let it in, drown in its power, let it consume her. Gritting her teeth, she fought it.

"Why?" Cian took a step forward, but Amaliya gripped his arm and yanked him back.

"Don't go near her," Amaliya hissed.

Cassandra stood at the ready, blades glittering while Eduardo hunched at her side, fangs bared. His powerful body was covered in a thick orange pelt shot through with black fur.

Bianca's perfectly-shaped pink lips smiled slightly. "Amaliya..."

The mere sound of her voice caused Amaliya to quiver. The power of the necromancer licked at her, arousing her even more, calling to her.

Out of the corner of her eye, Amaliya could see Rachoń edging away. Eduardo growled at the female vampire, lowering his body as he prepared to spring.

"I wouldn't move if I were you," Cassandra warned Rachoń.

Amaliya struggled to stand, her body now visibly quaking. Bianca smirked.

Cian shifted on his feet, his hand extending to steady Amaliya. She ducked away from him, inadvertently moving herself closer to Bianca. "Don't touch me!"

The dark power of the girl battered Amaliya's defenses and it took all her willpower to shut the other necromancer out. Her wrists still bleeding, Amaliya turned to face Bianca.

"Why does a girl from East Texas speak in an English accent?" she demanded.

Bianca's smile became almost serpentine. "You tell me."

"Where's my grandmother and my cousin?" Amaliya demanded.

The lithe girl in the stained white dress swayed on her feet, smiling. "Tell me, Amaliya."

"Where is my family?" Amaliya shouted at Bianca.

Bianca licked her lips. "Dead."

CHAPTER TWENTY-FIVE

With a scream of anger, Amaliya hurled herself at the young woman. She instantly realized it was a mistake. Bianca caught her, a triumphant smile on her face. "Always making mistakes. Always self-destructing. Tell me, Amaliya, what does death taste like?" Bianca crushed her lips against Amaliya's.

Instantly, Amaliya was flooded with the darkest of magicks. It filled her up and battered against her own power. It tried to overwhelm her mind and drag her into the abyss. Her body sang with need: the need for blood, the need for death, and the need for sex. Teetering on the edge of madness, hunger, and pleasure, Amaliya clutched Bianca to her. Their kiss was savage, full of hate, desire, and nameless darkest needs.

Amaliya wanted to drown in Bianca's power and rise again as her darkest bride.

No, as *his* darkest bride.

With a scream of rage, Amaliya hurled Bianca from her. Wiping her mouth with the back of her hand, she swayed on her feet. She briefly caught sight of Cian, held back by Cassandra and Eduardo. Understanding filled his horrified gaze.

Laughing, Bianca languidly licked her lips.

"How?" Amaliya gasped. "How?"

"Do you think I would die so easily? Did you think I would not find a way back from beyond the veil?" Bianca scoffed at her.

"The Summoner," Cassandra gasped.

"Yes," Rachoń admitted. "It's him. Or a part of him."

Bianca reached for Amaliya again, but she ducked away. "Come now, my delectable little necromancer. I have grand plans for you."

"Leave her be," Cian ordered, his voice ragged with hate and rage.

Twirling around to face Cian, Bianca narrowed her gaze. "I need to kill you. You don't amuse me anymore, Cian."

"Fuck you," Cian answered.

"You had so much potential, you know, to be my perfect offspring, but you could never quite shake off your mortality." Bianca tapped her foot on the ground. "Your adoration for the mortals is always your undoing."

"He's going to kill all of us," Rachoń said. "He's toying with us. Another game."

Bianca lifted her chin, her eyes amused. "Possibly."

Amaliya drew her silver blade. "I say we put him down so he never rises."

Lowering her head, Bianca frowned. "Really now?"

The dead broke free from their silent stances and surged toward Cian and the others. Amaliya uncoiled her power, her eyes flashing white as her own army of the dead rose out of the ground. Her dead blocked Bianca's minions.

"This is between you and me," Amaliya said in a grim voice. "Let the others go and face me."

"Do you really believe you can best me twice?" Bianca's voice was mocking and cold.

"Yes, I do, bitch," Amaliya answered.

Cassandra attacked in that instant, blades flashing. Bianca darted out from beneath the swinging daggers, easily evading Cassandra's assault. Ducking out from under what should have been a lethal swipe, Bianca smashed her fist into Cassandra's stomach, sending the woman crashing through a headstone.

Cian leaped at Bianca while Eduardo charged her on the ground. Amaliya surged forward, but a deft kick from Bianca sent Eduardo crashing into Amaliya, toppling them both to the ground. Pushing herself up with her hands, Amaliya saw Bianca pluck Cian out of the air and slam him into the ground. Lifting her hand, Bianca hissed. Before she could deliver a killing blow, Rachoń hurled a broken headstone at Bianca's head. The girl glanced up just as it struck, toppling her over.

"Cian!" Amaliya cried out, racing toward him.

Bianca rolled to her feet and caught Amaliya before she could reach Cian. Sharp teeth flashing, Bianca grinned. "Still attached to my wayward son, are we?" Bianca crushed Amaliya against her, fingers tangled in Amaliya's hair, drawing her head back and bearing her throat, holding her hostage. "Now, now, we must rid you of that bad habit."

Amaliya was vaguely aware of the two vampires and the coyote circling them, seeking a moment to attack again. Bianca's glowing eyes tracked the beings waiting to pounce. Amaliya felt The Summoner's power still pressing against her, trying to ensnare her.

"You and I will bring this world to its knees," Bianca promised.

"I'd rather die." Amaliya spat, then drove the dagger she had hidden in her hand into the chest of the girl.

Bianca gasped, releasing Amaliya.

Amaliya smiled triumphantly. "Told you I would kill you again." She waited for the vampire to fall, so she could slice off her head. A silver dagger through the heart would incapacitate her.

But Bianca didn't fall. Staring down at the silver dagger protruding from her heart, Bianca frowned. "When will you ever learn?" Taking hold of the hilt, the girl dragged the dagger free.

"No!" Rachoń gasped.

Amaliya gaped in horror when Bianca tossed away the dagger.

It was then that Pete stood up from behind a mausoleum and took aim at Bianca's head. Amaliya gasped as Pete's finger started to press the trigger.

A shadow abruptly unfurled from a nearby headstone and struck Pete from behind. The gun fell from his grasp before Pete tumbled over, a cry of agony issuing from his lips. The dark shape slid over his body then rose up to the height of a person. As though she was shrugging off a cloak, Etzli stepped out of the darkness and stood before them.

"Stop playing games and do what we planned," Etzli said sharply to Bianca.

CHAPTER TWENTY-FIVE

With a smile, Bianca answered, "I think you're correct."

Then all the graves opened and the world was filled with death.

Samantha knelt beside the small broken form at the base of a tree. Face down in the dry leaves, Innocente's body was still, silent, and empty. Samantha could feel that the essence of the woman was now gone, leaving only a shell.

"Oh, no," she whispered.

The male ghost hovered over Samantha. "It's all going to be all right."

Tears in her eyes, Samantha vehemently shook her head. "No, it's not. This is not all right."

"Don't argue with your elders," Innocente's voice chided her.

Startled, Samantha whipped around and fell on her butt. Innocente was standing behind her. Like the other ghost, she was luminescent, standing out sharply in the darkness.

"Innocente!" Samantha gasped.

"Samantha, you need to help Amaliya," Innocente said firmly.

"How?" Samantha gaped at the apparition of the woman with both relief and sadness.

"You're joined together. Her blood made you what you are. You can reach out to her and help her."

"I don't understand."

"Your magic will help her understand her own," Innocente insisted. Her form was growing hazy, but her voice was clear. "Amaliya cannot fight The Summoner by herself. She needs you!"

"But he's dead!"

"No, he's still among you. Just in a different form. Amaliya needs you, Samantha." Innocente bent over to rest her hand on Samantha's head. "You can do it."

As abruptly as she had appeared, Innocente was gone, along with the other mysterious ghost.

Sitting next to Innocente's body, Samantha wiped her tears with grimy hands. Afraid, but determined, Samantha closed her eyes. "Connected, huh?" With her eyes shut, it was easier for her to feel her own power tucked within her body. It stirred as Samantha mentally probed for any sense of a connection with Amaliya. The harder she concentrated, the clearer she saw in her mind's eye the pulsing power that linked her to the phantoms of the world. Within the miasma of silvery-gray power, she saw a darker thread interwoven with her own.

"There you are," she whispered.

In her mind, she gripped it tightly, focusing all her energy on that one thread. "Amaliya," she whispered aloud and in her mind.

There was no answer.

Forcefully directing everything within her on that one dark thread of power, Samantha again called out to Amaliya.

This time, she felt an answer. It was wordless, but she knew it was Amaliya.

"I need to help you," Samantha said. "I need to help you fight him."

Fear, rage, and sorrow filled the connection between them, but she could feel Amaliya's power surging through the link.

"Just hold on and I'll be right there," Samantha said.

The boiling power of Amaliya's necromancy poured through the bond, making Samantha gasp. "I'll be right there, I prom—"

Samantha didn't get out another word for the ground swallowed her and she vanished.

Chapter Twenty-Six

Amaliya was knocked off her feet as the ground beneath her exploded. Dirt, rocks, and chunks of the headstones hurled through the air. She fell into an empty grave as the dead rose in one great wave. Over two hundred stood before Bianca and Etzli.

Nearby, Cian gathered his daughter into his arms. Cassandra appeared groggy from a head wound, but it was a relief to see her alive. Eduardo stooped low, ears back, teeth bared at the dead. Rachoń, surprisingly, was still with them. In her hand was the dagger with which Amaliya had tried to kill Bianca.

Instead of attacking, the dead raised up their hands to Bianca and Etzli while sinking to their knees in supplication to the necromancer and vampire.

"Cian, you and your people stand down and we may let you live," Etzli said, her black eyes glittering.

Bianca wove her way through the dead, studying their outstretched hands.

"Why are you here?" Cian asked, helping Cassandra to her feet.

"He called to me and I answered," Etzli answered simply. She was dressed in a black dress that was split to her thighs on both sides. A belt around her hips was graced with daggers made out of bone. Amaliya had never seen her look so much like the blood goddess she claimed to be.

"But you're not his child," Rachoń said in disbelief.

"But I am bound to him by blood," Etzli responded. "Don't you remember my abduction oh so long ago? He bound me to him and showed me the glory of his ways."

Climbing to her feet, Amaliya felt hopeless in the face of Bianca's power and Etzli's appearance. If a silver dagger through the heart didn't even faze Bianca, how was she supposed to kill her? And Etzli's power was terrifying on its own.

Cian had told her horror stories about what Etzli was capable of.

"Does Santos know?" Cian asked.

"Santos knows what I want him to know," Etzli answered, shrugging.

Bianca tilted her head toward Amaliya. "Do you know what I want?"

"Your ring," Amaliya answered.

"Do you know why?"

Amaliya hesitated, then shook her head.

Bianca plucked a golden ring from the palm of a zombie and held it up for all to see. "Here it is." Slipping it onto her index finger, Bianca crushed the zombie's head. Then, as if that wasn't enough, she tore it apart, vengeance in her face.

"Not to kill them," Bianca said, gesturing toward the defiant vampire and his comrades.

"So much for not killing us." The sarcasm in Cian's voice made Amaliya slightly smile.

"Who should we kill first?" Etzli asked. "Cian? Rachoń? Or their pet dog?"

Eduardo growled, edging toward the Aztec princess.

Amaliya.

Studying the area, Amaliya realized no one had called her aloud. She glanced at Cian, but he was crouched low to the ground, the obsidian blade in one hand, watching their enemies, preparing to strike. Cassandra also had her blades drawn and looked far more alert, though blood still trickled from her brow.

Maybe they could kill Etzli, but how would they kill Bianca?

Again, Amaliya heard her name, but this time she realized it came from within her. Trying to remain alert to her surroundings, Amaliya let her mind sift through her power. The blackness of her necromancy was tangled with the remains of the witch's black magic, both edged with the fiery red of Cian's powers. But there was something more buried in all the layers. It was silvery and throbbed with power. Mentally grasping it, Amaliya heard Samantha's ardent whisper in her mind.

I need to help you. I need to help you fight him.

As Samantha's voice floated through her mind, Amaliya saw the armies of the dead attack Cian and the others. Instantly, she sent out her power, unleashing it, pulling the dead to her through her spilled blood.

Bianca gasped, her fury assaulting Amaliya, but Amaliya resisted. Concentrating on her link with the dead, Amaliya leashed them to her, calling them to her side. Bianca fought with her for control, her hiss of anger sizzling in the air.

Amaliya was dimly aware of Eduardo gnashing his teeth and tearing into dead flesh. She heard the clink of knives clashing and smelled Cian's blood spilling into the air. Amaliya wrestled the dead from Bianca only to have them called back.

"Come to me!" Amaliya said through clenched teeth.

Cian and Etzli spun through the air, clashing in an aerial battle above the

CHAPTER TWENTY-SIX

heads of the zombies. Eduardo ripped through the zombies, trying to fight his way to Bianca.

Amaliya dug her fingers into the earth. "Come to *me*!"

To her shock, Samantha spilled out of the ground next to her, coughing and gasping.

"Sam!"

"Bitch!" Samantha spit up dirt, then her eyes widened at the spectacle around her.

Etzli battled Cian and Rachoń at the same time, twisting and thrusting through the air. The tiny woman fought savagely, slipping in and out of the darkness like a wraith. Her daggers were made of bone and each cut was deep. She was a whirlwind of violence and Amaliya could barely track her with her eyes. Each time Etzli drew blood, it was a fountain that arced through the air. Cian had once told Amaliya that Etzli could summon blood from the very bodies of her enemies. Now she was witnessing it with her own eyes. Blood rained down on the zombies below as Cian sent Etzli howling into the darkness with a swift stroke only to have her reappear behind Rachoń. Cian grabbed Rachoń's arm and flung her aside, Etzli's killing blow missing.

Cassandra, meanwhile, fought her way through the zombies, slashing her way through creatures that were looking more and more human and exerting supernatural strength. Bianca was imbuing them with her power, making it increasingly difficult for the coyote and dhampir to fight their way to the necromancer.

Amaliya sent out her power like a net and caught the zombies within it. Again, she turned them against Bianca.

"I have them!"

Rachoń fell to the ground, her slashed throat pouring blood into the ground. Gagging, the vampire pressed her hands to her wound, trying to heal, but her blood arced into the air toward Etzli. The blood goddess was enshrouded in a halo of blood. Cian managed to slice off one of her hands, the bone dagger spinning into the night. Etzli screeched with pain.

"Oh, my God!" Samantha gasped.

Amaliya felt Bianca once more drag the zombies away from her control and she cried out in frustration. "I lost them again!"

Eduardo let out a pained yelp from somewhere amidst the zombies while Cassandra clambered onto a mausoleum, claiming the high ground in the battle with the undead.

"I'm supposed to help you!" Samantha shouted at Amaliya.

"How?" Amaliya demanded. "How?"

Samantha hesitated, then grabbed her hand. "Our connection! If you can drag me through the fucking ground to your side, it has to be something powerful!"

Amaliya felt the link between them soar the second they touched. Samantha's power was ghostly and beautiful. It easily meshed with Amaliya's own power, wrapping around it. Amaliya could see it clearly in her mind.

"I see it!" Amaliya gasped.

"Me, too!" Samantha's voice was awed.

The glittering darkness of Amaliya's power wove together with Samantha's sparkling ethereal mist. Interconnecting the two women, a beautiful tapestry of their magicks shimmered between them. It was then that the purple miasma of the witch's black magic broke free.

"What's that?" Samantha exclaimed.

"The spell...I got it!" Amaliya exclaimed. "I know what to do!"

Abandoning her struggle with Bianca for the zombies, Amaliya closed her eyes and concentrated on the spell. In her mind, she imagined it pushing it out of her body and spreading it out to cover the graveyard, the farmhouse, the hotel, the gas station and the edges of the town. A great dome of purplish-black power, shoving back her enemies. Repulsing them, driving them away.

Bianca's scream was one of fury.

Amaliya opened her eyes to see Etzli and Bianca caught in the wave of the spell. It snatched up both of them and hurled them to the ground. Instantly, Amaliya felt the zombies return to her control.

"Rest," Amaliya whispered.

The zombie horde instantly sank into the earth, leaving the graveyard strangely empty. Still gripping Samantha's hand, Amaliya stood. Cian floated above the graveyard, bloody, but alive. Rachoń trembled on the ground, Etzli's blood magic releasing her and allowing her to heal. Eduardo was covered in wounds. Collapsing, his body shifted into that of a man, allowing him to heal. Staring at the two women laying on the ground, Cassandra warily crouched down waiting to attack.

"What just happened?" she asked.

"Watch," Amaliya told her, then fed the last of her power into the spell.

Simultaneously, both Etzli and Bianca were jerked to their feet and slid along the ground as though gripped by a great hand. Their faces were eerily blank of thought as they were swept away into the darkness of the night.

"What just happened?" Cassandra gasped.

Cian set down on the ground, glancing upwards at the shimmering spell, then at Amaliya. "How?"

"The spell that witch cast the night of the accident. I swallowed it into my power. Samantha helped me...uh...vomit it up... kinda," Amaliya answered.

"Was that what that purplish stuff was?" Samantha asked.

"Yeah. I think it was caught inside of me, but now it's...free." Amaliya let go of Samantha's hand just before Cian swept her up in his arms. He kissed her mouth tenderly.

"You're amazing," he whispered against her lips.

Amaliya sighed with contentment.

"A spell?" Cassandra leaped off the mausoleum and landed next to Rachoń.

"A repulsion spell," Rachoń said to Cassandra. Healed now, she knelt beside

CHAPTER TWENTY-SIX

the dead vampire. His body would soon be nothing more than dirt. "Instead of casting it on humans to keep them away, she cast it on The Summoner and Etzli."

"How long will it last?" Cassandra glanced around warily.

"Till sunup. That's how long they usually last," Cian answered.

"Oh. That's good then." Cassandra sheathed her daggers and touched her bleeding head gingerly. "Who's that?"

"My cousin, Prosper. They murdered him," Rachoń answered, her voice pained.

"Pete!" Amaliya gasped, realizing she had forgotten him. She yanked away from Cian and scrambled over the broken headstones to where she had seen him fall. When she found him, she was surprised to find Jeff at his side trying to staunch the blood flowing from his chest. He had pulled off his own shirt to try to stop the bleeding.

"Jeff?"

"I can't stop it," Jeff said, his tone defeated. "I think she hit something major. An artery or something."

Settling on her knees, Amaliya leaned over Pete. She could see his blue eyes had a hint of life left, but not for long. Resting her hand on his forehead, she felt tears on her cheeks.

"Pete, I'm so sorry," she said.

Samantha crouched next to Jeff and covered her mouth. Sorrow filled her expression.

"He wanted to help restore you to human," Jeff explained though Amaliya didn't ask.

Stroking Pete's beard with her fingers, Amaliya stared into his compassionate blue eyes. She could see his love for her glimmering in their fading depths. Blood bubbled on his lips and words he tried to whisper were lost in the gurgling of his last breaths. He had hurt her so badly that night in the Dixie Motel, but now as she studied his sweet face she wondered how she had ever been mad at him.

Taking his hand, she held it to her cheek. "Thank you for trying to save me," she whispered.

"He just wanted a life with you," Samantha said in a voice fraught with emotion. "He wanted to make it up to you for rejecting you. He was just so afraid, he didn't understand."

"How do you know that?" Amaliya asked, glaring at Samantha. The words the woman had uttered hurt more than she wanted to admit.

"I can hear his voice as he grows closer to..." Samantha trailed off, studying Amaliya's stricken look. "Do you want me to not tell you?"

"No, please, do." Amaliya cast off her dark thoughts. She kissed Pete's hand and held it to her lips. "Tell me."

Samantha nodded, her hand finding Pete's other hand. Holding it gently,

Samantha closed her eyes. "He says that he's so sorry. That all he ever wanted was to be with you. He wants you to know that he has no regrets about trying to save you." Samantha wiped at her own tears. "He says...he says that he only regrets not growing old with you and watching your children grow up."

Jeff wrapped an arm around Samantha to comfort her.

Amaliya found it hard to speak, but she forced out the words. "I'm sorry, too, Pete. That would have been wonderful. A perfect life." It was a lie, but one she would say in this final moment to give him comfort.

As Pete's last breath escaped his lips, Samantha whispered, "He says he loves you."

Pressing a kiss to Pete's lips, Amaliya whispered, "I love you, too."

And then he was gone.

"I'm so sorry, Amaliya," Samantha said, meaning it.

Amaliya wiped away her tears with the heels of her hands. "Where is my grandmother and cousin, Jeff?"

"Sergio is in the truck. He got knocked out," Jeff replied.

"And my grandmother?" Even as she said the words, she knew the answer.

Jeff shook his head.

Amaliya sobbed and covered her face. "He killed her out of revenge."

"I think so. Yes," Jeff said, lowering his eyes.

"I'm going to find a way to fucking kill him. And he won't ever come back!" Amaliya swore bitterly, anger filling her. "He'll fucking stay dead!"

Cian watched Pete's passing from the other side of the cemetery. He didn't want to intrude, but he still heard the sorrowful farewell between Amaliya and Pete through Samantha. Cassandra lingered at his side, also watching, but saying nothing. Rachoń ignored the scene, burying Prosper's remains with her bare hands. Eduardo sat naked on a tombstone staring at the sky.

"So The Summoner is back," Cassandra said at last.

"Yes," Cian said. The grimness of the moment tainted his voice.

"And he has the ring again."

"Yes, he does," Cian sighed.

Cassandra pivoted toward him. "So what did we accomplish tonight?"

"You delayed the inevitable," Rachoń answered, smoothing the dirt with her hands into a mound. "And discovered the truth."

"Which is basically that the big bad necromancer is back from the dead in the body of a hot chick and we're all going to die fighting him and his Aztec bitch-vamp," Eduardo summarized.

"You missed something," Rachoń said, standing and wiping her hands on her jeans.

CHAPTER TWENTY-SIX

"What's that?" Cassandra asked.

"Etzli was wearing the same ring, too," Rachoń replied.

"Fuck me," Cassandra grumbled.

"Can I? And your girlfriend, too?" Eduardo teased.

Cian knocked Eduardo off the headstone with a punch to the jaw. Eduardo sprang up, growling, but didn't attack. Sulking, he slid back onto his perch.

Looking a little impressed, Cassandra said, "Thanks, Dad."

"Don't say that unless you mean it," Cian said crossly.

Startled, Cassandra said, "Okay. So what do I call you?"

"Cian," he answered.

"Okay, Cian."

He looked into Cassandra's eyes and knew he would not hurt her. Eduardo's crass remark had sparked inside of him something that had long been missing from his internal makeup. He had felt a father's protective love for a second. It had felt wonderful.

"Wait," Rachoń said, looking mystified. "You have a kid?"

Cian slightly smiled at Cass as she grinned back. "Yeah. Isn't she beautiful?"

"So I'm an aunt?" Rachoń lifted her eyebrows in disbelief.

"If I forgive you and don't kill you." Cian regarded his vampire sister thoughtfully.

"You can't blame me for fulfilling his last desire. Vengeance against the one who killed him."

"Then Etzli and Santos could have killed me, taken Austin, and began their quest to dominate Texas and Mexico."

Rachoń shrugged. "That's what she said they wanted. I told her I didn't care how it went down after Amaliya was dead."

"And now?" Cian arched a brow.

"Honestly, I want that asshole dead. He killed Prosper and he would have done worse to me if you hadn't shown up. I..." Rachoń fell silent.

"Now you know how it feels to be his pawn, huh?" Cian knew his manner was barbed, but he couldn't help it. "He played you perfectly through Bianca. And it wasn't you he turned to, but Etzli."

"Maybe he's right," Rachoń said, lifting a shoulder. "Maybe I'm too attached to my family for his tastes. He never liked split loyalties. I always made sure he never saw mine."

"Until now."

She nodded.

"So are you in?" Cassandra asked.

"What do you mean?" Rachoń tilted her head.

"Those rings tear the veil," Cian explained. "The veil that holds back the creatures of the pit and the darkness that devours all."

"Fuck me," Rachoń gasped.

"And if The Summoner wants the rings, your family won't be very safe for long," Cassandra continued.

"He never told me about any rings," Rachoń said, her betrayal evident for all to see. "He didn't trust me."

"So are you in or not?" Eduardo asked, showing his teeth.

Rachoń slowly nodded. "Yes, I'm in."

Cian extended his hand to her, and Rachoń it took with a nervous smile. "This is going to get messy, isn't it, Cian?"

"You have no idea," Cassandra muttered.

"It'll be fun," Eduardo said confidently. "Until we die."

By the time they left the graveyard, the story they agreed upon to tell the police was simple. Ethan had hoodwinked Pete, Sergio, and Innocente into believing that Amaliya was alive and that he would take them to her. Instead, he had tried to kill them in a black magic ritual. Sergio, in a rage, managed to overpower him and break his neck. Drugged, Sergio had passed out, not waking until morning when he drove to the nearest town to inform the authorities.

The police would find the camper stuffed with bizarre occult items and a folder full of stolen police records. If they were lucky, the police might even believe that Ethan Logan was the true mastermind behind the Satanic Murders.

Between Rachoń's vehicle and Alexia's, the vampire hunters, the dhampir, the witch, the vampires, and coyote returned safely to Austin, regretfully leaving Sergio behind to deal with their cover story. Having missed the battle, Sergio felt it was the least he could do. It had been difficult to leave Innocente and Pete's bodies behind in the graveyard.

When they left, Cian had to forcibly carry Amaliya away from Innocente's body. Strangely, it was Samantha who gave Amaliya the greatest comfort as they rode back to Austin. Holding Amaliya's hand, Samantha told her about Innocente's appearance and the mysterious ghost who had helped her.

"What did he look like?" Amaliya asked, her face streaked with blood tears.

Samantha described her ghostly helper in as much detail as she could remember.

With a sad smile, Amaliya nodded. "It was my grandfather. He came for her."

Curling up in Cian's arms, Amaliya clung to him the whole way home.

PART SIX

Two Weeks Later

CHAPTER TWENTY-SEVEN

The back room of Jeff's occult bookstore was even more cramped than usual. Extra chairs had been brought in from other rooms inside the shop and it was very crowded around the table.

Jeff took his usual position at the head of the table. He was amused when Cian and Rachoń sat on either side of him, angling their chairs so that it appeared they were also at the head. Amaliya sat at Cian's side, followed by Samantha. Whatever animosity had been between them was gone now. They chatted with each other in soft voices, waiting for the meeting to start. Benchley and Alexia had their usual seats, though both were still immensely grumpy over missing the big battle once again. Sergio and Eduardo sat next to Rachoń, while Cass and Aimee sat at the opposite end of the table. Cian's daughter and the witch had shoved the chairs together so they could snuggle into each other.

Jeff felt awkward every time Cass looked at him. They had a history they had yet to divulge to anyone and he wasn't too sure how Cian would take it.

But there were more important matters to discuss.

"We have a full house tonight. Talk about performance anxiety," Jeff said, trying to break the ice.

The somber expressions around the table informed him that he had not succeeded. It was two weeks since the death of Pete Talbert and Innocente Ottmer. They had anticipated a big media blitz after the deaths, but the police had kept it very hush-hush. Rachoń suspected that maybe Ethan's old contacts or family had worked their usual magic to keep it suppressed. The group had stayed apart from each other during that time. Only Jeff and Samantha had attended Innocente's funeral.

There had been concern about Etzli or The Summoner attacking in the aftermath of the battle. As a precaution, each of their homes was now heavily warded by Aimee's spells. Jeff was grateful to finally have a witch in their midst.

"Cut the chit chat. How fucked are we?" Cassandra asked with her usual lack of tact. She was clad in jeans, beat up Converse, and a Spider-man shirt. In contrast, Aimee was wearing a long green maxi-dress adorned with Celtic designs in gold.

Jeff rested his hands on the book in front of him, dreading what he was about to tell those gathered in front of him. "I'm not sure."

"The Summoner is not going to give up," Amaliya said. The dour look on her face was one that he was not used to seeing. It was hard for all of them to see the pain etched into her face, but she had lost two loved ones to The Summoner. She had Jeff's complete sympathy and support. He didn't take the sharpness in her voice personal.

"We're not sure what he's planning yet, either," Rachoń pointed out. "Or do we?" She looked significantly at Jeff.

"Tell us what you found out," Cian said, trying not to sound like he was ordering Jeff about. "Tell us why you called us here."

Jeff felt the intense scrutiny of those gathered and squirmed around in his chair. The usual joviality that accompanied these gatherings was gone. There was no joking, no playfulness. Everyone looked somber and a bit frightened. Benchley was staring at his bitten-down nails and Jeff hadn't seen him smile once since that terrible night. When Benchley wasn't cracking a bad joke, the world felt a lot gloomier.

Jeff took a deep breath. "Okay, where to start. I...uh...took that photo that Cass and Aimee took of the ring they stole and did a lot of research. I had to call on several overseas resources and really dug deep into my dad's works." He paused for effect, but saw that everyone was looking annoyed that he wasn't just getting to the gist of it.

"What's he not saying?" Benchley asked Samantha.

"I have no clue. He hasn't told me yet either." She glowered at Jeff. "He's being all mysterious."

Jeff sighed. "I'm trying to lay a foundation here for my discovery."

"We just want to know what it is!" Amaliya snapped.

"Okay, first off, how did The Summoner get into Bianca? I figured that out with Samantha's help. When The Summoner died, there were a ton of ghosts around the hotel and graveyard according to Roberto."

Cian arched his eyebrows. "Roberto?"

Jeff nodded. "Samantha saw his ghost the night it all went really bad. Roberto told Samantha that he tried to escape the town, but couldn't. When he was slingshotted back to the Hotel, the ghosts were gone. Rachoń, meanwhile, told me she found Bianca, the night The Summoner died, resurrected and already fully in control of her powers in the graveyard where she was buried."

Rachoń gave a curt nod, agreeing. "I should have known something was

CHAPTER TWENTY-SEVEN

wrong."

Jeff quirked an eyebrow. "Well, hindsight is always 20/20. I firmly believe that The Summoner consumed all the ghosts in the surrounding area after his death. He used their ectoplasm to travel to Bianca's body and claim it. Just like Amaliya, Bianca is one of his necro-vamp offspring." Jeff let his words sink in. "I don't know if Bianca was a mad fledgling, or rebirthed brain dead, but The Summoner implanted himself inside of her. He then waited until Rachoń set her plan in motion to begin implementation of his own."

"To get his ring back?" Cassandra asked.

"I think to get his ring back and Amaliya under his control." Jeff glanced at Amaliya, who shrugged. "He wants you. That was very apparent that night in the cemetery. And I think it might have to do with the rings."

"Is this the fucking *Lord of the Rings* now?" Benchley grumbled.

"One ring to rule them all!" Alexia said, pounding the table.

"Actually, thirteen rings to tear down the veil between our world and the abyss," Jeff corrected.

"Thirteen?" Aimee's eyes widened, looking at Cassandra with concern. "What the hell?"

"We hid the one we stole. The Summoner has one. Etzli has one," Cassandra said. "Who has the other ten?"

"I don't know, but I do know where they came from." Jeff flipped open the book in front of him and displayed a photo of a painting. It was a dramatic rendition of Lucifer falling from the heavens. "So, long ago, there was a war in heaven and Lucifer was cast out. When he fell, he hit the earth. More precisely, he landed in the Yucatán Peninsula."

"Huh?" Benchley gawked at Jeff. "Lucifer? Hitting Mexico? How do you know that?"

"I think he means Chicxulub, the meteor that hit like sixty-five million years ago," Sergio said incredulously. When he noticed everyone looking at him curiously, he said defensively, "We keep *National Geographic* in the bathroom. You know...toilet reading?"

"That's what tabloids are for," Alexia grumbled.

"Sergio, you're absolutely right. But Chicxulub wasn't a meteor, it was Lucifer," Jeff said excitedly.

"Wait!" Samantha glared at him. "Since when do you believe in Lucifer? You were all against me saying the devil is real."

"Well, since I found out about the rings, I have to say I now believe, okay?" Jeff felt annoyed by the interruptions. He hated to admit that he was pretty excited to share his newfound information.

"So Lucifer lands in Mexico and what does that have to do with the rings?" Aimee asked.

"His sword," Jeff replied. "His sword was in Mexico."

Cian lifted his eyebrows as he turned to stare at Jeff. "In Mexico? Where

Etzli is from?"

"Lucifer's sword was found by the Mayans. They believed it was the weapon of a fallen god and built a temple to house it. The Spanish conquered the Mayans, took the sword and the myth around it and delivered it as a gift to the Catholic Church." Jeff paused for dramatic effect.

"They gave the Catholic Church Lucifer's sword?" Eduardo snorted. "That's pretty stupid."

"Actually, it makes sense," Alexia interjected. "It would've been made in heaven. It may have been his sword, but it could've been considered a holy relic."

Jeff nodded enthusiastically. "It actually was, Alexia. It was made of pure gold with precious stones in the hilt." Jeff held up the photo again. "See. Just like this. So, someone in the Vatican decided that it would be a great idea to melt down the sword and create rings out of it. Well, originally, they wanted to make a crown, too, but when the blacksmith melted the sword it lost mass. In the end, he only had enough gold for the rings. The jeweler made thirteen rings: one for the Pope, and twelve for select archbishops."

"Does this sound like a horror movie in the making or what?" Eduardo joked.

"Does it ever," Cass grumbled.

Benchley chewed on his thumbnail. "Totally Exorcist material."

"So what happened to the rings, Jeff?" Amaliya's blue-gray eyes were demanding and a little cold.

"Well, they made the wearer go crazy. And realizing what was happening, the Jesuits collected the rings, dividing them up among thirteen devout priests and sent them out all over the world to hide the rings," Jeff explained.

"And somehow the vampires found out about them," Rachoń added.

"Yeah. About a hundred years ago they became a hot commodity among the vampires," Jeff agreed.

"About the time that The Summoner was holed up in some Mayan temples in the Yucatán Peninsula," Cian sighed.

Rachoń looked down at her hands, her face pensive. "That was when he kidnapped Etzli."

"She's been in on it all along," Cian agreed.

Jeff fidgeted in his chair, not sure how to impart the last of his information. "So, uh, well, lots of different hunter groups have been tracking down the individual rings over the years, but no one knew they were all connected. Not until now. The rings all ended up with different names and different legends, but when Cass and Aimee stole the ring from the Master of Dallas and then connected it to The Summoner, it all became clear."

"He wants the rings. All of them," Amaliya exclaimed, shaking her head.

Rachoń sat back in her chair and tapped her chin with one finger. "The Master of Chicago just went missing a week ago."

"We need to find out if he had a ring." Cian drummed his fingers on the table.

CHAPTER TWENTY-SEVEN

"Have any more gone missing?"

"But why now?" Samantha asked. "Why would he make his move now if he knew about the rings a hundred years ago?"

"The end of the Mayan calendar," Benchley said in a low voice.

"Oh, shit," Alexia whimpered, covering her face with her hoodie.

"Oh, c'mon. That's a bunch of bullshit," Sergio griped.

Benchley snorted. "It makes sense! What if that date is significant for another reason? What if it has to do with these rings that used to be a sword?" Benchley stared intently at each person at the table in turn. "Think about it. What if the Mayans figured out that on that date if the sword is used properly, it could bring destruction down on us?"

"But why destroy the world? What does The Summoner get out of that?" Amaliya protested. "He seems real intent on living."

"He has always been thwarted by the sun," Cian spoke up. "Always. From the beginning of his existence as a vampire, he has always been confined to the night. Maybe he wants to eliminate his ultimate enemy. The sun."

"Rip open the veil to the abyss and darkness consumes the earth," Rachoń whispered in a fearful voice.

"But he'll let out all the demons, the monsters of the pit..." Alexia's voice faded. "Of course, he'd love that."

"So he wants to destroy the world," Cassandra said, slightly shrugging. "Great."

Aimee looked several shades paler and her hand clutched Cassandra's tightly. "So we stop him."

"But how?" Sergio asked. "We're just a bunch of...uh..."

"Fuck ups? Rejects?" Amaliya offered.

"Speak for yourself. I'm pretty awesome," Eduardo retorted.

"Some vampires will help him, you know," Rachoń said grimly.

"And you?" Cian stared into her eyes.

Rachoń shook her head. "I love my family. He was right about that. And some members of my family aren't vampires. I don't want them to die."

"What about you?" Sergio asked Cian. "Do you want an eternal night?"

Cian said simply, "No."

"I say we send out what we know to the hunters and get a coalition going. We need to track down these rings and keep them from him," Cassandra said, thumping the table with her fist.

"If we do that, he'll know that we figured out what he's up to," Amaliya said, her hands nervously combing through her long hair. "He'll come for us."

"He's going to come for you anyway," Samantha said, resting her hand lightly on Amaliya's shoulder. "At some point, he'll come for you, because it's obvious he tried to make you and Bianca for a reason. Now that he's in her body, he's going to be coming for you."

Amaliya looked at Samantha worriedly. "What do you mean?"

"He must need another necromancer to help him pull off whatever he means to do," Samantha answered.

"She's right. Why else would he have tried to make you and Bianca?" Jeff closed the book gently and sighed. "It makes perfect sense that he needs you."

"So we have pieces of his puzzle that he will come for," Cian said.

"Yeah," Jeff answered.

"Then we'll be ready for him," Cian said firmly.

"We create a coalition then." Rachoń's jaw set with determination. "And we stop him."

"We have no other choice," Cian agreed.

"We fight," Cassandra said firmly.

"Until we die," Eduardo said with a flash of teeth.

"Or win," Aimee amended.

"Like Buffy and the Scoobies," Samantha said in a perky voice.

Jeff gave her an amused smile and she grinned at him.

Taking Amaliya's hand, Cian gazed into her eyes. "Nothing will take you from me."

Pressing her lips to his fingers, Amaliya nodded. "I won't let him take me."

"So let's get to planning..." Jeff said, and ignored his own wildly beating heart.

Epilogue

Amaliya stared across the treetops toward the sparkling Austin skyline. Safely ensconced in their new home in the Bouldin Creek area south of downtown, Cian and Amaliya were adjusting to their new digs. Amaliya rather liked the modern-style three-story home with its blocky exterior. The flat roof doubled as a deck that allowed her to gaze toward the building that had been her home for a brief, but lovely time.

Smoking a cigarette, she glanced down into the dark street below. Eduardo was somewhere down there patrolling. The streets were much quieter and darker than the busy downtown area and she was still adapting to the stillness.

Voices drifted up from downstairs. Aimee and Cassandra were doing dishes after their dinner. Amaliya hadn't been surprised when Cian had taken them in. The couple occupied one of the bedrooms on the second floor. Though the women seemed wary of the vampires at times, things were slowly warming between all of them. Amaliya had been amused to find Cassandra and Cian playing pool in their new game room earlier in the evening. They were both competitive, but their playful jibs had made her smile.

She heard the door open behind her and smelled Cian's cologne. He had been on the phone for the last hour. Cian had attempted to warn Santos in hopes of recruiting him eventually to their cause, but the vampire Master of San Antonio would not listen. Amaliya really didn't care if Etzli ended up killing the jerk.

Cian slipped up behind her and wrapped an arm around her waist. She rested against him, relishing his touch. His soft kisses on her cheek made her smile.

"You're always so beautiful in the moonlight," Cian said, his voice husky in her ear.

Putting out her cigarette, Amaliya nuzzled his cheek. "Stop trying to seduce me."

Their new bedroom didn't have the retractable walls of their former home, but it did have reinforced doors and heavy metal shutters that covered the wide windows. Amaliya rather enjoyed having an actual bedroom to sleep in, even if her clothes were strewn all over the floor. It was a habit that drove Cian crazy.

"I can't help myself." Cian kissed her cheek again and then rested his chin on her shoulder. "How are you tonight?"

In the aftermath of her grandmother and Pete's deaths, Amaliya had fallen into a deep funk. It was hard to fathom how two people who loved her so deeply could die when she remained alive. She still struggled with accepting that reality. Pete's final words through Samantha still haunted her. His sentiment had been lovely, but he spoke of a dream she could have never shared with him. He had died because he had believed that he could create a life with her. Pete had never known that she wanted to be a vampire and that she loved Cian.

That truth ate at her.

"Better," she said, wondering if it was a lie or not.

"Pete did what I would have done." Cian brushed his lips against her shoulder.

Amaliya wondered again if he could actually read her mind. "It doesn't make it any easier to know he died trying to save me and make me mortal when that's the last thing I want."

"We choose to do incredibly brave and sometimes stupid things out of love."

"The life he imagined for me never would have happened, even if I hadn't been changed into a vampire."

"Sometimes, when a man loves a woman, he dreams foolishly."

"Oh?" Amaliya lifted her eyebrows. "Do you dream foolishly?"

Cian turned her about in his arms and locked his hands behind her back. "I dream of a time when we are not facing death, but enjoying life. I have a little fantasy in my mind that I cling to when things are dire."

"Oh? Tell me."

Laughing, Cian kissed her lips lovingly. "Do you really want to know?"

"Uh huh." Amaliya slid her fingers under his shirt to stroke his skin.

"Okay, here it is." Cian fastened his intense hazel eyes on her face. "I dream of you. With me. Forever. No one ever comes between us and we experience the beauty of the eternal night side by side. We never part ways, but always find solace in one another."

Amaliya touched his cheek lightly, his words sending a thrill of terror and pleasure through her. "You mean forever..."

"I have been in love many times, Amaliya. I have tried to hold onto those loves only to lose them because of the choices I made. But it is different with you. It has been from the beginning. The same way you choose not to run away, I choose not to push you away. I have always betrayed or hurt the ones I love out of the selfish need to ensure my own survival at all costs. But when I look at you, I know I would die for you."

EPILOGUE

Covering his mouth, Amaliya whispered, "Don't say that."

Cian pressed his lips to her palm, then drew her hand away. "I will say it, because should I die in defense of you, I want you to know it is because I love you and would do anything for you."

"Like Pete," Amaliya sighed, lowering her chin and staring at his chest.

Tucking his fingers under her jaw, he lifted her face. His hazel eyes gazed into hers. "What is your dream?"

The pain that flitted through her was brief, but she accepted its cause. She loved Cian with all her heart and knew what she chose could result in both of them dying. If she was wise, she would run away and spare him, but she knew she couldn't. To live her life without him was to not live at all. "My dream..." she said in a voice husky with emotion "...is forever."

The smile on Cian's face warmed her heart even as her blood turned to ice.

"And I will destroy anyone or anything that comes between us and that dream coming true."

Cian touched her cheek, his eyes clearly reflecting her own determination. "I understand."

"No, you don't, Cian." Amaliya said, her voice rough with pain. "Because I will destroy the world if I have to…"

To be concluded in

Pretty When She Destroys

2014

Author's Note

It's been a long journey to this second novel in the *PRETTY WHEN SHE DIES* trilogy. When I wrote the original novel back in 2007, it was for a writing challenge. The idea was to write a complete book in two weeks. The idea for *PRETTY WHEN SHE DIES* had been knocking around in my head since it was born in a terrifying nightmare a few years before. I had always wanted to create a novel based on that dream. I decided to take advantage of the challenge and finally write my modern day vampire novel.

Three weeks later, I had exceeded my target word count for the novel and had my complete vampire novel. It would take much longer to revise the novel and shape it into the story that was finally released in November of 2008. It wasn't until just before the first book was published that I realized it was part of a much bigger story, a trilogy in fact.

Since I was just starting out in my Indie Author career, I thought it would be fairly simple for me to write the subsequent sequels the following year. I even announced the coming of *PRETTY WHEN SHE KILLS* in 2009

Then two factors prevented this from happening.

First, *PRETTY WHEN SHE DIES* barely sold in its first year of release. In fact, it wasn't until 2010 that the book started to sell briskly and garner solid reviews. At the time of its release, people were just being gripped by *TWILIGHT* fever and vampires became the staple of YA and Paranormal Romance novels. *PRETTY WHEN SHE DIES* did not fit the desires of the reading public until *True Blood* appeared on HBO.

Second, my zombie trilogy, *AS THE WORLD DIES*, took off like a shot, gathering rave reviews, landing on "best of" lists, before being snatched up by genre publishing giant Tor. My life became consumed with the revision of the zombie trilogy and all other writing projects were set aside.

It wasn't until this year that I felt the outcry for *PRETTY WHEN SHE KILLS* and the sales of the first book indicated that it was time to finally write the sequel. With the *AS THE WORLD DIES* trilogy on bookstore shelves and my next deal with Tor pending, I sat down in the beginning of summer 2012 at my desk and returned to the world of vampires, necromancers, and zombies.

It was wonderful writing about Amaliya, Cian, Samantha, Jeff, and all the rest of their crew. I'd missed them all so much. It was also a blast writing about the city I live in and sharing it with the readers. I promise that the third book will not take so long to be released.

I hope this story thrills, terrifies, and excites you as much as it did me.

Love forever,
Rhiannon Frater
August 2, 2012

ABOUT THE AUTHOR

Rhiannon Frater is the award-winning author of over a dozen books, including the *As the World Dies* zombie trilogy (Tor), as well as independent works such as *The Last Bastion of the Living* (declared the #1 Zombie Release of 2012 by *Explorations Fantasy Blog* and the #1 Zombie Novel of the Decade by *B&N Book Blog*), and other horror novels. She was born and raised a Texan and presently lives in Austin, Texas with her husband and furry children (a.k.a pets). She loves scary movies, sci-fi and horror shows, playing video games, cooking, dyeing her hair weird colors, and shopping for Betsey Johnson purses and shoes.

You can find her online at rhiannonfrater.com

Subscribe to her mailing list at tinyletter.com/RhiannonFrater